Get out of here,

a voice whispered in Digger's head.

It had been a long time since he'd been around children. They scared him. Here at the nursery school he could smell their chalk and crayons, hear their voices.

"Mr. Clayton?"

Hearing his name stopped his train of thought. He looked in the direction of the voice. It was the teacher, Erin Taylor, with her long legs, ponytail and a soft lipstick that drew his attention to her mouth.

Digger's breath all but stopped. After Josh died, after the divorce, he'd never expected to feel that way again. But Erin Taylor had done it with just one look.

Digger mentally shook himself. He'd been down this road before, knew where it led, how smooth it appeared. But this road led to places no man should have to go, through fiery rivers of pain. You either drowned…or survived—alive but scarred.

Digger had survived. He had the scars to prove it. But he could not do it again. His trip through hell had been one-way.

A second time would kill him.

SHIRLEY HAILSTOCK

is the author of seventeen novels and novellas. She has received numerous awards for her work, including the Holt Medallion, the Barclay Gold Award, the Waldenbooks Bestselling Romance Award and a Career Achievement Award from *Romantic Times.* One of her books made the Top 100 Romances of the 20th Century list. Shirley is working on her third novel for Silhouette Special Edition.

Shirley's books have appeared on *Blackboard* and the *Library Journal* Bestseller Lists. She is a past president of Romance Writers of America, and loves to hear from fans. You can write her at P.O. Box 513, Plainsboro, NJ 08536 or browse her Web site at www.geocities.com/shailstock.

SHIRLEY HAILSTOCK

A FATHER'S FORTUNE

Silhouette Books

Published by Silhouette Books

America's Publisher of Contemporary Romance

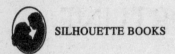

SILHOUETTE BOOKS

ISBN 0-373-81110-1

A FATHER'S FORTUNE

Copyright © 2003 by Shirley Hailstock

This edition published by arrangement with Harlequin Books S.A.

® and TM are trademarks of Harlequin Books S.A., used under license.
Trademarks indicated with ® are registered in the United States Patent
and Trademark Office, the Canadian Trade Marks Office and in other
countries.

Visit Silhouette Books at www.eHarlequin.com

Printed in U.S.A.

To Allison Kelly of Romance Writers of America,
because she cried when I told her I sold this book.

Chapter One

What was he doing here?

James "Digger" Clayton climbed down from the cab of his truck and stared at the building and yard. There had to be a mistake. A white picket fence, gleaming so brightly it rivaled the sunny afternoon, stood in front of him. Pushing the gate open, he clenched his teeth as he verified the number on the note in his hand against the scripted numbers on the Mexican tiles hanging above the center porch.

This was the right place, at least the place his dispatcher, Sarah, had sent him. And she knew better. Swinging his gaze up and down the street, he looked for another address. There were no other structures on this side of the street. The other side backed up against a development of contemporary cookie cutter houses, molded out of sand-colored stucco. This building at least had character. It was a big Victorian mansion with turret rooms. Cornflower blue with white gin-

gerbread trim, he wouldn't have been surprised to see Hansel
and Gretel running about the front yard.

Digger looked down at his dusty work boots then across
the crowded yard. Sarah had screwed up royally. She knew
better than to send him to a place like this. Squeals rang out
in the clear warm air, the sound wracking through his insides
like a rusty knife ripping raw flesh. He froze, unable to move.
Pain's hand swelled around his heart—squeezing memory
through his veins. His breath all but stopped. Sweat popped
out on his neck, and his arms were suddenly leaden and
heavy.

The yard was full of them—laughing, running, zigzagging
in unpredictable patterns, spinning around like tops of bound-
less energy. Digger had to dodge as they scurried around
him. He moved from side to side, trying to keep his balance
as they rushed around without order or purpose.

His brain told him to run, get away from here, but his feet
felt as if they were lodged in cement. He couldn't budge. He
should never have gotten out of the truck, driven away the
moment he saw them. He could have Sarah call and apologize for him. There was no way he could work here. He tried
to force his legs to move, but they were weighted. Digger
looked down. There *was* a weight holding him back—about
forty pounds of brown eyes, braids and small even teeth.

A child, a little girl, clasped her arms around his right leg.
Both her feet stood on one of his. She held onto him like a
detachable doll. She smiled up at him, her eyes bright and
happy in a face that would be hard not to love.

"Hi," she said.

Digger's heart accelerated. He closed his eyes and
clamped his teeth down hard, forcing back the memories that
tried to seep through. Shock waves rocketed through him. He
locked his knees, his hands balling into fists. He hoped the
tension in his body would stem the horror inside him. He
stared down at the little girl. She smiled at him. He didn't re-

turn it, yet he was unable to take his eyes off her. If it weren't for the child, if it weren't for forty pounds of innocence clinging to his trouser leg, her eyes trusting him, her smile as big as the sky, he wouldn't be able to stand on his own.

"Sam, come here." Someone called to her. Digger shifted his gaze. The child's teacher pulled the small hands from his dusty, jean-clad leg. "I'm sorry," she apologized. "She's very friendly. She meant no harm."

"I'm Sam," the little girl said. "What's your name?"

Digger swung his attention between the child and the teacher. He wondered if the perceptive young woman saw his discomfort. She had blond hair and light brown eyes. He guessed she was about eighteen, and she looked like the poster-child for the clean cut American teenager.

"May I help you?" she asked, lifting the girl in her arms. Her action was obviously protective. She turned slightly away as if he might be a possible criminal and she was checking her escape routes.

"I'm Digger Clayton. I have an appointment with Erin Taylor."

"Digger?"

"James Clayton, Clayton Construction." Most people knew him as Digger. He often forgot to use his given name.

"Oh." She smiled, a little embarrassed. He could see relief in her eyes. She'd obviously decided he wasn't there to do harm to her or any of the children. "That's Ms. Taylor over there." She pointed to a door at the far end of the building. A woman wearing navy blue Bermuda shorts and a yellow T-shirt walked toward the door. She didn't just walk. She seemed to glide, her pace unhurried and graceful. Her hair was held in a ponytail, which she pulled free as she walked. The shirt stretched across her back as graceful arms moved right and her head moved left. Digger was reminded of a ballet. He hated ballet, but something stirred inside him. He liked what he was looking at. And that was a surprise.

"I believe she's expecting you," the young woman's voice pulled him out of his dream.

"Thank you," he said.

She brushed the little girl's hair and walked back toward a group of kids standing inside a circle and playing with a ball.

"Bye," the little girl said. She waved her fingers. Digger's tongue stuck to the roof of his mouth.

He started to move toward the door where Erin Taylor had disappeared, but kids suddenly burst around him, through his legs, in front and behind him, hampering his movement. Digger jumped out of the way as they screamed with laughter. He waited a moment, more to compose himself than to allow the children to disperse. He hadn't been here five minutes and already he wanted to leave. He should head for his truck, he told himself. He should call Sarah on his cell phone from the comfortable security of the Bronco's cab. And after he reamed her out for sending him here, she could call the long-legged Erin Taylor and make his apologies. He wasn't interested, not in her job and not in her.

Her, he thought. He hadn't even seen her face. How could he be interested in a body wearing shorts and a tight T-shirt? Yet he didn't go to the Bronco. One unencumbered step followed the other on the path that led where he didn't want to go, shouldn't go.

Inside, it wasn't as bright as the yard had been. Digger stopped a moment to let his eyes adjust. The noise level inside was so different from outside that he shook his head to make sure there was nothing in his ears. He stood on a polished brown floor. Scuff marks were evidence of running, skidding children. Bins had been built into the walls. Most were closed, but a few stood open revealing redheaded dolls, tubs of Lego, board games, plastic bats and toys of all varieties. Small colorful chairs and tables were grouped on carpet circles, books lay askew in movable racks near the windows.

Get out of here, a voice whispered in his head. It had been a long time since he'd been around children. They scared him. But he knew this room. He could smell the chalk and crayons, almost hear the voices—

"Mr. Clayton?" Hearing his name stopped his train of thought. "Are you Mr. Clayton?"

"Digger," he said without thinking. He looked in the direction of the voice. It was her, long legs and ponytail. She'd put her hair back in the rubber band. It was straight and falling down her back out of sight. In this light it looked black, but he'd seen the reddish highlights in the sun. She wore little makeup, only a soft lipstick that drew his attention to her mouth. Whatever had moved him earlier repeated itself. He took a side step to dispel it. There were no soft curls to frame her face, as they'd done just moments ago. Yet her beauty struck Digger. Her cheekbones were high. His mother had always wanted high cheekbones. She said they added stature to a woman and gave her a timeless, classic appearance as she aged. He could see that in Erin Taylor. Her eyes were brown, darkly highlighted by long lashes, the kind rainwater or happy tears clung to.

Digger's breath all but stopped. It had been years since a woman had taken his breath away. Marita, his ex-wife, had done it the day he met her. He'd been surprised to find his reaction unchanged, long after Josh died, long after the divorce. But thankfully a day had come when he didn't wake reaching for her, thinking of her and hurting for his loss.

He hadn't expected to feel it again, would have fought it if he'd known it was a possibility. He hadn't known. And Erin Taylor—ponytail, Bermuda shorts, long legs and dark eyes—could do it to him with a look.

Digger cleared his throat and mentally shook himself. He'd been down this road before. He knew where it led, how smooth and wonderfully straight it appeared, how the trees lining the road were green and healthy and the grassy median was rivaled only by the yellow brick road and the Emerald City in the distance. But appearances were deceptive. This road led places no man should have to go, through fiery rivers of pain, across lava rocks of despair, inside vats of gin and Johnny Walker Red. You either crashed and burned, drowned…or survived—alive but scarred.

Digger survived. He had the scars to prove it. They were deep and heavy. He could not do it again. His trip through hell had been one way. He'd used his one and only ticket. There would be no doing it again. A second time would kill him.

If he hadn't already decided to let this job go, Erin Taylor would be enough to cap his decision. Digger hadn't thought he would ever react to a woman this way again. It surprised him that without a word spoken between them he could…want her. *Want*, that was the only way he could describe it. But it was a need he would not act upon.

"I didn't expect you until six," she said.

Her tone told him she liked to run things on schedule. "I finished another job earlier than I thought…" He stopped. He was explaining. Why was he explaining? Why did he feel like he had to? With one sentence he was back in school and she was the teacher scolding him.

"We'd better talk in my office. The kids will be coming in soon to get ready for their parents to pick them up."

She turned and went down a hall that had classrooms on either side. Digger saw brightly colored paper flowers pasted on the windows. On the bottom of one door were photos of smiling children attached to a green felt background. Everywhere he looked there were the echoes of children.

He followed her into an office. It was child-proofed. The furniture was smooth, unadorned by carved surfaces that small hands and feet could climb on. The desk was free of such things as pencils and scissors. There were a few coloring books and along the side was a bin with more toys. These he could see were broken. Maybe she had someone who would repair them or maybe they were being stored to prevent accidents.

She took a chair behind the desk, but he remained standing.

"I'd like to add the rooms along the back side of this building," she began.

"I can't do it," he said. "There's been a mistake."

"Excuse me, aren't you a builder?"

"I'm a carpenter." He never pretended to be anymore than he was. He had been a builder once. But that was before time ended.

"Your office told me you could build anything."

"I can, but not here."

"Here?" She stood up. He watched her go on the defensive. "What do you mean here?"

"This is a school."

"It's a nursery school." She nodded.

"I don't work around kids. They're too unpredictable. No one can determine what they will do next. They get in the way, cause accidents."

"I'll make sure—"

"You can't do that." He stopped her before she could say how she could keep reins on the kids. "No one can. No one knows what they'll do from one second to the next. I don't work around them."

She dropped her shoulders. "Why did you come here, Mr. Clayton? I told your secretary this was a school. I gave her the name and address."

"She didn't relay that information. She only gave me your name and the address. I thought this was a house that needed another room."

"Technically it is. It used to be a house, but we changed a lot of it."

"I know," he said. The outside still looked like a Victorian, or the semblance of one. It was really a puzzle house, having had many additions over the years. The inside had no resemblance to the small, high-ceilinged rooms of the early nineteenth century. Walls had been removed to make a larger space, and desks and chairs took the place of humpback sofas and heavy tables. "There have been several additions put on at different times." He looked around the room, up at the ceiling, in the corners. He'd noticed the wall joints as he looked over the building from the outside. The roofing had colored differently, forming a demarcation line that any good builder would notice. "This area," he indicated the space where they now stood. "Wasn't part of the original building."

"It was added ten years ago."

Quickly, he tried to calculate her age. She looked to be in her late twenties. Ten years ago she'd have been a teenager, probably like the blond girl he'd met earlier. It meant she was his age or younger.

"Were you here then?"

"I only bought it three years ago," she said. "I used to help out here when I was a teenager."

He confirmed his estimate of her age.

"Don't you like kids, Mr. Clayton?"

Not especially. The words were so automatic he almost said them aloud. For some reason he stopped. He couldn't tell her he didn't like kids. Most of the people he knew believed it, but he couldn't tell this teacher a lie.

"Liking kids has nothing to do with it. I value my business, and I don't want it hampered by unnecessary accidents."

"I see," she said as if some understanding had come over her. "If insurance is a problem I wouldn't want you to work around the children either. I thought you were fully bonded."

"We are," he said quickly. Digger should have left it there, but he went on, not able to allow anyone to cast a negative light on the business he'd put his sweat into. "There is nothing unethical about Clayton Construction, *nothing*."

"Then I don't understand."

"You don't have to understand," he said a little too harshly. He took a breath. "Just leave it. Find another firm. They'll probably do a better job for you than I could. And I'm very busy."

"I don't understand your attitude."

"Attitudes are like opinions. We're all allowed one. Good day, Ms. Taylor."

Erin had never been so frustrated in her life. She had the money for the addition. It had taken her years to save it, and the extra room was sorely needed with the number of applications she received and a waiting list that grew ever longer. So what was Digger Clayton's problem? Why wouldn't he build the two rooms she needed?

She'd hoped to have the addition completed before the fall weather came and school opened again. An influx of new students always came in September. She needed time to order and receive furniture, have those new felt-pen boards installed and decorate the walls. Clayton Construction had come highly recommended. She had four other estimates, but Clayton's recommendations were superior to any of the others. No comment had been qualified. She needed to be sure there would be as few problems as possible and no need to recall the builder once the job was done.

"Digger Clayton does it right the first time," she'd been told, over and over.

This Digger Clayton was hiding something. There was more to his reluctance than he'd told her. Erin was sure of it. She wondered why. What had happened to him? She'd seen the interest in his eyes, interest in her, sexual interest, man-woman interest, but then he'd closed down. The way he looked away from her…the transformation was almost physical.

She'd felt the attraction, too. While he'd spent a good minute appraising her, she couldn't help but notice the rush in her system when she found him standing in the common room. Men looked at her all the time, divorced fathers picking up their kids or enrolling them, eyed her with overt interest as if they were sizing her up to be the next Mrs. Whoever. Married men smiled and gave her that untouchable-but-interested look. She was aware of her appearance and the male reaction to it, but it had been a while since she'd reacted in a similar way.

Digger Clayton was handsome. In another time he'd be the muscular gladiator or the rugged cowboy herding steers north to Oklahoma. Today his silver horse had the power of two hundred and fifty of its brethren. His body was toned with muscles that spoke of hard work and days in the sun. She had the urge to touch them, run her hands over his skin and find out if he was as hard as he appeared.

He had dark eyes with disturbing depths. They were sad and haunted instead of happy and inviting. While he stood in front of her she'd wanted to lift his face as she'd do a child's and soothe away the hurt. But she hadn't touched Digger Clayton. She'd let him walk out, watched his retreat, sorry the battle between them had ended so quickly. She would have enjoyed fighting with him. And she'd have enjoyed the making up, too.

Digger sat in the dark. He hadn't bothered to turn on the lights when he got home. There was no need. He knew with or without the lights the trigger had been pulled. He could no more stop the memories than he could stop a speeding bullet.

He saw the crane moving. Saw himself in the driver's seat as if this was some giant cinema with only one patron. The boy stood off to the side, away from danger, out of harm's way. He lifted his hand and waved to Digger, his tiny fingers opening and closing. He smiled a little boy grin, toothy, trusting, loving. Digger smiled back and waved. His heart was full each time he looked at the boy. He didn't know it was possible to love someone as much as he loved Josh.

Then it happened. The crane started to slip sideways. He switched his attention to the machine. Frantically, he worked the controls, turned the wheel, trying to make the mammoth machine respond to his will and turn toward more solid ground. It slipped more, tilting. Digger bit deep into his lip, fighting the beast, cursing the laws of physics, denying everything he knew about the center of gravity, weight distribution and all the formal laws that kept objects upright and adhered to the ground. He fought, cursed, shouted at the machine. Still it defied him.

The left side pitched upward. Cries came from the ground, drowned out by the roar of metal lifting unnaturally into the air. Digger would never forget that sound. It wailed, almost cried out. He fought the forces opposing him, but deep down he knew he would lose.

Then the unthinkable happened, the unbelievable. Digger almost didn't see it, wished he hadn't seen it, but he couldn't look away. The boy was there, screaming to him, moving toward him, running on his little legs. As the giant creature rose in the air the boy came, mounting a rescue mission, trying to get to Digger, to help *him*. Then the three-year-old registered danger and turned to flee. Digger prayed the boy's legs were strong enough, prayed the ground was sure and he'd be able to clear the area before the machine tumbled over in the soft, wet earth. Digger cried for it, prayed to God for mercy, a miracle, help.

In a second his heart lifted. Jeremy, his foreman and best friend, had Josh. He ran down the hill, swung the boy up in his arms and turned toward safety. Jeremy would do it. Digger prayed. Even in this dream state seven years later, he rooted for Jeremy to change history, change the circumstances, rewrite what had happened.

But there was no time. Digger lost his hold. He fell. The giant machine crashed seconds later. He couldn't see Jeremy and Josh. He expected to feel the weight of the twenty ton crane crush the life out of him.

But it didn't.

He'd been luckier than hell, the doctor would tell him later. Many people would tell him how lucky he was to survive. They were all wrong. They didn't know the price of survival. They hadn't had to punch through the night, fighting unseen monsters of the dark, screaming through his dreams and trying without success to relive sixty seconds of pure terror. They didn't wake each morning and force themselves to put a foot on the floor and get up. They didn't meet sympathetic stares or hear the sound of silence that accompanied his entrance into a room. None of them knew.

And he hoped to God they never would.

The open case of the crane had fallen over him. His body had instinctively balled into the fetal position, and the cage completely insulated him, as if it were some huge hand that protected him from the safety of death. Inside the cage he lay untouched, uninjured, unscratched, *alive*.

Jeremy and the boy weren't as fortunate. The monster found them four feet from safety. Tears ran down his face, no matter how he tried to forget it. No matter how long between intervals, it was always there, the memory, the unreality, the helplessness, ready to spring up and torment him.

Going to that school, seeing the young child who'd grabbed his leg and Erin Taylor had brought this on. He hadn't let himself think about the accident in years. As long as he stayed away from children he could control the pain. As long as they weren't part of his daily routine he could function. He could see them on the street, drive by them along the roadway and not think of the accident, not immediately call the memory to mind. But he wouldn't be part of the nursery school project. He wouldn't allow Erin Taylor's beautiful eyes or the way she looked pulling her hair loose influence him. He had to remember the road. The bad road. The days and months of dying he'd done to find his way back to ground he could live on.

He was sure, he told himself, with absolute certainty, that he'd never have to see her again. Life would return to routine in the morning.

And he'd read the riot act to Sarah.

The last child left the school at five-thirty two days after Erin's encounter with Digger Clayton. She looked forward to an early night. Dinner and a bath were all she had on her evening agenda.

Dressed in a robe, she put on some light music and sat down on the sofa. The estimates for the addition lay on the coffee table. She didn't pull the papers forward. They needed to be looked at and she needed to decide on another builder if she wanted her plans completed on time. But she was restless.

Looking around the room Erin wondered if she'd spend the rest of her life here. After her tiring day at work and her bath she should be ready for bed. Yet her mind found fault with everything around her, something she'd been doing a lot of lately. That was probably why Digger Clayton had irritated her.

She'd been attracted to him, and she didn't like it. After Kent Edwards walked out of her life she'd vowed not to get involved again. It was just going to be her and the school, but now, tonight, the life of an old maid schoolteacher seemed so nineteenth-century. She found no comfort in her decision. After her relationship with Kent broke down she'd been emotional, but she didn't see how she could go through another relationship knowing the outcome would be the same.

No one wanted to simply date. This was a community of couples, families, children. Soon the dating would get serious and she'd have to cool it or reveal her secret. Then, it was hit the road time. Her phone never rang again.

Now she'd met Digger Clayton. He aroused feelings in her she liked, but she clamped down on them. There was no need to think any more about him. He obviously didn't like her or the kids at her school. And she lived for her kids. They were her lifeline, the only children she would ever have. After the amusement park accident when she was seventeen, there was no chance of her ever having a child of her own.

A tear slipped from her eye. Erin immediately wiped it away. She sniffed and looked at the papers. There was no need to spend time crying. She could not change the past. That was the way the cards had fallen. She could live with her lot. She smiled, thinking of Sam and Jerry and Crystal and all the other kids that came and went. She lived with their colds, their finger paintings, stories of monsters and what happened at dinner the previous night. She loved it. There were so many kids that needed loving, and they gave her the same hugs back that she gave them. Only *she* could kiss their hurts away. Unfortunately, they couldn't kiss hers.

Leaning forward Erin spread the estimates out on the table in her living room and stared at them. She had four, more than enough to make a decision. She thought she would get one from Digger Clayton, but he hadn't even let her present her ideas.

What was the real reason he'd refused to do the job? There had to be something more than what he'd said. She didn't think it was her. For a moment he'd shown genuine interest in her, but then he'd backed off. He said it was the school. What was wrong with the school? Schools had additions put on them all the time. If everyone thought like he did no schools would ever be built.

Her job now was finding another builder. She'd thought it would be an easy endeavor once the money had been raised, but she was finding that money didn't move the world, at least not this section of it. If Digger Clayton didn't want to do the job, she couldn't very well force him. Although she'd favored him, based on the testimonials she'd heard, she still needed an estimate to make sure it was within her budget. He'd seemed the best man for the job. She never imagined her decision would be met with hostility.

Or that the hostility would be packaged so well.

She sighed and pulled the papers even closer to her, discarding thoughts of Digger and how well she thought his clothes fit. She had to make a decision.

Erin shook herself, trying to clear her head of the image of Digger Clayton. What kind of name was that anyway? His real name was James, but she thought Digger fit him better. She remembered the look in his eyes when he saw her. She'd become so hot she was sure he could see her breasts pointing through her T-shirt. She could almost feel his eyes digging through the material.

He hadn't said a word, but he'd closed his eyes to her. She went back to looking at the estimates and reading the notes she'd made on each company. They were good, but none of them said "he does it right the first time."

She knew the comment referred to his carpentry, but she couldn't help wondering if it extended to all facets of the complex and enigmatic Mr. Clayton.

Chapter Two

Digger saw her the moment he pulled into the lot of the local building supply store. As always, the parking lot was full of do-it-yourselfers angling carts of 2X4s or panels of Sheetrock. Building supply was mainly a man's store. There were plenty of women who could plumb a wall, install roofing or build a new addition, but this was a place frequented by men.

Erin was wearing light blue jeans and a short-sleeved sweater that stopped at her waist. It wouldn't matter where she was or what she wore, Digger thought. She would stand out. Here, she stood out even more, as if she were dressed in a ball gown surrounded by dirty road workers.

She lifted a box from her cart and leaned over. The short sweater revealed a patch of brown skin. Digger drew in his breath. Her cart was full of flat boxes that looked heavy. His first instinct was to rush over and help her, but he checked himself, remembering his vow to stay away from her. She represented complications, and he didn't need complications in his life right now.

Or ever.

He climbed down from the cab of his truck as she reached for the second box. He couldn't do it. His feet were walking toward her before his mind could stop them.

"Let me help you," he said, taking the box she struggled with and storing it in the van that had the school's name and logo painted on the door.

"Hi," she said with a smile.

Digger's grasp on the box faltered. It fell with a clunk to the floor of the van.

He knew this wasn't a good idea. All she did was smile and he'd lost it.

"Bookcases," he said, covering his embarrassment. The box had a picture of a bookcase on the outside and heavy thick printing with the dimensions of the contents.

"The ones we have need replacing. I'm afraid they might fall apart while a child is reaching for a book. Or roll away and cause someone to fall."

"Safety first." He quoted the anthem of all construction workers.

She nodded, applying the same slogan to children.

"These have to be assembled." He placed the third box in her van.

"I know. I figure I'll tackle them tonight after the children leave."

"You." He hadn't meant to imply she was incompetent. These things would be easy to assemble using only a screwdriver. But she looked so soft. He saw her with a child in her arms not sitting in the middle of wood parts, screws, tools and preprinted instructions.

"I'm sure I can do it," she said.

"I meant…I mean, I thought you'd have a handyman or someone in maintenance do it for you."

She laughed. "We're not that large an operation. I have a ground crew to take care of the grass and shrubs and I have a service that cleans the floors and windows. None of those people are employees." She paused. "I'm sure I can get them assembled before Monday."

Digger looked at her. She was capable. There was no reason to believe she couldn't do it. He didn't want to volunteer, didn't want to see her again. He should end his conversation with her now, close the door to her van and say good day, but something inside him forced the words out.

"What time does the school close?"

"The children are gone by six. Why?"

"I'll come by and do them around seven."

"That's not necessary."

He wasn't sure she was protesting. Even if she wasn't he should grab the chance to back out. Yet he didn't. "I have all the tools, and you want to make sure the screws are tight enough to hold the unit together."

"Of course, but—"

"I'll see you at seven."

He walked away, taking her empty cart and not giving her time to protest further. He also didn't give her time to talk him out of it.

And he had no idea, why he was forcing himself into her company or why his heart danced at the thought of seeing her again.

Digger opened the door at seven. The place was quiet and empty. He sighed, relieved that there were no kids present. Setting his toolbox on the floor he realized he hadn't been completely sure he wouldn't find the place full of uncontrollable bodies weaving through the halls. She had told him the children would be gone, but until he actually saw the emptiness he hadn't believed it.

Digger had barely straightened to his full height when he

heard a giggle. He automatically stiffened and turned at the same time. Out of nowhere the little girl—Sam—barreled across the floor. She gave him no time to get out of the way before she tackled his leg. The forty-pound missile nearly toppled him over. She looked up with a happy smile, unmindful that she'd nearly upended him. He guessed this was her normal method of greeting people since it was the second time she'd seen him and the second time she'd put her little arms around his leg. Digger couldn't quite decide what to do with her. He stood in place with tension stretching his muscles. He was still looking down when Erin joined them.

She pulled the child away and held her hand. As she straightened, Digger let himself inhale. He smelled her, taking in her exotic scent mixed with a flowery perfume. The combination intoxicated him. It had been a long time since he'd been near a woman, especially one who looked like Erin; one who made his heart flip over and robbed him of the ability to think with God-given logic.

"Hi," Sam said, her eyes wide and dancing. Digger nodded at her. He found his throat too dry to speak. Clearing it, he looked at Erin.

"I thought the children would be gone by now."

"All except Sam." She glanced at the child. "Samantha Pierce." The smile she gave to Sam softened Erin's face. Digger found himself wanting her to turn that smile on him.

"Her parents are attending a program tonight. Her father works at the university and there is a faculty gathering. I agreed to keep her until it's over." She bent down and lifted the four-year-old. "Sam, this is Mr. Clayton."

"I already met Mr. Satan." Her voice was light, but her tongue heavy.

"Why don't you call me Digger? Everyone does."

She turned her head and looked at Erin, her eyes and mouth opened in anticipation. This was obviously against the rules.

"It's all right," Erin told her.

"Digger," she said with a big smile on her face. She looked as if she'd graduated from kid to adult and couldn't wait to test her new level. "My name is Sam. It's short for Samantha Yvette Pierce. Sometimes my daddy calls me Sy. He takes my two first names and *really* shortens them." Digger could tell she'd recited this litany before.

She hadn't mastered pronunciation yet. She had a slight lisp, which she'd grow out of in time. Digger found it cute and endearing. It made him watch her and listen. Her fractured language reminded him of Josh's attempts to say certain words. Digger looked away. He didn't want to remember Josh, and he couldn't look at Erin. Even after such a short acquaintance she'd found the key to his chemical code. She was drawing him to her, even against his will. Without that pull he wouldn't be here tonight, and his stomach wouldn't be curling into a hard knot.

"Samantha," Erin interrupted her, stopping the runaway conversation. Erin turned to him. "We were just having something to eat. Would you like to join us?"

Refusal was on the tip of his tongue. He was here to put together bookcases. He needed to minimize his contact with Erin and Sam. So why was his head bobbing up and down? Why did he seem paralyzed in the presence of someone he'd met only twice? Erin smiled, and he knew the reason.

She turned, leading the way toward the main room. A large box of pizza sat open on one of the child-size tables. Digger stopped. His six-foot frame wouldn't fold up small enough to fit into a toddler chair. Erin moved the box and plates to a standard table. Sam got several books from the rack and put them on her chair, an act she obviously performed with practice. Digger found himself wondering who else had had dinner with the two of them. A momentary streak of jealousy ran through him. He refused to name it. Sam raised her arms up to Digger indicating he should pick her up.

"Ms. Taylor says climbing is dangerous," she explained in her child's voice. "I could slip and fall. She says it's too dangerous." She pronounced the last word slowly, articulating all the syllables as if she had just learned the sounds.

Digger lifted her onto the stack of books. She was light, weighing almost nothing. He'd forgotten how weightless a child could seem. Almost as light as air. Oh, God, he thought. This was a really bad idea. He wanted to hold her close. For a moment he wanted to pretend she was Josh.

Erin set a plate and slice of pizza in front of Sam and slid a lidded plastic cup of soda next to it.

"Help yourself," she told him as she placed a paper plate before him.

Samantha took care picking up her pizza. Her fingers were unsure on the awkwardly moving slice. Digger stopped himself from helping her. She took a bite and chewed. "Do you have a little girl?" she asked with her mouth full.

Digger heard the question as he slipped a slice of pizza toward his plate. It stopped in midair. His hand shook, but he got the pizza in place and pulled the plate back. He looked at Sam. Tomato sauce increased the size of her mouth, outlining it as a clown would put on makeup. Expectant eyes looked at him.

"No, Sam, I have no children." His voice sounded strained. He had no children, no one at all.

"Why not?" She took another bite. The bread in her hand fell through her fingers and missed the plate. She negotiated it off the table and held it.

"I'm not married." He seized the easy answer. It would be years before she understood the true methods of pregnancy and childbearing. For the time being he could answer her simply. He was aware of Erin listening to their conversation. She had said nothing, but he could feel her presence next to him. From the corner of his eye, he saw her flip her hair over her shoulder. It was no longer in a ponytail, but fell in curls about her shoulders.

"Eddie's mother has Eddie." Sam applied her own brand of logic to his answer.

"Samantha, you know Eddie's mother was married," Erin said.

Sam nodded, her head bouncing up and down in an exaggerated effort. "But she's not married now."

Erin glanced at him unable to dispute a four-year-old's truth.

"Why do you want Mr. Clayton to have a child?"

"Digger," she corrected, her big eyes looking as if Erin had forgotten the covenant the two of them had agreed to.

"Why do you want *Digger* to have a child?"

"So I could play with her."

"Sam, there are plenty of kids for you to play with."

"Not now," she said lifting her plastic cup with two greasy hands and drinking.

Erin gave him a helpless look. Digger picked up his cup and drank, too. *Not now,* he thought. There was nothing he could say.

"We have a lot of toys here." Sam changed the subject with a speed equal to her attention span. She set her cup down with care, showing how she had been taught to place it at the top of her plate, out of danger of being knocked over. Digger watched the small act. He remembered teaching Josh that procedure. A long time ago.

"I have a lot at home too," Sam went on.

"A lot of what?" Digger asked. He'd lost track of what she was talking about.

"Toys," she said without annoyance. "I have a Barbie doll. She has her own car. It's red. But it doesn't look like yours."

"Mine is a truck," Digger said, following her train of thought. "It's silver."

"Do you like silver?" She pronounced it as "filver." "I like yellow."

Erin pushed her chair back and stood up. "It's time to

wash your hands," she told Sam. Sam didn't argue. She let Erin lift her off the books and steady her on the floor. Erin nodded to him as they walked away.

Digger watched them leave the room. He finished two more slices of pizza. She was a cute kid. He smiled at her questions before depression squeezed his heart. Josh had asked the same kind of questions. He hadn't been as old as Sam. He would never be that old. He would never ask Digger about other children or catalog his toys.

Pushing his chair back, Digger cleaned the table, closing the box of leftover slices and disposing of the plates and empty cups. Sam's place was marked by a clean circle ringed with crumbs, tomato sauce and discarded bread. How often had he seen that same ring? Using a napkin, he wiped the ring away, eradicating his thoughts with the swipe of a thin piece of paper.

Turning away from the table, he searched for the bookcases he was here to assemble. Retrieving his toolbox from the place near the door, he went to work. He had accounted for all the parts and laid everything out when he heard Erin and Sam return. He was kneeling, screwing a base and side together with a screw gun when he heard the quick running steps of the child.

"Samantha!" Erin called.

The steps continued without hesitation. Digger looked over his shoulder. He saw her coming.

"No!" he shouted just as Samantha Yvette Pierce rushed toward him without a thought for the danger. He dropped the screwdriver and grabbed the child out of the air as she launched herself toward him. Together they fell backward.

Digger's arms closed around Sam in a protective posture as the two of them skidded across the scuffed, but polished floor. She was a lightweight child, dressed in pink pajamas. Her face scrubbed, her braids swinging. He held onto her for just a minute after the motion stopped, savoring the smell of her hair, the scent of the children's soap Erin had used to bathe her, how light she was as she lay on his chest. Digger squeezed her to him. His eyes closed as he held her, taking in the scent of childhood and the promise of happy times. For just a moment, he thought. He wanted to remember the feel for just another moment. It had been a long time.

A very long time.

Erin ran over and kneeled beside them. "Are you all right?" she asked. Sam pushed herself up and giggled. To her it was a game. Tiny hands pressed against his chest. Erin pulled Sam away.

Digger needed to get up, but he couldn't move. He lay on the floor, fighting the demons in his brain, the emotions in his throat and heart and the need to shout. Erin looked at him with concern. A hollow, weightless cavern replaced the space where the child had lain. He felt as if more than this child had been pulled from him. His heart had been pulled from his chest.

Sweat broke out on his forehead and, for a moment, there were no workable muscles in his body. Erin touched his arm, ran her hand along his exposed flesh.

"Digger?"

He reached over and placed his hand over hers. "I'm fine," he said. But he wasn't. He remembered the accident.

"I'm sorry," Erin apologized. "She's very fast. I had her hand, but she just took off."

Digger sat up. His breath was shallow, and he hoped Erin didn't notice how shaky he was. Sam still smiled at him as if she'd done something wonderful.

"I know how fast they can be." He gave the kid a quirky smile and looked at Erin to let her know he was all right.

He could see the questions in her eyes. There were hundreds of them. He would answer none. Again, she touched his arm, comforting him. The child sat between them. Digger looked at Erin, concern in her eyes. She broke the link between them by looking down at Sam sitting on her knees.

"If we're going to get these cases done, I'll have to put Sam to bed. There are cots in the other room," she explained.

"It's not my bedtime," Sam chirped, her head craning to look at Erin.

Erin smiled and kissed the child's head. "It's close enough. Digger has work to do and by the time you brush your teeth it'll be time."

"Can't I stay and help Digger?"

Erin shook her head. "Digger is used to working alone." She looked up at him, not for confirmation, more for reassurance that her intuition was correct. She could tell he was uncomfortable.

"I'll be gone until she falls asleep," she said.

Digger thanked God she was going to leave him alone. He waited for the two of them to move back before getting to his feet. Erin stood, too. She gave him a searching look then walked away holding Sam's hand.

Sam giggled as she skipped along, looking over her shoulder. "Good night," she called.

"Good night, sweetheart."

They disappeared through a door at the end of the hall. Digger wiped the sweat from his brow on his shirtsleeve. Taking a deep, steadying breath, he leaned over and fought his memories. Then he went to work on the bookcases with greater zeal than he'd planned. Putting the cases together took little mental ability, although he tried to concentrate on flathead screws and fitting part A in part B. Still, the task left his mind free to concentrate on other things.

Erin.

He didn't dare think of Josh, but he couldn't stop his thoughts about the nursery school owner. She'd touched his arm and warmth had flowed through him. The concern in her eyes was real. He was glad she couldn't read his mind—or his feelings.

Easy to assemble furniture was just that—easy. There was

no real reason for him to be here, no reason other than long legs and a ponytail. She wasn't wearing a ponytail tonight. Her hair was down. Soft curls framed her face exactly as he knew they would. This was dangerous ground. The hazard of children—and what he felt happening to him each time he looked at Erin Taylor.

Half an hour later Digger pushed the first completed book-case back and forth to test the wheels. It rolled easily. Then he applied the safety brake that held the non-skid wheels in place.

Erin Taylor took safety seriously. He was glad of that. From what he'd seen, everything in her school was designed to keep kids happy and safe. Padded corners, separate areas for different age groups, they showed her awareness of the potential hazards. He knew it didn't matter how conscientiously anyone prepared, there were times when nothing worked. He had firsthand knowledge of the inability to change events as they happened. Children reversed directions like lightning streaking through the sky. And no adult could anticipate the transformations.

He heard the door open and Erin return. He was glad for the distraction. Her appearance stemmed the whirl of his thoughts, which could only spiral downward.

Erin carried a small toolbox. From his position on the floor he watched her approach. Time and motion slowed until he could examine every moment in detail. Her arms and legs moved in rhythmic contrast to each other, like a model walking down a runway. The sway of her hips tantalized him. The soft bounce of her breasts aroused him. Erin Taylor had no idea what effect she was having. But he was definitely reacting. Cardiac arrest couldn't be more painful than trying to force his body into a state of rest.

Without a word she slid one of the bookcase boxes away from him and opened her toolkit. Digger was watching her and not what he was doing. He banged his finger with the hammer he was using to tap safety covers over screws.

"Ouch," he yelled and gripped his sore finger.

Instantly, Erin was at his side. "Let me see it." Her hands closed over his.

"It's okay," he said, turning away from her. Pain throbbed under his fingernail. He clenched his teeth, holding it back.

She followed him around. "Open your hand," she said quietly, but firmly. She pried his fingers back and inspected his finger. His heartbeat pulsated in his finger, but it wasn't discolored. She raised his hand and lowered her head at the same time. Her lips kissed the sore hand tenderly.

Digger groaned. Pain took a back seat to the rioting emotions that racked his body, starting with his finger. Heat flooded his bloodstream like a shot of a narcotic. His entire body felt the effects of a hot, dizzying blast. The air around him heated, liquefied.

"Why did you do that?" Digger asked, his voice lower than usual, slower than usual.

"I'm sorry. I wasn't thinking."

"Thinking about what?"

She let go of his hand. Hers fluttered about in the air as if she couldn't decide what to do with them. She clasped them together and stared straight at him. "We have minor collisions here all the time. I just reacted the same way I do with the children."

"You kiss their hands?" She looked nervous, her hand pushing through her hair, but he wanted to know she felt something for him.

"A kiss to take the pain away." She gave him a shaky smile. "You'd be surprised how much a kiss can do."

She meant it to be light, but Digger heard the meaning underneath. Without thought he raised his hand, the sore one. He smoothed his knuckles lightly along her jaw. She didn't move, but her small gasp wasn't lost on him. He was holding his own breath. The moment spoke loudly in the quiet room. He leaned forward, his mouth opening. Her hair swung against his hand. It was as soft as a breeze, but it stopped his forward movement. He looked at her face. His gaze settled on her mouth. He wanted that mouth on his. He wanted to devour her. He could smell the heated scent of her, but…he knew better. He knew the road. Knew where it would lead.

Dropping his hand he stepped back, walked away, left her. He went through the door and out into the soft air of the evening.

Erin didn't follow him outside. Instead she completed the last two bookcases alone. While he'd had his hand on her face she couldn't move, couldn't breathe. She needed to collect herself. The chemistry between them was volatile. She knew the fuse to the dynamite was short. If he hadn't left…

When she finally went outside he was gone. His truck was nowhere in the lot or on the street in front of the school. Disappointed, Erin returned to the building.

Digger's tools lay discarded on the floor. Erin packed them up and closed the case. She set it on the porch by the front door, in case he returned over the weekend to retrieve it. She stood there staring at the starry night.

What had happened in there? she asked herself. He'd hurt his finger. Why did she kiss it? She hadn't thought about it. It was a reflexive action, the same thing she would have done for any child. But Digger wasn't a child. And her action took on so much more meaning when he questioned her about it, when she'd held his hand and realized she was shaking. Around them the room had receded. She heard her heartbeat, thudding in her head. She was sure Digger heard it. Then he'd leaned forward, and she knew he was going to kiss her. She wanted him to. She could almost feel his mouth on hers. But he'd stopped.

Erin should be glad he'd found his senses. She obviously hadn't found hers. She couldn't get involved with him, with anyone. It would lead to disaster, and she would be the one hurt. It was best to keep her distance. She was glad he refused to build her addition. She would call Allorca Construction on Monday morning and offer the job to them.

She needed to get the addition built with as little disruption as possible. It was a good thing that Digger left, she reminded herself. It was a good thing that he hadn't kissed her. It was a good thing that she didn't have the memory of his mouth on hers. It was a good thing that, for the rest of her life, she wouldn't carry around the knowledge of what it was like to kiss Digger Clayton.

Chapter Three

The wheels grated against the concrete with each glide of Erin's feet. She roller-bladed regularly, at first to keep in shape and relieve stress, then for the freedom it afforded her. Blading was one of the things she and her best friend Gillian did together. Erin cut through thick, hot air, her arms and legs scissoring. She usually loved skating, reaching that point where her blood was infused and her mind free of thought. She found it hard to reach that point today. Digger was at the forefront of her thoughts and no amount of endorphins could replace him.

Perspiration poured over her face, down her arms and rolled off of her legs. Her sports top was completely soaked, and she could feel a diamond of wetness from the waistband of her shorts to her legs. Her hair, pulled into a ponytail to keep it off her neck, was heavy with wetness.

She pushed on. They had gone their usual route and farther. Erin skated as if she were trying to outrun the devil on a pair of single-cased wheels.

"Erin, stop."

Gillian's voice broke Erin's concentration. She swung around, skating backwards, using the brake on her blades to finally stop.

"I can't go any farther." Gillian's body was shining with perspiration. Her shoulders drooped, and her knees turned inward. She looked done in. Her hair was plastered to her head and sweat poured down her body as if she were melting. Her face, usually a blushing pink, was red with exertion. "I have to rest."

Fatigue settled over Erin like a blanket. She was suddenly so tired she didn't think she could remain standing. Erin looked around for some place shady. She was wearing a baseball cap but needed to get out of the sun. Cobblersville had plenty of open space, parks for kids, grassy areas for picnics and small ponds and lakes. They were out of town, past the city limits and on a road leading to a residential area. There was nothing around except the tree-lined street and open fields.

"We can't just stop," Erin said. She continued to move and Gillian followed her. Erin slowed considerably and skated until her heartbeat was normal. Then she moved onto the grass and the two of them sat down. Resting was a blessed relief.

Gillian pulled her water bottle from the belt around her waist and took a long swallow. Erin did the same. She felt as if every bit of liquid had been squeezed out of her.

"All right," Gillian said, her voice still breathy. "What was that all about?"

"What?"

"What?" Gillian mimicked. "You know what. You haven't skated this hard since Kent Edwards bit the dust. And I'm sure you've extended the quota for that leg." Gillian glanced at Erin's left leg, which had been hurt in an accident years ago. Exercise was good for her, but overdoing it could force her to limp. "So what's happened that's forcing your emotions into your skates?"

"Nothing," she said. They had been friends since Gillian came to Cobblersville six years ago. Both of them fresh out of college and looking for their first jobs. While Cobblersville wasn't a thriving metropolis, Gillian was a nurse and had come to take care of her aunt. She stayed on after her aunt died. Erin had been here all her life.

"This is Gillian." She placed a hand on her breast and cocked her head to the side. "Not some stranger who walked in off the street. Or fell onto the grass from exhaustion."

Erin took another sip of her water. The air was drying her skin. She felt it cooling. She knew it was a short-lived experience. In moments the relentless Texas sun would be baking them.

"There really is nothing to tell."

"You don't work out like that over nothing. So this *nothing* must be a someone, and I'll bet it's a man."

"I don't have time for men."

"You should make time."

"You only say that because you are in a solid relationship. I can remember when you—"

"We're not changing the subject here," she interrupted. "I want to know what happened to you." Gillian paused, but cut in before Erin could speak. "Don't even start with the nothing again. You don't skate like the fires of hell are licking your heels unless something has happened. So tell me who he is."

"He?"

"Yes, *he*."

Erin knew there was no use trying to keep it from Gillian. They had shared every secret since the two of them met.

"It's less than you think."

"Go on," Gillian prompted.

"You want to read romanticism in my actions."

"I admit, I do."

"It's not love, Gillian, just frustration."

"What do you mean?"

"I had a builder come by Friday night."

"What did he look like?"

"What difference does it make what he looked like?" Digger's face and body dressed in tight jeans jumped into her mind.

"If it makes no difference, why didn't you answer the question?" Gillian raised her eyebrows. Sometimes Erin could almost hate her. "What did he look like?"

"It's not his looks. He wouldn't even talk to me. He was like some throwback from the fifties."

"Chauvinistic?"

"No, not that."

"Take charge, unwilling to listen?"

"Kind of…" Her voice trailed off. "He doesn't like kids, doesn't want to be around them. He refused to even hear what I wanted for the building."

Gillian sat up straight. "So get another builder. You have several estimates already, right?"

Erin nodded. "I plan to call one on Monday."

"So why are you upset?" Gillian prompted.

"I'm not upset."

Gillian shifted, pulling herself up on her knees and resting her body on the back of her legs. "Let's start at the beginning. What does he look like?"

Erin didn't have a choice. She described the muscular, broad-shouldered man with sad dark eyes, remembering the wave of heat that went through her when he got close. She told Gillian everything that had happened with Digger, from him showing up at the nursery school Friday afternoon to him leaving in the middle of completing the bookcases last night. She left out the almost kiss and the abrupt manner in which he'd retreated.

"And you're attracted to him." Gillian stated when Erin finished.

Erin thought of denying it. She knew Gillian would see through her lie, but more important she knew it *was* a lie. That was what frustrated her. She was attracted to him, but she knew how men thought. Despite their verbal contention that they didn't want to be tied down by commitment, they wanted the same things women wanted. They wanted marriage, children, family. They wanted stability and offspring. She couldn't offer those.

Her emotions and needs hadn't changed with the accident that robbed her of the ability to produce children. Her emotions weren't removed with her uterus. But she was forced to repress them. And repression was painful.

Digger Clayton freed those emotions, and made her want what she couldn't have.

"Yes," she finally answered. "I am very attracted to him."

The weekend had been miserable. Erin had skated with Gillian both Saturday and Sunday and both times her friend had brought up Digger. While Erin wanted to forget him, he appeared in her consciousness without invitation. She'd relived the time in the nursery school over and over, wondering what he was thinking and why he left without a word. As a result, she had done little, except decide to call Mr. Allorca of Allorca Construction on Monday. At least she'd narrowed her search and could proceed.

Finding a new project was not going to get Digger's almost kiss out of her mind, but on Sunday afternoon she decided to shop for the school. She did it every week, usually on Monday during the children's nap. Shopping today meant she'd stay at the school tomorrow. She had plenty there to keep her busy. She wouldn't be able to think of anything except the children's welfare. She wished she had someone to take care of *now*. Sam was a handful, but she would keep Erin busy if she were here.

Slipping into the van Erin headed out of her driveway toward the local supply store across town. As she pulled on to the highway and moved into the next lane she heard it—a horn blaring. The car came from nowhere—straight for her.

She had no place to go. The shoulder was closed and the entry ramp had run out. As she slammed the brakes, screeching tires sounded in her ears. She fought the wheel for control, turning it right and left in the small amount of space she had. The other vehicle traced a drunken path along the blacktop. She desperately tried to avoid hitting the car. Where it had come from was a moot point, but it was headed directly for her van.

Erin smelled the acrid odor of burning rubber as she passed the closed shoulder and tipped onto the gravel a second before the car connected with her van. Stones pecked the outside of the van as she came to a halt without touching the other vehicle. She took a breath and rested her head on the steering wheel. Shaking, she closed her eyes. Her heart pounded and her legs and arms seemed heavy and rubbery. Her breathing came in short gasps.

Someone appeared at the door, yanking at the handle. The door was locked and didn't budge.

"Are you all right?" a man shouted.

Erin raised her head and sat up. Her hair obscured her face. Pushing it back she turned to the window and looked directly into the eyes of Kent Edwards.

This day couldn't get any worse, she thought and rolled down the window.

As soon as she assured Kent she was fine and that there was no need for an ambulance or the police, Erin pulled away. She got off the highway. She was too shaky to negotiate cars and her jangled emotions at the same time. Stopping, she parked the van along a side road. Her heart pounded, and her hands shook. Memories of the old accident came back to her, the one in which she'd damaged her leg. It wasn't a car accident back then, but the fear of losing her life forced itself through the cracked door of her past. Erin waited until she was calm and rational and able to drive. Naturally a careful driver, she took her time when she started the van again.

What luck, she thought. Bad luck. Of all the people to have a near miss with, why him? The whole thing had rattled her. First Digger, then Kent. She'd been so eager to get away she'd forgotten to ask why he'd swerved into her lane. It was too late now. Erin took a deep, calming breath.

When she'd met him, she'd thought Kent was different. He was good-looking, beautiful almost. He was in real estate, owned his own company and had gotten into the market at just the right time. New companies were moving to Texas and needed facilities with Internet capability and satellite links. He'd made a name for himself and plenty of money.

Erin had met him at a party and fallen head over heels. He'd said all the right words. Wined and dined her in the tradition of Galahad. He'd told her many times how he was not the usual type of guy. He'd even said he didn't want children. He'd been perfect.

Almost.

Erin couldn't have been happier when he asked her to marry him. He'd planned the perfect romantic evening—dinner, wine, soft music—and then the question, along with the appropriate opening of the ring case. She'd said yes and during the course of making plans for a super wedding, the type of wedding he wanted, she heard him mention children.

"Children? I thought you said you didn't want children." Erin and he were in the middle of looking at china patterns. She had been surprised that he was so traditional. Unlike most men, who wouldn't get near a department store, Kent was into all the details of living. She should have seen the clues, but in the blurry midst of wedding fever, she hadn't seen it, hadn't wanted to see it.

"When did I say that?"

"Months ago, when we were talking about the nursery school I want to buy."

"Erin, do you know who else was there?"

She thought a moment, then listed the names of the other people who had been in the small group at the Sullivans' party.

"Amy Sullivan was standing there."

She stared at him. That wasn't an explanation.

"She can't have children."

"So no one is supposed to mention them in her presence? Kent that's silly. Amy Sullivan loves children."

"Of course she does, and I thought it would be less hurtful if I didn't mention wanting them in her presence."

"So you want to have children?"

"Of course I do. I come from a large family. I want three or four kids."

Erin had been sitting. She got up and walked to the window. The sun was shining brightly, the trees were brilliantly green. She'd found the ideal man. Everything should have been perfect, except there were huge menacing clouds obscuring her future. She'd been disillusioned, believing what she heard, wanting to hear it, so much so that she'd never questioned his comment, never brought the subject up. Had she known all along? Hadn't his lifestyle, his interest in the details of a house, the furnishings, china patterns told her he wanted the perfect life, a storybook life, with wife, dog, minivan and 2.2 children?

"Erin, what's wrong? You want to buy a nursery school. Don't you want children of your own?"

He was standing behind her. She could feel his heat soaking into her. At another time she would have stepped back into his arms, inviting his affection. This time she turned to face him and backed away into the small space available to her. She knew what his reaction would be.

She pulled his ring from her finger and handed it to him. He looked at it but didn't take it. "I didn't know. I thought you meant it."

"You're talking in riddles."

"Strange you should say that." She was amazed at how calm she was. "I never said anything in your presence I didn't mean."

"Tell me what you're talking about."

"I can't have children," she announced.

His reaction was as expected, yet this time it hurt her more than anything else ever had. She wanted him to take her in his arms and tell her they could adopt, that having her in his life meant more than having children. There were plenty of children who needed families. But he said none of the words she wanted. She wanted him to be different, to be the man of her dreams. To understand.

He said nothing, his face closed, frozen in a solid mass of surprise, indecision and retreat. He opened his hand, and she dropped the ring in it.

Erin had left him standing in his office and hadn't seen him again until today.

She turned on to East Porter Street. Passing the school, she noticed Digger's toolbox still sitting by the front door. Erin didn't stop. Thoughts of Kent and the accident were replaced with thoughts of Digger. Children seemed to frighten him. He was uncomfortable around them, yet when Sam had launched herself at him he'd held her as if he didn't want to let her go. He'd cradled her in his arms, even smelled her hair. She pulled her mind away from him. She didn't want to carry the case around in her car. She didn't want to touch anything Digger had touched. She needed to keep as far away from him as possible. No matter what he said to the contrary, Digger would be just like Kent—he'd want marriage and all the trappings. She couldn't provide the trappings.

Staying away from him was more than simple self-preservation. A day-care center teacher needed to be careful too. Her personal reputation was tied to the school's. Erin had always wanted to own a nursery school. She loved the children and they were more important to her than anything, including any feelings she might have for Digger Clayton.

Erin parked and concentrated on what she needed in the store, saying the names of products to keep her mind on the task. She usually had a list, but it was lying on her desk at the school, waiting for her Monday routine to begin. She picked up two cases of drink boxes and placed them on the bottom of her cart. She added a box of hot chocolate, and systematically selected the things she needed for the week. Cereal and oatmeal. Little Alice Wise came in every morning asking for cinnamon raisin. It was her favorite—this week.

Erin liked this store. It provided one-stop shopping and was large enough that she wasn't running into neighbors conversing in the aisles. She didn't want to do that today. Kent, the accident and Digger were all she could handle. She grabbed a case of paper towels and added them to her treasure trove.

"Erin."

The voice was deep, dark and paralyzing. Erin went still. She didn't turn or move. Digger was behind her. This wasn't *that* small a town. There were at least 10,000 residents living in Cobblersville, Texas. Prior to a week ago she had never set eyes on Digger Clayton and now she couldn't drive ten miles without running into him.

She turned to face him.

"About Friday night—"

"It was nothing," she said.

He wasn't wearing dirty work clothes or jeans as he had been when he left her last. He had on a suit. In work clothes he was strong and masculine, in a suit he was devastating. His tie hung loosely around his neck. The white shirt, heavily starched, contrasted with his dark coloring and somehow brightened his skin and dark chocolate eyes. Erin couldn't believe how good he looked or how weak her knees felt. She blamed it on her encounter with Kent's car. Maybe she should have taken more time before coming to the store. A few more minutes sitting on that road and she'd have missed Digger altogether.

"I'm sorry. I don't usually act like that with clients."

"I'm not one of your clients."

"I don't usually act like that."

"I'm sure you don't." She wanted to get away from him. There was no need for this conversation. "Why don't we just forget it. Nothing really happened." And that was the problem, she admitted. She had *wanted* something to happen. He had wanted it, too. The fact that it hadn't happened left her frustrated and unable to concentrate. She knew her attraction for him was a bad idea. It could only hurt her in the long run. Yet when he'd bowed his head Friday night and leaned toward her, she could only move toward him, which was exactly what she wanted to do this very minute.

She turned around and grabbed the handrail of her cart. Digger walked to the side. He looked down at the contents she'd chosen.

"Some of the kids don't get a good breakfast," she answered his silent question.

"And you provide it?"

"They need a good meal." She lifted a coloring book. Under it was a puzzle book. "Sam loves these."

Digger stared at them, then looked away as if he were reminded of something, some painful memory. Erin remembered thinking his eyes were sad. She wondered what he'd seen in the items she held.

"What about your addition?" He changed the subject. "Have you hired someone to do it?"

Erin felt relieved and concerned at the same time. She wanted to ask him questions about the books she held, why he avoided looking at them, but she kept quiet on the subject. The addition was a safer topic. The less she knew about Digger Clayton the better. She didn't need to get involved in his life or know what made him happy or sad. She had her own problems, taking on his was more than her thin shoulders could handle. His shoulders were much broader. Let him weather his own problems. The thought was easy, but she found her heart overruling her mind.

"Allorca Construction," she finally answered.

"Allorca?"

She nodded. "They have the best estimate, and the reports I've received are adequate. I plan to call first thing tomorrow morning."

Digger didn't say anything. The look on his face was blank. Erin wondered what he thought. Did he have an opinion on her choice? Did he approve or disapprove of Allorca Construction? She wanted his approval. She wanted to know that this was the right decision. While she was sure of him, especially after seeing the bookcase he'd put together for her, she wanted to know that his construction firm approved of Allorca. But she didn't get that feeling.

"Is he a good contractor?" she asked.

"He does a lot of work around the area."

He hadn't answered her question.

"I'm sure you'll have no problem with him," Digger said flatly.

"Thank you," she said. There didn't seem to be any reason for her to continue talking to him. Friday night he'd built more than a bookcase. He'd erected a wall between them. It was a strange wall. She didn't know him well. She'd had only two encounters with him, one which ended in an almost-kiss. But she felt as if he were an old lover, one with whom she had unfinished business or tons of baggage.

They had nothing in common except the extreme chemistry that drew her to him. She looked him over one more time, taking in his features. He looked great in the suit. She wondered where he had been. Church? To his parents' house for an early dinner? Did he have living parents? What about sisters and brothers? She knew nothing about him, only that he wore no wedding ring. She'd noticed that the first day.

"I should be going. I want to drop this by the school today." He stepped away from her cart. "I noticed your toolbox is still on the step where I left it. I put it out front. I thought you'd return…to get it." She added the last so he wouldn't misinterpret her comment. She had wanted him to return.

"I'll get it on the way home," he told her.

Erin nodded and moved away. She knew he watched her, watched every step she took until she finally turned the corner and moved out of his sight. Only then did she breathe.

Damn, Digger thought to himself as he watched Erin walk away. What was wrong with him? How could she get under his skin without doing a thing? He tried to tell himself he'd overreacted Friday night. It hadn't been that big of a deal. His finger hurt, but he'd banged it much harder in the past. Yet when she held it, touched her mouth to it, he'd lost his reason. Her head had come up, her eyes all liquid, her mouth slightly wet, he could do nothing but touch her. Kiss her. Yet he'd held back. He thought he'd managed to stop before any real damage had been done. But the damage was there nevertheless.

He'd seen Erin walking into the store as he was returning from his sister's. Digger had grown up in foster care. He had no real family, not a blood-connected family, but his foster family had been a happy one. He'd kept in touch with all of his sisters and brothers.

Luanne, his oldest sister, moved to Cobblersville a year ago and reinstituted the Sunday dinner that had been traditional in his foster family when they'd all lived in Houston. Today he'd pleaded a headache and left early. He hadn't had a headache. He was thinking of Erin, Friday night and what her mouth would feel like. He wasn't good company.

On the drive back he'd seen Erin's van pulling into The Warehouse, the place to get any and everything as long as you bought it in large quantities. It was the perfect place for Erin to pick up supplies for her school.

The school. That was another problem. Digger turned toward the exit. She'd chosen Paul Allorca to build the addition. Digger knew the man's work. He'd worked with Allorca when he'd first come to Cobblersville. Allorca's work was adequate, but only adequate and Digger'd had some real run-ins Paul over work that was a little substandard. Eventually, Digger had quit and started his own firm.

Outside, the sun was bright and the day was beautiful. He removed his jacket and hooked it on his finger, then slung it over his shoulder. People moved about him with huge carts of food, clothing and computer supplies as he went toward his car. He hadn't driven his truck today. He rarely worked Sundays unless they were grossly behind schedule. Sundays he spent with his sister or playing basketball with his friends. He'd left home in his sporty Dodge Intrepid. It sat three spaces from Erin's van.

He reached it, opened the door and threw his jacket on the passenger's side but didn't climb into the driver's seat. He stood inside the door, his arms resting on the roof of the car, and looked at the title written on Erin's door. The school and Allorca crowded his mind.

Crossroads Country Day School. Intertwined with the letters were the smiling faces of children. One of them had braids that reminded him of Sam. He couldn't help comparing the boy in blue jeans and a striped shirt to Josh. Digger took a deep breath and closed his eyes. With the heels of his hands, he squeezed the sides of his head. The headache he hadn't had at his sister's was now real. He could feel it as surely as the heat burned the hot, packed earth.

He opened his eyes and squinted at the bright light reflecting off the hoods of parked cars. He didn't know how Allorca worked now, but he was fairly certain their practices were the same as they had been in the past.

The nursery school.

Children.

Suppose one of them got hurt? Josh came to mind. Digger knew what it felt like for a child to get hurt, for a child to die. What if it happened again while the room was being constructed or even afterward? How would he feel? Could he let it happen? On purpose? Could he let her pick this construction company without telling her of the practices Allorca used? Was it his obligation? He hadn't worked for Allorca in years. He had no idea how the company ran today. Maybe a foreman handled the jobs. Maybe her plans weren't complicated. It was a room. Digger knew all there was to know about adding onto an existing building. He also knew if it wasn't jointed correctly it could cause an accident. Or if he used substandard materials. Or watered down cement mixture. There were a hundred things that could go wrong and each of them could cost a child his life.

He moved his hands off the car. The roof had heated up past the point of comfort. The best thing he could do was get in the car and leave.

Digger glanced sideways as he heard a cart approaching. He turned, facing Erin squarely, unsure of what he'd say or do. She stopped behind his car. Her cart was full of the stuff he'd seen in the store and more. The sun was behind her and it turned her loose hair into a reddish halo.

"What's the estimate?" he asked, not intending to do so. She told him without a thought. She didn't ask why he wanted to know, just gave him the number with an expectant look on her face.

"I'll do it," he said.

She nearly smiled. He saw the twitch of her lips going upward before she reigned them in at the last moment. "Are you sure?" she asked.

"I'm positive," he snapped, angry with himself for wanting to save every child in the known universe.

"What changed your mind?"

Digger stared at her, through her, back to another time and place, another life. Then he said one word.

"Josh."

Chapter Four

Two rooms along the back, she'd said. That was all the information Digger had to work with. He walked around the building, checking the sketches he'd drawn and discarded. The school was an interesting building. He wondered who'd built a Victorian puzzle house in Texas. He'd lived on Texas soil all his life, hardly ever left it. Only for his honeymoon when he'd taken Marita to New York and once to Los Angeles after he graduated from high school.

Most of the houses in Cobblersville were ranch-style; sprawling structures that pulled in all the countryside they could. People in Texas loved to spread out. Erin's school was no different. It was huge in both directions, upward and outward, and that gave it a castlelike appearance as it sat alone on the block. Digger had sketched it from memory and tried to add rooms to the rear that would enhance the building and provide functional space for the children.

He needed to talk to Erin. He'd been putting it off for a

week, ever since he'd agreed to construct her addition. He needed to ask her what she wanted, what the space should look like. He hadn't seen her since they spoke in the parking lot of The Warehouse, but she hadn't been away from his mind in all that time.

Digger laid his pencil down. The drawing could be totally wrong for her style or needs. He had to go talk to her. Checking the clock on the office wall he realized the school should be empty now, except, possibly for Sam. Digger smiled at the thought of the little girl. She was impulsive and totally free. Hurling herself into his arms had made him remember how much he missed having a child around.

Digger drove to the school. He parked in front, the same place he'd parked on his initial visit. He got out of his truck and walked to the back, checking his plans against the current structure. He'd built rooms before, added on to houses and businesses, finished basements, remodeled kitchens and bathrooms, but this was the first Victorian and the first school.

He had to keep the look of the place, the puzzling aspect that made him want to smile when he saw it. He was sure parents liked it. It gave the whole place a fun look.

Digger wondered if that had been Erin Taylor's thought when she took over the place. He wondered how many of the renovations had been hers.

"Digger?"

He'd walked around the building and was standing at one of the side doors when he heard Erin's soft voice. He stopped, taking a moment to compose himself before looking up. He knew he wanted to see her. Yet he'd avoided her for a week. He'd worked on her plans and waited until she should have been gone for the night before coming here. Over the past week he'd wondered if he'd react to her the same way he had upon seeing her the first time *and* the last time. Now he knew.

She was standing on a porch, looking at him. There was no smile on her face, nothing he could read in her eyes.

"You look great." The words fell out of his mouth without the benefit of having his brain in gear. She wore a white dress that made her skin look darker. Her hair was swept to one side of her head with curls that dropped down to her shoulder. She wore eye makeup and lipstick the color of red roses. Digger immediately thought of kissing her, taking that red color onto himself and tasting all the wonder beneath it.

"I have a date," she said.

"What?" He hadn't meant to sound as if a date was incredible. She looked incredible, and a jealous streak flashed through him. She was off-limits. He knew that. He'd told himself he didn't want to have a relationship with her or any woman. He'd been anaesthetized after Josh and Marita. The cuts were bandaged over. He wouldn't open them to the air, no matter how beautifully packaged that air came.

"A date," she repeated. "Did you come by to see me?"

"No… Yes." She confused him. He hadn't expected to find her here, but when he did he looked for the ponytail and shorts, instead he found a siren. "I need to talk to you about the addition."

"Now?" She started down the stairs, her hand resting on the wide wooden railing that bisected the stairs.

"I drew some sketches, but after looking at the building, I'm not sure they will work."

"May I see them?" She sat down on the steps and reached for the papers in his hands.

"What about your date?"

"He'll wait."

Digger knew he was fishing for information. He wanted to know who she was going out with. He'd hoped it was a girlfriend, one of the kids' mothers, but her dress didn't say home-cooked meal. It said, dinner and sex. Actually it said, skip dinner. Go straight to sex.

"Digger, can I see them?" She was still holding her hand out for him to pass the rolled up sheets of paper to her. He pulled his thoughts back and handed them over. She quickly unrolled the pages. "These are great," she said. "I like the way you included the trim and gave the room lots of windows."

He sat down next to her, leaning over to view where she pointed. She smelled good, a flowery scent that reminded him of spring sunshine.

"I wasn't sure what you had in mind."

"Maybe we should get together tomorrow, and I'll tell you what I need."

"Tomorrow." He remembered her date and his throat tightened.

"How about dinner?"

"What?" Had he heard her?

"I have to be here all day. I thought we could go over the plans during dinner, but if you're not available…"

"That's not it," he interrupted. He hadn't expected to be invited to dinner. "Where would you like to eat?"

"Since we have the plans…" she looked at the papers. "These are very large pages. Why don't we meet at my house. I can't promise you home cooking, but it won't be pizza."

She smiled, and he knew she was remembering the impromptu dinner they'd shared.

"Where's Sam?"

"She left hours ago."

"She seems like a happy little girl."

"She is," Erin said. She turned to him. She was only inches away. His eyes focused on her mouth. Her tongue came out and licked her lips. His mouth dried. He wanted to wet it, wanted to lean forward and kiss her. For a long while they didn't move. Digger felt as if there was a thin wire between them, holding them in position. Then Erin shifted her gaze to the papers in her hands. She rerolled the plans and handed them back. She stood up, and Digger stood with her.

"I have to go now or I'll be late."

He looked at her admiringly. The dress had only small, pencil-thin straps holding it up. It fit her waist where a wide belt cinched it. Her waist was no bigger than the span of his hands. From the waist the dress hung to her knees in a wide circle. Her legs were bare and her feet were spared the bare ground by a few scraps of leather.

"I think I'll look around a little more. It'll help when I'm working on the plans."

"Do you need to get inside?"

"Not tonight."

She smiled one more time and turned to walk away. She'd only taken three steps before Digger called her name. "Erin?" She turned back. "About the bookcases."

"I finished them," she said.

"I want to apologize." He thought she'd say something but she only waited for him to continue. "My conduct…I mean…I usually don't…" He thought she would stop him. He was uncomfortable and nervous. "It won't happen again."

She nodded quickly and turned again. He watched her walk away. Like the ballet dancer she'd first reminded him of, her movements were balanced and purposeful. He kept watching until she cleared the corner of the building and was no longer within view.

Digger tried to concentrate but his mind kept going to Erin. Who was she dating? Where was she going? It shouldn't matter to him he told himself. He looked at the building, looked at the plans, thought of the crew he would need. And of the children.

The thought accosted him as surely as if it were an intruder. He had to make sure she understood when he talked to her tomorrow night. She had to know that under no circumstances should any of the children ever be allowed near the construction. He'd make sure to set up sturdy fences, not just construction fences, but those designed to keep curiosity seekers, like wide-eyed children, safely out.

* * *

Digger rang the doorbell of Erin Taylor's house on Lefred Street. She lived in one of the oldest neighborhoods in Cobblersville, built in the 1940s when lumber and labor were cheap and plentiful. The wood-framed ranch sprawled in the center of a double lot. It was landscaped with several varieties of cacti and hearty plants that thrived in the desert heat of southwestern Texas.

This is *not* a date, Digger told himself. He wasn't showing up on his girlfriend's porch and sitting nervously in her living room under the scrutiny of her father. This was a business meeting. He was here to talk about work. So why had he changed clothes three times before deciding on khaki slacks and a short-sleeved shirt of pale blue? Digger couldn't remember the last time he'd worried over his wardrobe. He'd brushed his hair and shaved, even put on cologne.

But this was not a date.

It felt like a date. His mouth was dry. His heart was beating fast, and he couldn't wait to see her again. Yep, this felt like a date.

Erin opened the door. Digger had prepared himself to see her, he thought. He'd talked to himself in the mirror, told himself how he would react when she opened the door, how he would act, what he would say and do. The lecture was fruitless, preparation useless. The speech might as well have been delivered about some other person, not the one standing before him with her hair pulled behind her ears and flowing down her back, not the woman with long brown arms extending from a sleeveless orange blouse and the tight-fitting jeans that drew his attention to legs as long as a carpenter's ruler.

"Come in." She gave him a wide smile. Digger said nothing. He crossed the threshold and followed her, watching her dancer's movements. Jerking his gaze away, he examined the way the place was constructed. Sturdy walls with plenty of light and space. The living room was comfortable with two overstuffed sofas, upholstered in a yellow floral print, that faced each other over a large wooden coffee table. "Dinner is almost ready. Why don't you have a seat?" She gestured toward the sofas.

"I brought some wine." He held the bottle up for her inspection, switching the plans he carried to his other hand.

She smiled. He didn't know if she liked wine. She was a nursery-school teacher and as much as her movements could stir a statue, she might be conservative.

"You can open it and pour a couple of glasses," she said.

He followed her into the kitchen. It was large and bright, with pale blue walls. Floral curtains hung at the windows. The pattern matched the cushions on the chairs at the table. The smell of baking bread and cooking meat combined with a slight sweetness and made his mouth water.

She handed him a corkscrew and went through a door that led to a formal, but darkened, dining room. She didn't turn on a light, coming back a moment later carrying two cut-crystal wineglasses.

"I thought you said you couldn't cook." Digger took the glasses and set them on the counter.

"I said don't expect home cooking."

"What is this?" He screwed the opener into the cork.

"This is experimentation. I don't do it often." She smiled.

Digger relaxed. The cork came out of the bottle with a soft pop and he poured the wine into the two glasses. He handed Erin one. She put down the scoop she was using to turn a flat stick of butter into flower rosettes and accepted the glass. Her hand touched his and Digger felt the warmth of her fingers. She looked up then and his eyes caught hers. He couldn't look away, didn't want to look away. He wanted to go on looking at her bright eyes, at her thick mane of hair and the way her blouse moved up and down as she breathed.

Digger inclined his glass and touched hers. The crystal

clinked. The sound broke the tenuous bond that held them in place, although he didn't know how he was going to drink. The look in her eyes had him holding his breath.

Erin took a sip and quickly put the glass on the counter. She turned to the stove and pulled out a tray of bread.

"Is there anything I can do to help?" he asked.

"Grab the salad and put it on the table. It's in the refrigerator." She kept her head down, giving her full attention to the task at hand. Digger had the feeling she'd felt the same connection he had.

She snatched up and quickly dropped the burning hot biscuits into a basket lined with a blue towel. In a few moments she and Digger were seated in the kitchen alcove, the food spread out before them. It was a feast. Except for his sister's on Sundays he never got a meal this abundant.

"Did you always want to be a nursery-school teacher?" he asked, cutting into the half-inch steak that was broiled exactly the way he liked it. She'd said the meal wouldn't be home cooking, but the steak was perfect, the salad fresh and crisp, the bread hot and buttery and the side dish was twice-baked yams instead of the standard white potato.

"I like kids, but I was studying to be a psychologist."

"Why did you switch to teaching?"

"I worked at the school as a teenager." He remembered her telling him that. "When I got out of college I worked part-time there helping out until I could get a real job."

"I take it a real job never came along?"

"Kathryn Hamilton, the former owner, suggested I take some teaching courses at night. I did, and three years ago she had an accident and was forced to close the school. I thought of all those parents who'd have to find immediate placement for their children."

"So you offered to buy it?"

She nodded. "I had no money and I doubted that any bank would give me a loan, but they did and Kathryn accepted the small offer. She has a good heart and knew that the school provided a service that needed to continue."

Erin added more wine to her glass and refilled his. Digger took a bite of the sweet potatoes. He loved them. He normally ate them candied or served as a pie. His foster mother used to make a pudding of them for holiday meals. Erin had baked them, scooped them out of their jackets, added some spices he couldn't identify and put them back into the shells, then baked them a second time. They were delicious.

Digger usually ate on the run, restaurants and take-home meals, grabbing whatever was convenient. He didn't cook for himself, nothing more than bacon and eggs and the occasional spaghetti with store-bought sauce. Once or twice he'd tried his hand at chili, but more often than not he'd change his mind about cooking long before he turned on his range.

"What about you?" Erin's voice brought him back to the table. "How did you get into construction?"

"I never wanted to do anything else." He'd wanted to be an architect. He liked designing and building, seeing his creations come to life in glass and steel. But then— His thoughts were headed toward a closed door that he didn't want opened.

"Nothing else?" Erin asked.

"What?"

"You've wanted to be a carpenter since you were a small child?"

"I built a lot of things with Lego."

She laughed.

"I'm serious," he said. "They were my first real building blocks. I built houses, restaurants and skyscrapers. Once I built the entire downtown area of Dallas. It was six feet high, twenty feet wide and made entirely of Lego."

She raised her fork with a piece of juicy steak on it, but stopped short of her mouth.

"What was it for?"

"There was a new mall opening, and I did it for the exhibition. It drew more crowds than the stores."

"I bet it did. I would take my kids to see something like that. They can relate to Lego. How old were you when you did this?"

"Twelve."

"How long did it take?"

"Three weeks of doing nothing other than going to school and building the city. Bryan Towers, the Hyatt Regency Hotel, the Plaza of the Americas, etc., etc."

Her eyebrows raised in appreciation. "I'd like to have seen that."

"It was in the newspapers, and I have pictures. I'll show them to you sometime."

She ate her meat. Digger realized what he'd said and reminded himself for the tenth time that this was not a date. Even though it had the look and feel of a date, it wasn't. Yet he'd just made it seem as if they would see each other again in some social setting. That wasn't going to happen. He knew better than to let her—or anyone—get under his skin. He was strictly a one-night stand type of guy. He didn't want entanglements. And she represented them all: a big sprawling house, home-cooked meals, children running around. He could see himself in this picture and he couldn't be part of it. He'd tried marriage. It hadn't worked. It had almost killed him with grief when it all fell apart. He couldn't do it again.

"How about some coffee and dessert? Or would you like to finish the wine?" Erin lifted the bottle.

"Coffee." He needed a stimulant not a depressant.

She got up and sliced a cake. He watched her. Her ballet-style movements were rooting themselves in his consciousness.

"Did you ever study dance?"

She stopped and looked at him, holding a slice of cake over a plate. "Why do you ask?"

"You move like a ballet dancer."

"Do you like ballet?" She placed the slice on the cake plate, her eyebrows raised.

Her voice was low and sexy when she asked the question. Digger hated ballet, but he wanted to tell her he liked the way she moved. "I've only seen a couple."

"And you didn't like them?"

"I found the stories hard to follow. But the dancers had nice legs."

She was wearing pants, but she looked down at her own legs. She understood what he meant. "Thank you," she said.

"You're welcome."

"I never studied ballet. The only dancing I do is teaching the children a few line-dance steps. It's fun for them and helps their coordination."

She returned to the table and set the plates down, then poured coffee for two. Digger dug into his cake, giving it his full attention. It was moist and as delicious as the rest of the dinner.

"Your experiment worked," he told her when she sat down again.

She laughed. He liked the sound of it. "I really can't cook," she told him.

"I can tell." He took another bite of the cake with a smile.

Erin's face sobered. "People said very good things about your work." Her eyes turned serious.

"I pay them to say that."

She didn't laugh, but sipped her coffee. "I don't think so. They know I run a school and that I was very concerned about the addition."

"We aim to please."

"You say that lightly, but I know you mean it with all the sincerity of someone who is proud of his craft."

"You got me," he said. He wasn't good at taking compliments. He didn't often work with women. Men didn't compliment, at least not in the same way. They pointed out what they liked, discussing sections of the structure or the uses for the added space. Women talked about the man. Erin's compliments were going places he didn't want them to go. She was approving of him and his past performance, his reputation. Small businesses thrived on a good reputation. Yet from her he felt it was personal. And he'd drawn the line at personal.

"I won't embarrass you any further. Why don't we take the coffee in the other room and go over the plans."

He agreed. The sooner they got to the plans, the better it would be for him. He should get out of this situation, out of a house that was more than furniture and walls. The place had Erin Taylor written on it as surely as if she'd painted her name on the walls. Her serenity was in every room, displayed in the color schemes. Her softness could be felt in the cushiony carpet and the sofas with pillows and stuffing that he could sink into. The pictures on the walls had been chosen with specific care and one table in her living room held the photos of people who had touched her life. Some were children, others adults.

Digger wished they'd met at his office or even in the school, but it was too late. They were here, in her house, where he'd been fed and where he couldn't keep his eyes off her.

Digger met her at the kitchen door and took a tray with a small urn and cups of coffee from her. He could smell her perfume as the tray changed hands. Unconsciously he took in the heat of her body as it transferred to his.

Erin led the way. She went through the living room and opened French doors that led into a small office. There was a large desk and bookcases and a couple of chairs.

"Sit it there." She pointed to the corner of the desk and Digger set the tray down. "I had some ideas for the addition. I sketched them on those papers.

Digger went behind the desk and sat in her chair. He pulled it in, then pushed it back when his feet encountered something on the floor. Reaching down he pulled out a stuffed bear.

"It's Sam's," Erin said reaching for it. "She stays here sometimes."

"Oh?" His brows went up. He shouldn't be surprised. Sam had been at the school with Erin. If he hadn't come by that night, they'd have waited for Sam's parents here. Digger realized he'd conditioned himself not to think of children after seeing them. There was a time when the sight of a three-year-old had caused him physical pain. He'd overcompensated by removing children from his mind.

He remembered Sam. A ball of energy as unpredictable as lightning, she was impossible to forget. He pulled the papers closer to him and began inspecting them. Erin poured coffee in fresh cups and set one near him. She pulled a chair next to him and looked at the pages. The space behind the desk was small and Digger could feel her closeness, smell her scent and wondered how he would concentrate on lines and angles when curves were all he could see.

He thought he was past this, that after Marita left him he was dead to any other woman, but Erin was proving him wrong. Just thinking about her aroused him. Having her this close was slow torture.

"I know these aren't as professional as yours, but I did them to show what I had in mind."

"They're good," he complimented her. "Very good. Normally people don't know what they want. They have no sense of dimension or size. All they know is they want more space." He looked at the three pages she'd drawn. "You've taken the existing building and added a structure that makes sense and stays within the style of the present architecture."

Erin smiled and blushed a little. The office was well lighted, but not as brightly as the kitchen had been. Here she looked warmer, seductive. It could be the wine, he told himself. That could be the reason her face looked flushed and her cheeks were slightly darker than the rest of her skin.

Digger felt more relaxed than he thought he would. He knew she wasn't reacting to him, she was the one who made *him* nervous. Looking at her he saw so much that was forbidden. He could never have what she represented. He'd had his chance at love and family and he'd failed—to the detriment of three people. He wouldn't try to relive it, replace the lost life. It was not replaceable. He'd learned that the hard way.

Erin slid in closer. "The kids like sunlight," she was saying. "They do better on sunny days. I thought adding a room with huge windows would bring the outside in, even when it was cold or rainy."

Digger nodded. She'd reached across him to point out the sides of the drawing where the windows were located. Her arm brushed across his and he clamped his teeth together to keep from sighing at the wave of pleasure that passed through him.

He had to get a grip on himself. This was ridiculous. He didn't know Erin. He hadn't had more than a few conversations with her. He'd known Marita for years before the two of them started dating, before he felt more for her than friendship. With Erin the feeling had been almost instantaneous. He knew he had to fight it for her protection as well as his. There was only heartache at the end of that road.

"I had a problem trying to keep the Victorian look of the outside of the building." She pulled a piece of paper from the bottom. This showed the structure from the outside. It included the proposed addition.

Digger turned toward her. She was close. Closer than he thought. He could see her brown eyes and point out the flecks of dark green that were indistinguishable at a distance. He could smell coffee on her breath and for an instant he wanted to taste it, but not from his cup or hers. He wanted to drink from her. He cleared his throat, hoping it would also clear his mind and said, "You're keeping the puzzle aspect."

"Puzzle?"

"Haven't you noticed it looks like a puzzle?"

He got up and retrieved his rolled up plans from the coffee table. He walked slowly back and forth, giving himself time to get his emotions back in check. Erin lifted the coffee cups out of the way as he spread one of the pages on the top of the desk. "Look at it," he said. "This looks like a huge puzzle piece." He ran his finger over several lines that, when taken together, resembled a jigsaw cut. Then he repeated it several times.

Erin laughed. "I never noticed that."

"You've drawn it perfectly." He pulled her drawing next to the one he'd produced. They were very similar. "Would you like this area here to be larger or more round?" He pointed to the left side of the building, the side on which he'd discovered her standing the night before.

"I don't know."

"I'll show you what I mean." He took a pencil from his pocket and redrew her straight lines into curves.

"Can I afford that?"

"I'm not sure. I have to develop a workable plan and then determine if it's within budget."

"How long will that take?"

"Give me a week."

She nodded.

"May I take these with me?" He indicated her pages.

"Sure." She shrugged.

"I'll combine yours with mine and see if I can come up with something you'll agree to." He began gathering the pages and rerolling them. As he extended his arms she moved back. Digger saw her move out of the corner of his eye. He didn't know if he'd been about to touch her, but the thought made him want to.

He glanced at her. His glance took his attention away from the desk and he knocked over a picture frame. "I'm sorry," he said, grabbing it. He would have put it back, but he glanced at it and noticed Erin. "Is this you?" He pointed at one of the four young women in the picture. They were candidly arranged on the swings in a playground.

She moved behind him. "Those are my sisters and me. That was the day I got the loan and bought the school."

She smiled as if remembering something pleasant.

"Did they come to wish you well?"

She nodded. He felt her head move near his shoulder. He wanted to turn and put his hands in her hair. "Your hair was longer then."

Two of her sisters sat on the swings while she and the fourth one stood on the side of the seats, holding the chains and extending a leg into the air. Like balancing bookends their hair fell in straight panels toward the ground. Wide smiles were on the four similar faces. They looked as if they were having the time of their lives.

"I cut it a few days later. With all I had to do at the school it was easier to manage like this." Instinctively she reached up and smoothed her hair back from her face. Digger watched the gesture. Then he put the photo back. He thought of his sister and the fun they used to have as children. He'd never been part of a biological family. Despite the love of his benevolent and kind foster parents he'd always wondered about his real parents. He would never find out. They'd died in a car accident and the system had taken him.

"Would you like another cup of coffee?" Her voice was soft, tremulous as if she didn't want him to go.

He didn't want to go either. He wanted to stay and drown in those large brown eyes of hers. But he shook his head.

"I better get home. I have a few things to get done and several crews to contact for tomorrow's jobs."

"I understand," she said hurriedly. She stepped back out of his way, distant enough for him to notice the cool air that rushed in, containing none of her body heat.

"You must be tired, too," he said, holding the rolled up plans. "Your date last night," he reminded her when she looked confused. "Staying out late and having to be at work early doesn't leave time for sleep."

"I wasn't out that late," she explained. "Dinner and a play."

"What did you see?" Digger should leave this alone. He didn't know why he pursued it. It was none of his business. His business was concluded. He had her plans, understood what she wanted and why. He even had a budget to work with. Any other time he'd have shaken hands with his client and been on his way.

"A revival of *Cat on a Hot Tin Roof* at the Carver Auditorium. It was very good."

"Carver is in Austin."

"It's only a short drive," she defended. "I'm not tired at all."

Digger stared at her then dropped his eyes and shifted his papers under his arm. He'd heard a double meaning in her words. Was it really there? Was she asking him to stay and visit?

"Have you been to the theater recently?"

He looked up. Could this be an invitation? He shook his head. He was reading too much into innocent words.

"You said you don't like ballet. Does that mean you don't like plays either?"

"I wouldn't say that. I haven't been to the theater in years." He hadn't been since he and Marita split. He hadn't even thought of the theater—or any of the pleasures he used to enjoy. He had a regular crowd that got together for sporting events, going to see the Cowboys play or watching basketball on television. Plays were things you went to with a woman, and Digger had steered clear of women.

"Why is that?"

He shrugged. "Time."

"You do a lot of hard work. Your evenings must be for relaxation."

Anger flashed through him. "The man you went to the theater with, I suppose he doesn't do hard work."

"Oh, yes, he works hard, but he likes the theater and other creative ventures like art galleries and ballet."

That was it, he thought. He wanted to know who she'd been out with and, more than that, he wanted a few minutes alone with him. Digger knew he was in trouble. He was having too violent a reaction to her phantom date. Deciding to cut his losses, and possibly save face, he ended the conversation.

"I hear there's an entire season of seats still available. You might want to tell him."

Digger had seen commercials on late-night television for the remaining summer season. He couldn't remember for which theater, but he was sure Erin's lover of creative ventures could find out.

"I'll see you in a week then?" she asked.

"Or less."

She smiled.

He started for the door with her following him. "Thank you for the dinner," he said. "It was wonderful."

Erin opened the door and he went through it. He stepped down one stair and turned back. She was right in front of him, at eye level.

"There is one thing." He noticed her eyebrow go up. "When my crews start, there are to be no children around the site. Please instruct the teachers to keep them clear of the construction area. We're going to need to bring in digging equipment to clear the area and dig the foundation."

"I promise," she told him. "We'll be invisible."

"You couldn't be invisible if you tried," he answered without thinking. And then he did something stupid.

He ran his hand around her neck and into her hair. He let its thickness wrap around his hand. For a moment neither of them moved, neither of them breathed. Then he leaned forward and kissed her cheek.

Chapter Five

"How was your date?" Gillian asked the moment she opened the door of her four-bedroom ranch. Erin didn't even make it to the foyer before being interrogated.

"I didn't have a date," she said and pushed past her friend. Gillian's older brother Logan lounged in front of the television in the family room.

"Hello, Erin," he yelled, raising his hand with a can of cola in it as she passed on her way to the kitchen. Gillian's kitchen was the center of her home.

"Hi, Logan, what are you doing here on a Saturday night?"

"The big city got to be too much for me. I needed a break."

Logan lived in Austin and visited his sister often. He was tall and lanky and worked as a stockbroker. Gillian had tried to set Erin up with Logan, but the two of them never got any further than affection.

Still, once in a while, they went out. Like last week when he'd taken her to see the play. She and Logan were compatible; they both liked plays and music, but they weren't lovers.

"A break," she said. "I just think you're here to check up on Gillian."

"Not Gillian, darling. I'm here for you."

They both laughed, and Erin continued toward the kitchen.

"So, how was your date?" Gillian wouldn't give up. She placed a glass of orange juice in front of Erin. In the center of the table was a veggie tray with a bowl of dip. Erin popped a carrot in her mouth and chewed.

"It wasn't a date," she repeated.

"It was a business meeting." The sarcasm of Gillian's voice was easily detectable. "Did he kiss you good-night?"

"Gillian!"

"I guess that's a no."

"It is not."

"Then he did kiss you?"

"No…it's none of your business." She was confused. Digger had pressed his mouth to her cheek. Should she call that a kiss?

"Erin, you had a date?" Logan joined them. The program he was watching had gone to a commercial. He pulled a chair out and straddled it.

"Doesn't anybody here think I've ever had a date before?" she asked rhetorically. "And last night wasn't a date."

"I don't see why you don't date every night," Logan said, obviously complimentary.

She smiled at him. "Thank you, Logan."

"So tell me about this business meeting," Logan prompted.

"Tell me if he kissed you," Gillian said.

"That's none of your business."

"Of course it is. We're friends, best friends."

"But some affairs are private."

"So this is an affair?"

"You're twisting my words."

"And you're being evasive."

They glared at each other. Neither of them meant anything by it. They were friends, best friends as Gillian had mentioned, but Erin found it difficult to express how she felt. She didn't want to have these feelings, but like breathing she couldn't control them.

"What's wrong, Erin? Every time a man gets interested in you, barriers go up."

"Gillian, you know what's wrong." Erin's gaze swung between Gillian and Logan. "You know what happens every time I let anyone get close to me."

"We're not all the same, Erin," Logan said. He knew her story and he was one of the few men if not the only man who'd told her it didn't matter and meant it. "It's unfair to generalize."

"Too bad it didn't work with us," she told Logan, trying to lighten the mood. "You're the perfect man."

He took her hand. "Just say the word, and I'll marry you tomorrow."

"And divorce me the day after? No thanks."

They smiled, but Gillian didn't join the play.

"So you think Digger is different?" Erin asked, addressing Gillian. "That he will understand if I tell him I can't have children?"

"He might."

"And he might not."

"How are you going to know if you shut him out?"

"He doesn't like kids. He's only reluctantly doing the addition. I'm committed here. These children are my life. Getting involved with him can only end in heartache."

"He told you that? That he doesn't like kids?"

"Not exactly."

"What exactly?"

"He's told other people."

"How did he act at the school?"

She remembered Sam hurling herself into his arms. How his eyes closed and he hugged her to him, smelling her hair. And the look in his eyes, was that of...what? She didn't know. Hurt? Loneliness?

"Like a man who loves children." She smiled. "At least he likes Sam."

Gillian smiled too. "How could he not? She's a precious little girl."

"How did he act with you?" Logan asked.

She reached across the table for a broccoli bulb to hide the heat that rushed into her face. "He said I moved like a ballet dancer."

"Meaning he was looking at you from the waist down." Logan leaned over and looked her up and down. "Yep," he said again, using his favorite word. "You got good legs, but how could he miss those gorgeous breasts?"

"Logan!" Gillian admonished.

"Must not be a breast man," he continued as if Gillian hadn't spoken. Logan did this all the time. He liked the shock value. Erin didn't let it bother her. Logan was harmless. She liked him, loved him as a brother. With three sisters, Logan filled a void she hadn't known was there until she met him. He was the brother she'd never had and brothers often said things no one else was allowed to even think.

"And the hair," Logan continued. "If he never got as far as your hair, I say drop him and never date him again."

Erin burst into laughter. "I promise, Logan. I won't date him ever. I'll only date you."

Logan stood up. "Now that is a smart woman." He pointed both of his index fingers at her, then went to the refrigerator and got another cola. Holding it in the air like the Olympic torch he headed back to the family room and the television program he'd been watching. "Give him a chance, Erin," Logan threw over his shoulder. "He could be the one."

"How do you feel about him?" Gillian asked when they were alone.

"I've only just met him. I don't have any feelings."

Gillian stared at her, but remained quiet. The silence lengthened.

"Not even anger?"

"Why would I be angry?"

"You were the first time he came to see you."

Erin smiled. She thought of that day in her office when Digger refused her job out of hand. She was tired of explaining her requirements and seeing the expressions on builders' faces when she showed them her amateur plans. Then he walked in, James "Digger" Clayton. She hadn't expected the impact he'd had on her senses. He frightened her, and she was unprepared for his refusal.

"Erin…"

She looked up at Gillian. They had no secrets. Gillian was the only person she could completely trust. "He did kiss me," she said.

"What?"

"On the cheek. It didn't mean anything." She could still feel his hand sliding through her hair and the pressure of it pulling her forward before his lips touched her.

"Of course, it did," Gillian insisted.

"No, it didn't. And it's not going any further. We have a business relationship."

"He had dinner at your house. You baked a chocolate cake, for heaven's sake. We only share chocolate with people we want to impress."

"I did want to impress him…so he'd do a good job."

"Erin, why are you lying to me? And why are you lying to yourself?"

Erin closed her hands around the juice glass. The moment passed. Then she told her. "I'm scared, Gillian."

Her friend's expression sobered. "Of what?"

"Going through it all again. I hate it, Gillian. It wasn't my fault. I didn't have the accident on purpose. I didn't ask for the hysterectomy. But I've accepted it. There is nothing I can do about it, except steer clear of men."

"Erin, that's not the solution. It's unhealthy to go through life pretending there is not a man on the planet for you."

Erin blinked. She didn't like being alone. Her parents had been married for thirty-eight years. Her three sisters were all married with children and ecstatically happy. She was the only one unmarried and with no prospects. But Digger? Should she trust her feelings to him? Should she accept his glances, give in to her own, let him know that she wanted to take that kiss on the cheek and turn it into something else?

She wasn't sure. She'd hidden behind her condition for so long that it felt natural to repulse anyone's advances in order to protect herself. But she knew Digger had somehow already passed the safety zone.

When Erin arrived at the school two Mondays later the construction crew was there and working. The parking lot was completely blocked off and a heavy fence had been anchored into the ground. It surrounded the parking lot and a section at the rear of the building where the addition would replace part of the schoolyard. Backhoes and bulldozers stood in the space where she usually parked. Red dust and clay were attached to them like customized parts.

A crewman came up to her as soon as she got out of her van.

"You Ms. Taylor?" he asked.

She nodded.

"Jackson Wright, the foreman." He introduced himself and offered her his hand. Erin took it. It was calloused and large, reminding her of Digger's hand. It had been rough, but it sent tremors running through her.

"Where's Digger?" she asked, checking for him over the

massive shoulders of Foreman Wright, hoping to see him coming toward her.

"He's with another crew."

She was disappointed, but tried to keep it off her face.

"He wanted me to remind you about the children."

"I've spoken to the staff. We'll keep them away from the area."

He nodded. "Thank you. We set up a path for you." He moved back to indicate the new pathway the children should take. "I'm sorry about your parking lot."

Her mouth curved in understanding. Touching his hard hat he left her. Erin had known Digger's crew would start work today. She'd looked forward to seeing him. He'd come by the school briefly last week to show her the plans and get her approval. He'd taken her plans and added to them, giving her more than she'd asked for. He'd improved her straight lines with a few curves that provided more space for the children. Additionally, he'd drawn plans for the interior space with classrooms and built-in bookcases.

She'd been glad to sign off on them, but in doing so she'd eliminated any reason for them to see each other. She'd hoped he'd be here this morning. She'd planned to offer him coffee, maybe share it with him before he got started. But her plans were waylaid. He wasn't here.

She shouldn't have let Gillian talk her into giving Digger a chance. She couldn't risk her heart only to discover that a man who said he didn't like kids, really didn't like *other* people's kids, but wanted his own. She'd seen that happen. Parents who disapproved of everyone else thought their own offspring were darlings. Digger could be the same.

When he'd come to have her sign the papers for the addition he wouldn't even accept a drink. Thinking back over it, she remembered he was in a hurry to leave. Had their previous encounter put him off? Did he feel sorry that he'd kissed her? She was sure he did. There was no reason for it. They were having a business meeting, not a date.

It was good she decided, unlocking the front door, that he wasn't here. She needed to keep to her convictions. There was no place in her life for him. She had the school, and it took up all of her time. There was no need to bring anyone else into her life.

She went to her office, turning on the school lights as she went. She put down her purse and turned on soft music that filtered through the school. She liked to play it during the morning arrival period. The kids came in, some of them happy, some with tears in their eyes. Some had traumatic separations, every day.

Today the music was more for herself than the children. Thoughts of Digger were on her mind and her own decisions didn't help reinforce her confidence. They should have. They had in the past. But not today.

"Ms. Taylor."

She heard her name called in a high-pitched voice and knew Sam had arrived. Leaving the office, she caught the running bundle of joy and swung her around.

"Good morning," Erin said. "How are you today?"

"Fine," she said.

Erin looked at Sam's mother, an older version of the little girl. But Sam got her hair from her dad. Her mother's hair was long and straight, but her dad's was thick and vibrant like the little girl's.

"Good morning, Claudia."

"Hi," she said. "These are Sam's things." She held up a small pink suitcase. Erin put Sam down and took the suitcase.

"Why don't you go put your lunch away," Erin told the child, who immediately rushed away.

"We'll pick her up tomorrow after school," Claudia said.

"No problem," Erin told her. "We're going to make cookies tonight." Sam's parents had to go out of town for the day and would be back very late. Sam would stay with Erin overnight, and Erin looked forward to it. The child kept her busy. She was a nonstop chatterbox who asked questions all the time and loved to help Erin with everything. Sam especially loved to help bake. She made a mess, but Erin didn't mind.

"We'll see you tomorrow," Erin said. "Have a good trip and say hello to George."

"He's waiting in the car. There wasn't much room to park."

"I'm sorry. The construction will disrupt things for a while."

"Don't worry about it. The kids will love watching the builders."

Erin remembered Digger's warning. The kids had to be kept away from the danger of the site. Though they would be curious. Maybe she could get Digger to come in and explain to them what was going on. She'd call him and ask.

Sam came running back. "Give mommy a kiss, Sam." Samantha kissed her mother dutifully, then hugged her tightly. The two separated and Sam, holding onto Erin's hand, waved as her mother left.

"What are we going to do now?" the little girl asked. She was earlier than usual. The other teachers were due in forty minutes and the kids in an hour.

"How about we make some coffee for the men outside."

"Okay," she said. "But I can't carry any hot water." She shook her head from side to side in exaggerated slowness.

Erin smiled.

The day had been rough. Two teachers had called in sick and Erin had to combine their classes. Everyone appeared to be on a sugar high even though the parents brought healthy snacks and the amount of sugar was kept to a minimum. Erin seemed to run all day.

The noise outside and the new fence had the children's attention. They gravitated toward it as if it were a magnet. Erin was glad to close the doors and turn out the lights when the workday ended. She limped out of the building. Her hip was telling her the strain her day had caused. A beneficiary of the accident that had resulted in her hysterectomy was that her hip was pinned. When her days were especially grueling the limp that doctors said would be with her for the rest of her life reminded her.

She had worked hard at walking without it, spending hours in physical therapy and refusing to give in to the pressure to quit. She would prove the doctors wrong. She wouldn't walk with a limp. And if she didn't overdo it she could almost forget the limp was a part of her life. She would never ski or run a marathon, but she could live a day-to-day life, exercise in moderation and no one would have to know about the infirmity.

All day long she'd thought of Digger, looked for him during the controlled recess periods the kids had in the reduced play yard. He hadn't shown up at all. She should stop thinking of him. He wasn't her type. And the way she felt leaving tonight she didn't want to see him.

He wasn't interested in her anyway. If he was he would have come today. He wouldn't have been so quick to leave last time and the kiss on her cheek would have meant something, or at least have been the prelude to something.

Erin mentally shook herself. She didn't understand why she had such a strong attraction to Digger Clayton, but it had to stop right now. She'd told herself all the reasons a relationship with him wouldn't work. They were all good reasons. She had to put him out of her mind and go on with the important things in life.

"Put in now?" When Erin looked up Sam held the sifter full of flour precariously over a bowl. It was overflowing. The child's hands were covered in white, and she was ready to turn the handle.

"It's too full, honey. You need room for the flour to move."

Erin took the sifter and used a tablespoon to reduce the load to a manageable size for a four-year-old.

"Now?" she asked reaching for it.

"Now." Erin gave it back to her. The kitchen had a fine dusting of flour on the counter and a splattered pattern on the floor around Sam's step stool. The television played a videotape of *The Lion King*. It was Sam's favorite and she had insisted on bringing it into the kitchen when they'd started the cookies, although neither of them looked at it now.

The two had rested for a moment after dinner. Erin had taken a pain killer for her hip, but wished she could have come home, settled into a hot bubble bath and gone to bed early. Instead she and Sam were making cookies.

Sam turned the handle on the sifter slowly at first and the flour dropped like a powder into the stainless steel bowl. The room was pleasantly warm and smelled of cookie ingredients.

"Milk." Erin filled a measuring cup and transferred it from her large hands to the smaller ones of the child. Sam caught her lower lip between her teeth, the way she did when she concentrated. She poured the milk as if it were nitroglycerin and could explode at any moment.

Erin fed Sam the ingredients for chocolate chip cookies one by one, and Sam put them in the bowl, stirring until it got too hard. Then Erin showed her how to knead the dough into balls, and they broke off pieces and put them on the cookie sheets.

Two sheets went into the oven.

"We can eat all them tonight."

Erin laughed. "No, we cannot eat them all tonight. If we did that, we'd both have a tummy ache."

"I wouldn't," Sam said with confidence.

"I thought we'd take some of them to school tomorrow."

She cocked her head to the side then agreed. "Okay. I can give them out."

"I think we can arrange that."

They had just finished the third cookie sheet when the

doorbell rang. Erin looked up, and her heart started to pound. She wasn't expecting anyone. Gillian was on duty at the hospital and her other friends usually called if they were planning to come by.

The only other person who could possibly come was Digger. She wiped her hands and wondered what her hair looked like. Sam went running to the door. She wouldn't open it. Her parents had taught her not to do that. She looked through the side windows.

"Digger," she said excitedly and jumped up and down as if her best friend in all the world was standing on the doorstep. Erin's heart pounded harder. Sam looked over her shoulder to Erin whose hip faltered. She limped more when Sam spoke his name. "It's Digger. Digger's here," the little girl said as if Erin had failed to hear her the first time.

Erin opened the door. She tried to smile. She wanted to see him, but it frightened her that he'd come. Sam jumped into his arms.

"Hi," she said. "Making cookies in the kitchen. Want to help us?"

"Sam, you're getting flour all over him." Erin reached for the child, but Digger stopped her.

"She's all right. Flour washes out."

Erin stepped back and let him come into the room. She closed the door. They looked at each other for a moment. Then Sam remembered the batch in the oven.

"We have to look at the cookies," she said. Sam squirmed to the floor and took off for the kitchen at a run. Erin tried to rush, forgetting her leg in the wake of Digger's appearance. It was quick to remind her.

In the kitchen Sam stared through the glass door. Erin maneuvered slowly to conceal her infirmity.

"I think they're cooked," she told Erin.

She was right. Erin lifted the trays from the oven one at a time and placed them on the counter.

Sam peered over the counter, her nose parallel with the cookie sheet. Digger's hands curled around Sam's shoulders and pulled her back, out of harm's way. The little girl looked up at him.

"Would you like to help?" she asked in a rare case of completing a full sentence.

"Sam," Erin interrupted before Digger could say anything. "I'm sure Mr. Clayton didn't come by to make cookies."

"He's Digger," she corrected.

Erin remembered Digger giving Sam permission to use the nickname. She smiled at the child. "He's still here for something other than cookies."

"Oh, I'd like a cookie." He smiled at Sam as if the two of them had conspired against Erin. "I'd like that big one over there." He pointed to an odd-shaped cookie that resembled a small hand.

"Mine," she announced. "You can have it."

"Yours?" He feigned surprise, his eyebrows raising and his eyes opening wide. Erin felt a tremor run through her at the playfulness of the situation. "I can't eat yours. I'll take this one." He pointed again. Sam's smile covered her entire face.

"Ms. Taylor made that one."

Digger turned to face her. Erin met his eyes over the little girl's head. Sensation power-washed into her bloodstream. For a moment she held his gaze, then turned and scooped the cookie he'd identified as his onto a spatula. She transferred it to a saucer and handed it to him.

"Can I have mine?" Sam chimed in.

Erin put the big one on a small plate and took it to the table. She added a glass of milk. Every step she took was painful, but she refused to limp. She'd pay for the action later, but for too many years she'd seen the pity in too many eyes. If she rested she'd be fine. There was no need to reveal her secret.

"Was there something you wanted?" she asked Digger while the little girl ate. She moved the rest of the cookies to a rack and placed the sheet they had been working on into the oven.

Digger sat on a stool at the counter in front of her. He looked comfortable, as if he belonged there. The whole scene jelled in her mind. A flash so sudden she couldn't stop it. A perfect family, herself and Digger and a little girl. All of them sitting around the kitchen making cookies. The pain in her side dispelled the image. Erin nearly cried out the pain was so sharp. She pulled a stool up and rested on it, taking her weight off the floor and easing the discomfort.

"I came about the new rooms." Digger interrupted her thoughts and her pain.

Erin hesitated, waiting until she had her voice under control. She was thankful she had something to do to camouflage what had to be visible on her face. "Is something wrong with them?"

"Nothing upsetting. I just forgot to let you know about the fencing and the new entry areas."

"Your foreman explained it."

"I know it's an inconvenience."

"We'll adjust," she told him. "No one complained."

"Good," he said, taking a bite of his cookie.

"Would you like coffee?"

"Milk would be fine." He nodded toward the container. "These are very good."

"They were Sam's idea." Both of them glanced at the child who was absorbed by the television.

"They're my favorite," she said, pulling the last word out to show her love of chocolate chip cookies.

"While you're here I'd like to ask you something."

He raised an eyebrow.

"The kids were very curious today. We could hardly keep control of them with the construction going on." He stiffened. She noticed it and quickly added, "We kept them away from any hazards." He relaxed a little, but Erin felt as if that hadn't been the reason for his uneasiness. "I wondered if you would come by one day, when you're not busy, and give a class about how you add on to a building."

He said nothing, and it unnerved Erin. She picked up part of the cookie dough and rolled it into a small ball, placing it on one of the empty sheets. She continued this, making three more cookie balls. She couldn't stand the silence any longer.

"I know you're busy," she went on, saving him from having to refuse her. "It was just a thought. The kids have short attention spans, and they probably wouldn't understand…."

"It's not that," he said.

"I'm finished," Sam announced at the same time. "Can I have another one?"

"May I," Erin corrected her. Then she placed a second cookie on her plate. "No more tonight," she told her. "It'll be time to go to bed soon."

Erin returned to her task, looking at Digger who appeared to want to say something.

"What?" she asked.

He shook his head.

"So you came here to apologize for the fence and the walkway." She looked at him, but expected no answer. "You could have called and told me that. And Mr. Wright already apologized for you."

He dropped his eyes and lifted the glass of milk.

"But I'm glad you came by." He looked up then. Sam finished her milk and cookies and came over with the plate and glass. Erin placed them in the sink and used a napkin to wipe away Sam's milk mustache. The little girl went to Digger and stood next to his stool. She looked up at him. Erin knew what she wanted. She wasn't sure Digger did. But he seemed to get the message. He leaned over and lifted her into his lap.

Erin put another tray into the oven and took one out. The cookies smelled delicious. Tomorrow the kids would love getting a cookie as a snack. She hadn't forgotten today's display of chaos, but tomorrow she'd have a full staff to help control the excited kids.

"Digger, dig?" Sam seemed to have found something more interesting than the cookies.

"Sometimes," he answered.

"That your real name?" She changed the subject with the usual speed of a child's mind.

"My real name is Samantha Yvette Pierce, sometimes called Sy for short," he mimicked her. Erin recognized Sam's introductory speech. She must have said it to Digger at some point. The child's giggle was high and happy.

"Not your name." She pointed to herself. "My name."

"My real name is James Clayton."

He tickled her, and Sam's light voice filled the room. The two of them looked great together. Digger might say he didn't like kids, but his actions didn't confirm it. Sam could wiggle into anyone's heart. If James Clayton didn't want children around him he would have left right after he apologized. He'd fulfilled his reason for being here. Yet he'd stayed for cookies and still remained in her kitchen.

Erin didn't want him to leave. She should. His playing with Sam told Erin that she and Digger could have no relationship. *Give him a chance.* Both Gillian and Logan had told her that. She didn't think it was a good idea. So why was he here and why was she letting him stay? It was past time for Sam's bath. Erin had plenty of excuses to get him out of her house and she hadn't used any of them. She was thinking of his leaving the last time, when he'd kissed her.

Her knees went weak, and she turned away from the man and child and opened the oven door. The heat blasted her face contributing to the warmth that had already invaded her body.

The last batch went into the oven. The sink was full of trays and bowls. As Erin placed the cooled cookies in plastic containers for tomorrow, she broke one.

"Can I have it?" Sam asked. Then remembering she repeated, "May I have it?" And reached up.

"May I have it?" Digger asked. Both of them looked at her.

She handed half of the cookie to Sam. "You'll have to brush your teeth after this and get ready for bed."

The other half she gave to Digger. She said nothing to him, but the look in his eyes had her thinking she should repeat the phrase she'd just given to Sam, with innuendo.

Giving herself something to do, Erin turned back to the oven and removed the final tray. "I'll have to put her to bed," she told Digger as she transferred the cookies to the cooling rack.

Instead of saying good-night as she expected he nodded and set Sam on the floor. After a moment's hesitation, Erin took Sam's hand and led her away.

"Good night, James Clayton," the little girl called. She had a churlish smile on her face, although the words came out more like Ames Kaytin than Digger's real name. With time her pronunciation would improve. "See you in morning."

"Good night, Samantha."

Sam giggled as she skipped away. While Erin watched Sam brush her teeth she wondered about Digger remaining in the kitchen. Why was he really here? Why didn't he come to the school today with the crew? And why was her blood racing through her body just knowing he was a few steps away from her?

Sam chatted away in her own form of broken English while she played in the bathwater and put on her nightgown. She seemed fixated on Digger and kept asking questions about him. Erin answered her absently until one question caught her off guard.

"You and Digger could have a baby and I could play with her." Erin went still as Sam continued. "I'd be careful. I wouldn't drop her."

She looked so serious. "Sam, I explained about that."

Sam yawned as if she'd already dropped the subject. She dropped off to sleep almost the moment she closed her eyes. Erin left her to return to Digger.

She found him pulling the sleeves of his shirt down. The kitchen was clean. All the pans had been washed or placed in the dishwasher. The cooled cookies were in the plastic containers and properly sealed. The flour that had been on the counters and floor had been cleaned away.

"My foster mom taught me to clean up, even if she didn't teach me to cook," he explained.

"Thank you," Erin said incredulously. "I didn't expect anything like this." She spread her arms. "I'm impressed."

"I know you clean up at the school. I thought I'd help out here."

"Thanks. Sometimes after a long day I'm too tired to cook and clean."

"The kids seem really happy there and the teachers that I met."

"They are a good mix."

"And you like it?"

Erin nodded. She'd loved children all her life. "It's the power," she said.

"Power?"

"You'd be surprised what a look can do." She raised one eyebrow and showed him her menacing look. He laughed. "And peanut butter on crackers is a delicacy. The kids love it."

"Sam's a nice kid," he said.

"She is, and she's taken to you."

Erin went toward the door and he followed her. She switched off the light. The room was plunged into darkness and he was directly behind her. It was automatic for her to turn off the light. She was usually alone. Tonight the act turned the space between her kitchen and family room into an intimate setting. She should have smelled the lingering scent of sugar or the flour that had blanketed the air and coated the floor. But what her nostrils took in was Digger's cologne.

He was close behind her. All she had to do was turn around and he'd walk into her. She'd be in his arms.

Where she wanted to be?

She asked herself the question. There was chemistry between them. She'd known it from the first, when he'd come by to show her the plans. Each time he got near her lightning bolts shot through her veins. There was definitely something guiding her, urging her to let this happen. Only she was afraid.

Instead of turning toward him, she went into the family room. She and Sam had been in there before going to make the cookies. Her toys were all over the floor. Erin thought she should have taken Digger to the living room, but it was too late to change her mind.

"Have a seat," she said. She bent over and started picking up the toys. Digger reached down and helped her.

"Where do they go?" he asked.

Erin lifted the lid of a window seat and they dumped their treasures out of sight.

"Do you want to tell me why you really came by tonight?" Erin knew there had to be more to it than just that he'd forgotten to tell her about the fence and the path. "Is there something that has to be done which we didn't talk about? Something outside the contract that needs to be added?"

She sat down on the sofa, and he sat across from her in a wingbacked chair.

"Has that happened to you before?"

She nodded. "Although no one who recommended you said anything like that."

"That's not it. The contract is fine. The job will be done with the current agreement. There is nothing to add that we didn't talk about."

"So we're back to question A. Why are you here?"

He stared at her. "I wanted to see you."

He'd said it. He hadn't intended to speak. When he left home tonight after his shower, he thought he'd drop by, give her the apology and be done with it. Yet the situation looked so homey, the cookies smelled sweet in the air and she looked adorable. He just wanted to sit there and stare at her. Sam provided him with the opportunity.

"I wanted to ask you if there was anything about the site that hurt the children?" He hoped he covered himself with that.

"Hurt the children?"

"Like too much dust. Often we use water on big projects to keep the dust down."

"We didn't notice anything in particular. Probably as time goes by."

This was getting worse, Digger thought. Why didn't he just leave? There was no reason for him to stay. Something was poking into his back. He should take it as a signal to leave. Reaching behind him and between the cushions he pulled out a rag doll.

"Sam must stay here often." He held the toy in both hands, remembering the stuffed animal he'd found under the desk in her office the first time he'd been there.

Erin smiled. His heart fluttered. "A couple of times a month. I don't mind."

"You like kids?"

"I could hardly say no to that. I run a nursery school."

"I withdraw the question."

"I love children. They're so innocent and open. What about you?"

"In my business I don't come into contact with them often."

"I'm not talking about business. Don't you want to marry and have children?"

He hesitated. Why had he started this conversation? He didn't want to talk about marriage or children. After Marita and Josh he knew nothing would ever replace what he'd had.

"I don't think I'm the marrying kind," he said.

"That sounds like someone who's been destroyed in a relationship."

He hadn't expected her to be this perceptive. She worked with children all day, but he remembered she'd trained in psychology. Digger looked at his hands. He was still holding the rag doll. He put it down and stood. "I'd better leave. We both have to be up early in the morning."

Erin looked at the clock on the wall. It was a little after nine. Still early by his standards, but he didn't know her schedule. And he felt as if he were only treading water being with her.

She stood and walked with him to the door. She didn't open it tonight as she'd done the previous time he'd been here. Digger turned to her.

"You're limping."

"It's nothing." She tried to move normally, but he saw the effort it took and the pain on her face.

"You're in pain."

"Digger, I'm fine."

"Sit down," he told her. She stared at him for a moment, but didn't argue. "What happened?"

She stared straight at him. "I told you it's nothing. I just had a hard day."

"What do you mean a hard day?"

"I had an accident a long time ago. Every now and then my leg reminds me."

"What happened?"

"I don't want to go into it."

He didn't push her. He had his own secrets. "Can I get you anything, aspirin?"

"I've already taken a pain pill."

"It hasn't worked," he stated. When she said nothing he stood up. "Lie down," he said.

She stretched out on the sofa. Pain was etched on her features. Digger wanted to ease it. He dropped to his knees and took her hands. Their eyes met. Digger wanted to hold her, but he knew better. He didn't ask her to lie down to seduce her. He raised her hands to her face and dropped them, rubbing his knuckles against her cheek.

"Close your eyes," he said. Her lids fluttered down. She was lying with her back against the back of the sofa. Digger reached for the side she'd favored when she walked. She jumped slightly as his hands touched her. "Shhh," he quieted her and massaged her hip, his thumbs drawing small circles on the outside of her clothes. He widened the circles, feeling the warmth of her and hoping the heat of his hands was penetrating her skin and relaxing the muscles that forced her to limp.

She moaned slightly and Digger recognized the sound as pleasure, not pain. He switched the circles to a straight line, holding the waist of her jeans as he smoothed the surface from her hip to her thigh. This massage would be better with hot oil and minus the clothes, but he wasn't sure he could manage to maintain his dignity if nothing separated them except a long towel. He continued stroking her, changing directions and coaxing her muscles into submission. She relaxed under his hands. He felt her body soften and heard the low, throaty sound that had no name, but meant she was being helped, meant that she was trusting him.

Digger was trusted by his crews. He was trusted by his family and, once, he'd been trusted by his wife. It had been a long time since a woman had trusted him this way. It surprised him that it seemed important, that he needed that. He hadn't known it.

He glanced at Erin. She'd fallen asleep. Sleep was good. It was healing. He wondered what she had done today that made her tired. He wondered what had happened to her hip. She didn't want to tell him about it. But she did trust him.

Digger considered leaving her where she lay. She was comfortable and if Sam hadn't been in the house he might have done so. But Sam was down the hall, out of earshot, away from where Erin slept. He looked at the dark hallway and back at the sleeping figure. Digger stooped down and slipped his hands under Erin. She rolled toward him, toward his warmth. She smelled good, her perfume heated by her skin and forcing him to remember he wasn't here for seduction.

Erin opened her eyes, but they didn't focus. She put her arms around his neck and he lifted her into his arms. For a moment he stood holding her as if she were a child in need of comforting, while he was the one taking the comfort. It had been a long time since he'd held a woman in his arms. He cradled her to him, her head on his shoulder, her hair tickling his nose, her mouth only a few inches from his.

Digger finally moved. He carried her toward the bedrooms, where Sam slept silently. A night-light pointed the way to Sam. The door was open and Digger could see the foot of her bed and the small form under the covers. The house had three bedrooms and the first one he checked was a guest room. He found Erin's bedroom and entered the large space appointed in various shades of blue.

Lowering Erin to the floor he held her against him while he pulled back the comforter and sheet. He set her on the bed and lay her against the pillows. She wore no shoes. He put her legs under the covers and loosened the snap on her jeans before pulling the covers up to her chin. Then he ran his hand down her hair before he left the room.

He checked Sam. She slept the worry-free innocence of childhood. The two were fine. Digger went down the hall checking that everything was in order. He went to the kitchen making sure the stove was off even though he'd already checked it once before. The back door was locked and the windows were closed. The room was cooled by the air system, which appeared in perfect order.

Digger went through the front door, making sure it locked behind him and got into his truck. He turned the key in the ignition and backed down the driveway. His lights swung across the house as he turned onto the street and drove away.

For the first time in four years Digger wished there was someone waiting for him at home.

Chapter Six

Erin's internal clock woke her with a start. It was dark, and she was in her bedroom, in her bed, not where she went to sleep. She was fully dressed, too. Except for her shoes.

Digger must have carried her to bed. She lay back down, her lips curving in a pleased smile, her body warming to the thought. She didn't remember it. She pushed her hair back and listened for any sign that Digger was still in the house. She was usually a light sleeper, waking at the slightest noise. The last thing she remembered was lying on the sofa.

And Digger's hands.

She closed her eyes as delicious sensations washed over her at the memory of his hands stroking her leg. She'd only meant to rest her eyes when she closed them. It had to have been the grueling day tiring her out and the throbbing pain in her hip that made her relax under his hands. She'd lost herself in the dark room and the healing effect of the massage and fallen asleep.

Where was he, she wondered? Was he in the other room on the sofa? Or had he left? Erin slipped out of bed. Her slippers were still in the closet. She reached for the light next to the bed. The clock said five-thirty. The sun wouldn't tinge the horizon for another half hour. She padded to the hallway without shoes. Sam slept silently in her bed. She wouldn't need to wake up for a while.

Erin went to the family room. She'd walked these halls too often to need light to show her the way. The sofa was empty. Her shoulders, along with her heart, sank in disappointment. Had she really wanted Digger to be there? Asleep on her sofa? She was a nursery-school teacher and presently charged with the care of a small child. His presence would be outside of propriety, even in this day and age.

The kitchen was as she had left it. The sink clean, the dishes washed and put away, all vestiges of last night preserved only in her memory.

Erin put on coffee and began her morning ritual. She thought she would see Digger later today at the school.

But she didn't.

She looked for him all day, constantly checking what was going on in the yard, expecting to see his strong body among the many muscle-bound men. At ten o'clock she'd taken coffee out to the workers and casually asked Jackson Wright, the foreman, if Digger was due.

"He's usually around at the start of a job, but he's got a restoration over in Brentwood and they keep finding things that aren't in the plan." The big man laughed. "Digger loves making over old houses." He looked up at the Victorian. "I'm sure he'll get here soon."

He hadn't arrived by closing. Erin walked through the empty school. The other teachers had put the toys back in the bins. The place was clean, even the floors had been swept and the temporary cots stored.

Erin rested her feet on the desk and her head against the

back of her chair. It was after closing and the place was quiet, although in Erin's mind, the echo of shrilled voices never really left the place. The workmen had gone, and there was nothing outside but the setting sun and a gaping hole in the ground.

She should go home.

When the knock came on the door Erin jumped. She rushed toward it, thinking it might be Digger. She was hoping it was him. But she saw Gillian through the glass panel.

"What are you doing here?" Erin asked, pulling the door inward.

"I saw the van as I passed." They walked back into Erin's office. "Thought I'd stop and see how the addition was coming along."

Erin glanced at her friend knowing that was only an excuse. Gillian went to the window and looked out. Several pieces of heavy equipment had been parked in front of the hole as if they were protecting it. In the setting sun they looked like huge yellow bugs.

"How's Digger?" Gillian asked.

Erin tensed. She didn't want to do it, but she couldn't stop the reaction. A secret thrill ran through her. She recognized it as a growing attraction for the man. Erin knew she should suppress it, but the feeling was so wonderful she let it run wild. Taking a seat at her desk she stared at Gillian's back. "He wasn't here today."

"Is that why you're waiting?"

"I am not waiting."

Gillian turned around and took a seat across from Erin. The expression on her face said, "This is me."

Erin sighed. "I'm really not waiting," she told her. "I just didn't want to go home yet."

"Have anything to do with dinner last night?"

"How did you know he was there?"

"This is a small town." Gillian paused. "And it only has one hospital."

"Hospital?" Erin sat forward. "Did something happen?"

"He's fine, at least the last time I saw him."

"Which was?"

"Thirty minutes ago."

Erin waited for her to continue.

"He's got a sister. She had a minor traffic accident and was a little dazed. Her husband is out of town, and we tried to find her brother, but he didn't answer his pager. I didn't think to call your house until I noticed his truck when I was on my way home."

Erin dropped her eyes. Her face grew hot with embarrassment.

"Is she all right?"

Gillian nodded. "She was only shaken up, but she couldn't drive herself home. She was released late last night."

Erin felt a little guilty that he had been with her, administering to her pain, while his sister was in the hospital.

"So, how long did he stay?" Gillian asked.

"He didn't sleep there," Erin said.

"Pity," Gillian threw out as if it were an everyday occurrence to discover a man's truck outside Erin's house.

"I don't know what time he left."

Gillian sat forward with interest. "Don't stop at that."

"Yesterday was awful," she began, telling Gillian everything from the sick teachers to the limp. "I woke up in my bed. Digger was gone."

"And you've been waiting for him all day. This is good."

"I wanted to apologize to him."

"For what?"

"Being rude. Falling asleep on a guest."

"You didn't exactly fall asleep *on* him."

"Gillian, you are terrible."

"It's the hospital. I need a release valve when I leave there."

Erin stared at Gillian. She worked in the emergency room and even in a small town there could be trauma. "Are you all right?"

"I'm fine. Today was routine. We had a few burns, a guy who had a nail in his foot, a couple of teenagers who got their braces stuck together, two heart attacks, a serious allergic reaction and a woman hyperventilating when she discovered she was pregnant. Overall it was no big deal."

Erin was holding her heart at the images that surfaced when Gillian matter-of-factly described her day.

"Everything turned out all right I take it?"

"Perfect." She smiled brightly. "How's your hip today?"

"Back to normal."

"I suppose the massage helped."

She was back to Digger. Erin should be prepared for her friend. They had known each other long enough to be able to say anything to each other, but Erin was finding it hard to let her feelings out. She'd concealed them too long and while she really liked James Clayton, she was reluctant to let her heart really feel anything for him.

"Erin, what are you thinking?"

Erin changed the expression on her face. If there was anything there that Gillian could read, she wanted it removed.

"You said you saw Digger thirty minutes ago. Where was that?"

The smile on Gillian's face widened. "Down by the courthouse. I thought it strange since at this hour everything in the courthouse is closed."

"Maybe he has a job there, too."

"He didn't look as if he were observing the place. More like he was waiting."

For someone, Erin finished in her mind. She didn't own Digger. She barely knew him. It was a good thing he wasn't interested in her, she told herself. He would finish her addition or have one of his crews do it and they would both get on with their lives. It was for the best. She knew the consequences of thinking a man would be interested in her and her alone. Families didn't come with a marriage ceremony, they came when a child was produced. Didn't all the cards say "hope all your problems are little ones"?

She wished she'd hired the other construction company and that Digger was not in her life. But he was. He'd taken up residence in her mind and refused to vacate the space.

Three days later Erin still hadn't seen or heard from Digger. His construction crew worked steadily every day, but he never appeared. She continued to serve coffee to the men, and they were comfortable with her and some of them joked or asked her questions about the building. Not once did any of them mention Digger and neither did she.

After closing the school she went shopping. The stores in Austin were open late and she wasn't ready to go home yet. It had been fun to walk up and down the aisles of different stores and find treasures for the school that she couldn't find locally.

She turned on the radio for the forty-minute drive back to Cobblersville, and as she neared the school she decided to drop off her purchases now instead of bringing them in on Monday. The construction area parking lot was closer to the back door than going all the way to the front, so Erin turned in and stopped short as her headlights illuminated the dirt-stained truck that Digger Clayton drove.

Her heart began a thud that could rival an African tom-tom. He was here. Finding her coordination, she pulled into a space and got out of the van. She stood in the darkness, hearing only the ticking of the cooling engine. She scanned the ground, squinting into the darkness, trying to see him. She saw nothing, heard nothing.

Suddenly she thought of the huge hole they had made. Could he have fallen into it and be unconscious? Gillian's detailing of the emergency room cases flashed through Erin's mind.

"Digger," she called. Her voice sounded small in the vastness of the night. She moved away from the van, then remembered the flashlight. She grabbed it from the brace inside the door where it was always kept and switched it on, testing it for battery power.

Then she started walking. She'd changed shoes after school today as she always did. She found that working all day in one pair of shoes could cause her hip to hurt. Different shoes used different muscles in her legs and gave her greater strength. Consequently she was now wearing sandals with a small heel that sank into the soft earth.

She went on, calling Digger's name and shining the light over the area. She hadn't been around this side of the building. It wasn't close to the play area, and she couldn't see it from the street. She shone the light into the hole and could see water at the bottom. She wondered how much foundation they had to dig before they began to build walls. Were walls next? She'd asked Digger to talk to her classes, but he hadn't committed. She'd like to know some of the answers herself.

When she took her next step, Erin's foot sank into mud. She cried out involuntarily as she lost her balance. She finally righted herself and pulled her foot out. Her shoe was ruined. If it hadn't been for the strap around her ankle the mud would have eaten it completely.

She pushed it back on and continued, mud squishing uncomfortably through her toes. Where was he? she wondered. Why didn't he answer her? Again the thought of an accident flashed through her mind, and she kept going, seeking, expecting to find him facedown in that enormous hole.

"What are you doing here?"

The voice was angry. It came out of nowhere. Erin recoiled

and stepped back, unconsciously retreating from the danger. Behind her was nothing, only the open pit that could swallow her up. She grasped for something to hold onto. She knew there was nothing. Her hand closed over air. But Digger was faster than that.

Hard hands grabbed her torso, wrapped around her and pulled her back to safety. She was against him, breathing hard, her heart hammering in her breast. Her arms went around his neck and she hugged him, glad to be safe, glad he was there to prevent her fall.

She hung there in his arms for several moments, until she was sure she could stand, could push away from him, until she realized she didn't want to move. She raised her head and Digger looked down at her. There was a tenderness about him that quickly turned hard.

"You could have broken your neck," he ground out. "You've already had one accident. Do you want to do it again?"

Erin was stunned, not by his words, but by the way he pulled her into his arms and held her against him. She felt his breathing and could hear the rapid beating of his heart. She'd scared *him*. His arms caressed her close to him. She could smell the dust on his clothes and feel the trembling of his arms.

"Erin, you're driving me crazy," he said and pulled her closer. She heard the groan in his throat and in the next moment his mouth was on hers, devouring her. The kiss was raw, sexual, backed with desperation and need. Her arms wound around him. She forgot they were standing in mud, forgot the school, her reason for being here. All she could think of was Digger, being in his arms, with his mouth on hers.

His tongue tangled with hers as every part of his body aligned with the complementary parts of her own. He held her close, his hands running the length of her and returning as his mouth changed positions, drinking her in. Digger was taking his fill and she was giving, pouring out to him in the only way she knew how. She could feel the changes in him.

His hands found the hem of her short blouse and went under it. Rough skin raked over her smooth back. Sensation rioted through her, and she arched against him. His hands were like fire, hot and burning, searing her flesh and turning her into a mass of emotion, as pure as unharnessed energy. What was this magic? she tried to wonder, but she could think of nothing. Reason left her with the movements of his hands and his mouth. She gave up thought, gave up everything and let herself be carried away by tidal waves of delight that transported her to some paradise she had never before seen.

Erin didn't remember Digger breaking the kiss. She was too far gone. She clung to him as if her life depended on keeping contact with his body. Her breath was ragged, hard and audible. She heard it before she realized his mouth was no longer on hers, that the sensation of another world, a private world, their own world was gone. She returned to reality, to the mud, to the school and to herself, a woman with a crippled body.

"Let's get out of here," Digger whispered. His voice was gravelly. She shivered, feeling it touch someplace inside her, someplace that resonated a single note, like the plucking of a bowstring in her heart.

She limped next to him as they headed for the parking lot.

"Your leg?" he asked.

"It's my shoes."

He looked at her feet. They were muddy. With each step the earth sucked her feet toward its center. She had to force each step.

"They're ruined," he said.

Erin looked at him. "I know." She wasn't talking about her shoes. She knew her life had altered. With a single kiss. Just as suddenly as her accident. Only she had recovered from the accident. She wasn't sure whether she could ever recover from Digger.

"Sit here," he told her when they reached the edge of the lot. He brushed off the step of his pick-up and Erin perched on it. He moved in the darkness with ease, going to the hose that lay nearby and turning on the water. Erin realized he must have come here often or he wouldn't be so comfortable with the surroundings. Had he come at night? Had he been avoiding her? Was that what he meant when he said she was driving him crazy?

He came back and lifted one of her feet. He sprayed the water over the mud on her feet and shoes. It ran across the pavement and onto his work boots. He took no notice. The water was cold, but against her heated skin it felt exquisite. He removed her shoes and washed her feet. Erin bit her lip to keep from crying out. No one had ever touched her feet in such a sensuous manner. It might be unintentional, but his touch was far from impersonal. It was having an effect on her.

It ended all too soon. He walked away, taking the hose with him and turning off the water. When he returned he grabbed a towel from the case in his truck and dried her feet.

She laughed.

"Ticklish?" he asked.

She nodded. He continued his ministrations and then ran a quick stroke over the pad of her foot. She jumped, laughing.

"No one's ever washed my feet before."

Digger looked at her in the half-light. "You've had a lot of pain in your life, haven't you?" he asked seriously.

"No more so than anyone else," she answered.

He knew that wasn't the truth. At least not the whole truth. When he'd first seen her he thought she'd seen only the good side of life, home, a loving family, sisters who loved her and triumphed in her accomplishments. But on closer inspection, he could see the creases that life invariably etched into everyone. Erin Taylor had etchings just as he did.

"I wouldn't put those back on."

She glanced at her shoes. "I have another pair in the van." She started to get up, but he stopped her.

"I'll get them."

"They're behind the driver's seat."

He found them and came back. "There were four pairs. Will these do?" he asked.

Erin took them and put them on.

"Are they for your hip?" he asked.

She nodded, knowing he referred to the other shoes in the van behind her seat. People usually asked if she was a shoe freak. Digger was more perceptive than most.

"The other night you didn't want to tell me what happened to your leg. What about now?"

Erin took a breath and stood up. She rarely told anyone the details. Gillian knew, but the staff at the school and most of her other friends rarely saw her limp. Some of them didn't even know she'd ever had an accident.

"I was seventeen," she began. "Close to graduation and looking forward to college. It would be the first time I was on my own. I was going to a big city and couldn't wait for the experience to begin."

Erin walked, feeling the need to move. Digger fell into step with her. He took her hand and Erin felt reassured. She garnered strength from the small act of touching. "It was Senior Day, the senior trip. Do you remember your Senior Day?"

Digger nodded. "We went to an amusement park."

Erin swallowed. "We did, too. It was there that the accident happened." She stopped, taking a long breath. She hadn't relived the details in a long time, and she was surprised how vivid and real they appeared in her mind. It had been bright, sunny and not too warm. Perfect weather for a day outdoors, and unusual for April in Texas. They'd separated into small groups with specific times and places to check in with their chaperons, but for the most part they were on their own.

Erin was with Percy Sandford, Elaine Quinlan and

Mackenzie Patterson. Percy and Elaine had dated no one else since the first day of high school. Erin had dated several guys over the course of the four years. Percy and Elaine dragged Erin along with them when she wasn't seeing anyone. On Senior Day she and Mac were a couple. The two had started dating a few weeks before Senior Day.

"We'd spent most of the day riding, eating and enjoying our freedom. Then we decided to ride the roller coaster. The line was always long, and we'd waited all day. This one had three drops and a loop. The cars got stuck at the top of the third drop. We were on top of the hill for thirty minutes while the maintenance guys tried to find out what was wrong."

She looked at Digger. He still held her hand. Erin realized they'd been walking in circles around the parking lot. She was standing near his truck again and didn't remember getting there.

"You would have thought there would be panic that high up, a full carload of riders sitting on top of the park. There were a few people crying, a few silently praying, hoping we'd get down soon." Erin could see the entire scene clearly in her mind. "Someone made a decision to get us out of the cars and down to the ground."

"How?" Digger asked. She knew he hadn't intended to interrupt her. He'd patiently circled the lot while she talked. "Short of climbing up and escorting you down one by one."

"They brought in the fire department, but the park had been expanded and the hook and ladder truck couldn't get close enough to extend the basket high enough to reach us. They decided to climb up, as you said." Erin took another breath. She tried to distance herself from the story, let it be reported and not lived. "There were three men on the scaffolding when something came loose. We heard a huge noise and the cars bounced. The guys made hooting noises, proving they weren't afraid. The girls screamed. It felt like seconds later when the whole section came apart and we fell."

"Oh my God." Digger spoke lowly. He comforted her, pulled her into his arms and hugged her close.

"I was pinned under the metal skeleton for five hours. I woke up in the hospital. My parents were there. My hip had been crushed and the doctors said I would walk with a limp for the rest of my life." She skipped the pain and the necessary hysterectomy, unsure she could relate it impartially. "It took several operations to put me back together again and many months of therapy to teach me to walk, but I beat the odds. If I don't overdo it no one knows it ever happened."

Digger pulled her closer to him. His hand caressed her back and slipped upward into her hair. Someone always knows, he told himself. She would never forget the experience. It would linger in her mind forever. He thought of the crane he'd tried to control and how nothing he did kept it from toppling over.

"No one was killed," Erin continued. He'd felt her swallow and knew she took a moment to distance herself from the memory. "The kids with me had broken bones. There was one minor head injury. I was the only one in critical condition. I worked for hours to gain strength in my legs and walk without the limp. I can do almost anything anyone else can do."

She felt the need to explain that she was normal. The only way she lacked normalcy was in being able to bear children. Most of her friends had already married and started families. She had never done so.

Now with Digger's arms around her and the tantalizing smell of him clouding her memory, she found it hard to remember her vow was to stay away from men.

Chapter Seven

Digger wished they had someplace to sit down. The cab of his truck was too small and her van was filled from top to bottom with boxes. He was holding her, but she was supporting him. Her story brought back Josh's accident. The huge metal monster crashing down and stealing the boy's life and future.

Digger couldn't let her go yet. He threaded his fingers in her hair, feeling the smoothness of it, allowing it to cascade over his rough hands.

He could only imagine the pain she had been in. Five hours pinned under a mass of metal. He was amazed she'd lived through it. The weight of the metal beams and internal injuries should have killed her. She was lucky she could walk at all.

He could feel her breathing hard against him. Her story had been told with little emotion. Yet it was powerful for him in the wake of what he knew. He didn't like the idea of her lying helpless under so much metal or that she'd spent months in therapy trying to walk again. Even the daily effort of forcing herself not to limp took something out of him. He wanted to help her, do for her, carry whatever he could to make her burden lighter.

She was driving him crazy and there seemed to be little he could do about it.

He went on holding her until he was sure they were both back to normal. Her smell invaded his nostrils and he wanted to caress instead of comfort. He had to let her go. He could hardly keep holding her without wanting more. And soon he would take it.

He pushed her back to keep from acting on his thoughts. "Those boxes in your van, are they for the school?"

She nodded.

"I'll carry them in."

He started for the van, and she went with him. When she reached for the first box, his hand caught her arm.

"I'll do it."

Erin snatched her arm away. "Don't treat me as if I'm broken. I'm not."

Digger took her arms and smoothed his hands down them until he was holding her hands. "I don't think you're broken," he told her. He knew what she meant and knew, from her tone of voice that she'd been treated that way in the past. Erin had built up a defense by not telling the tale. Digger was glad she'd included him in the people who knew about her past.

"My mother taught me to be a gentleman. I was going to carry it because it looks heavy."

She looked at the ground. "I'm sorry. I thought chivalry was dead."

"Not in our family."

Digger lifted the heavy box while Erin carried the smaller packages. "There aren't more bookcases in here, are there?" he asked when they were inside and Erin told him in which room to store them.

"They're chairs. We needed some replacements."

He recognized the store name on the box. It was in Austin. "Do you want me to open them?"

"The teachers will do that. The kids love playing in the boxes."

A strange silence grew between them.

"About—"

"About—"

They both spoke at the same time. Digger wondered if they were going to say the same thing.

"You go first," he offered.

"About the other night," Erin said. "At my house. I wanted to thank you for massaging my leg and carrying me to bed. I apologize for falling asleep."

"Apology accepted. It had been a long day and you said you were tired. I barged in without an invitation."

"Very unchivalrous of you." She smiled. "But you redeemed yourself by carrying me to bed."

Digger knew he hadn't. Chivalry wasn't on his mind when he took her to her bedroom. He'd wanted to climb into bed with her and make love the entire night. He'd wanted to rake his hands through her luxurious hair and ravish her like some knight returning from war and finding his love waiting for him. Then he'd come to his senses.

"We'd better get out of here," he said, determined not to act on those thoughts.

Erin turned out the lights as they made their way back to the entrance. Digger walked her to the van and opened the door. Erin stepped up to climb inside, but he stopped her. She looked back. In the open doorway of the van they were very close. "You told me about a part of your life. Why don't I tell you part of mine over dinner on Sunday?"

He could almost drown in the smile that reached her eyes. "I'd like that," she said.

He bent and kissed her lightly on the lips. Neither moved

back as the kiss ended. When he spoke he could feel his own breath bounce off her mouth. "Dinner's at three. I'll pick you up at two."

She nodded. "What shall I wear?"

"Nothing," he whispered as his mind pulled up images of her naked. For a long moment they stared at each other. Digger didn't know who moved first. He wanted her in his arms, and she wanted to be there. Her arms wrapped around him at the same moment his took her. His mouth melded with hers, tasting her, kissing her as if he was a man famished.

This hadn't happened to him before. He'd wanted women before, had them, been married, but he'd never felt this helplessness, this madness to hold someone, kiss her until neither of them could think of anyone but the other. This was possessive, out of character and it felt so right it frightened him.

Heat enveloped him. His body grew hard against hers, seemingly harder the more she melted into him. Blood throbbed through his system, his heart pumping at three times its normal rate. He was close to tearing her clothes off and taking her right in the parking lot. He bumped against the van's door. The small act reminded him of where he was and the insanity he was contemplating. His mouth slid from hers, his head fell on her neck and he breathed in the scent that was Erin and only Erin, a smell so potent it threatened to overwhelm him.

She was well and truly driving him crazy. He was so near the edge now he might as well jump. Erin's arms slackened. They moved from his neck to his shoulders and over his arms until they reached his elbows. She was pinned to the van. He had to move back to give her room.

He lifted his head. Neither spoke a word. Words were not necessary. He needed some room though, some thinking room. He stepped back, separating them, taking his body from hers. Air rushed between them, a place it had not been able to reach a moment ago. It was warm, but not as warm as the heat between them. It felt as if an arctic breeze had swept in.

"Good night," Digger whispered. His voice was almost unrecognizable. It was filled with a passion.

Erin climbed in the van and, with a wave, drove away. He walked to his truck. On the ground were her shoes, wet still, ruined. He scooped them up as if he were lifting her and put them in his truck.

Nothing was something Erin couldn't handle. Digger hadn't called or contacted her since Friday night in the parking lot. It was nearly two o'clock on Sunday. He was due to take her to dinner soon and she still hadn't decided what to wear.

It would have helped if she'd asked where they were planning to eat, but at the time her mind had been otherwise engaged, not to mention her body. Color and heat suffused her at the memory of Digger holding her, kissing her so baldly in the parking lot. She didn't think the neighbors were looking. Even if they were, few could have seen anything with the helpful absence of any kind of moonlight. What surprised her was her reaction to him.

She'd been disappointed to leave in separate cars. She'd wanted to invite him home, to her house and her bed. Only the inability to speak had kept her from doing it.

Erin returned to her closet, which she'd always thought was spacious, but could find nothing appropriate in it. She had shorts and sundresses, countless T-shirts, tops and blouses, but what should she wear? She was running out of time.

It was the shoes that decided her. Erin looked down and spotted a pair of sandals. She knew she had to wear them. One decision made. Now all she needed was something to go with them.

When Digger arrived she opened the door wearing a light

blue pantsuit. Digger had on a suit. He looked wonderful. Her breath stuck in her throat when she saw him. He smiled, that devastatingly handsome smile that made her forget to speak. She'd forgotten how impressive he looked. It seemed he was more handsome in today's light than she'd remembered.

"I'm underdressed," she said instead of hello.

"No, you're not. I'm changing clothes at my sister's."

"Your sister's?"

"Yeah, that where we're eating."

Erin felt deflated. "You never mentioned a sister."

"We have dinner at her house every Sunday."

"We?" This was getting worse, she thought.

"Usually it's just her, her husband and me."

"But today your whole family is there."

"How'd you know?" He seemed genuinely surprised.

"That's how it works," she muttered under her breath.

"Ready?"

"I have nothing to bring."

"Bring?"

Men, she thought. "When you go to someone's house for dinner, you should bring something, a casserole, a pot-luck dish…something. You brought wine the first night you came here."

"Don't worry about it. We don't stand much on ceremony."

"Why didn't you say we were having dinner with your family?"

Erin regretted the question as soon as she saw his face. He was obviously remembering what they had been doing when he invited her to dinner.

"We don't have time for you to make something. I'll just tell her what you told me—you can't cook. She'll understand."

Unable to refuse, Erin followed him out to the car she'd seen him driving that day in The Warehouse parking lot, when he'd agreed to complete her addition.

The drive to Digger's sister's was short. Erin didn't have much time to ask questions.

Luanne Rogers herded her brothers out the back door. She took a bowl of punch and set it on the patio table. The day was perfect. The humidity was low, and it wasn't too hot. They would be able to relax outside instead of being forced to stay in the air-conditioning to remain comfortable.

Owen, Brad and Dean had been in and out of the pool several times since breakfast. She'd had to remind them that this was not a pool party, and she expected them to be dressed for dinner. She wasn't expecting formal wear, but bare chests and tight trunks were out.

She approached her family as they sat around the yard engaged in spirited conversation.

"Digger is due soon and remember he's bringing a guest."

"A woman?" Rosa asked.

"Of course a woman," Dean said. "What did you think he'd bring?"

She made a face at her brother. "Since he and Marita—"

"I don't want anyone to mention Marita this afternoon," Luanne ordered. "And for heaven's sake don't bring up Josh."

"I thought he was over that?" Owen said.

"You never get over that," Brad put in.

"I meant Marita." He gave his brother an angry look.

At that moment Digger arrived. He came around the side of the house. Next to him stood the woman they'd all been waiting to meet.

"Hi everybody," Digger called.

"Wow," Dean said. "She's certainly *not* Marita."

"Put your eyes back in your head little brother," Rosa muttered. "She's too old for you, and Digger saw her first." She looked at Owen. Admiration was on his face, too. "That goes for you too, Owen."

Owen got up. "She's not too old for me."

* * *

"Hi, I'm Owen Clayton." A tall walnut-colored man a head taller than Digger reached her first. Erin shook his hand as the other four members of Digger's family arrived. Erin knew she wouldn't be able to keep their names straight.

Digger introduced them. "Owen is the oldest. He beats me by fifteen days. He lives in Dallas and is an architect."

"And one of these days Digger will come back to Dallas and be my builder."

Digger didn't say anything, but gave Owen a strange look. Erin didn't understand the family dynamics, but, like all families, there was more under the surface than any outsider could ever learn. She did believe there was love between the brothers, especially if Owen wanted Digger to work with him. But in Dallas. That was two hundred miles away.

"This is my sister Luanne and her husband Mark Rogers. They live here in Cobblersville." Erin shook hands with both of them.

"Thank you for inviting me to dinner." Erin remembered Gillian telling her Digger had a sister. She must be the one who had the accident last week.

"We're glad you could come," Mark said.

"Luanne works for Child Welfare and Mark is an oil geologist. He consults with all the big oil companies." Digger turned to a young man of no more than twenty. He had sandy hair and sandy colored skin. "This is Dean. He stays with Owen in Dallas, but attends college in California. He's studying filmmaking."

"That sounds very interesting."

"You'd be a great subject—"

"Dean." Luanne stopped him. Then a young woman stepped forward. She was beautiful. Erin thought she looked familiar, but couldn't place her. She had straight black hair, clear skin that was enviably smooth. Her nose was straight and her eyes bright and clear, although they held a bit of challenge.

"I'm Rosa Clayton," she said. Her voice was soft, but it had a confidence that spoke of experience.

"Rosa is a model. She lives in New York and gets her face plastered all over bus stations and subways," Dean said.

Erin placed her then. She'd seen her face in fashion magazines. "It's a pleasure to meet you."

"Finally, this is Dr. Brad. He lives in Philadelphia and flew all the way here just to visit the family."

"That's wonderful," Erin remarked.

He nodded, but said nothing.

"What do you do?" Rosa asked.

"I own a nursery school." She glanced at Digger. "Digger's company is adding some rooms for me."

"Is this the one on East Porter Street?" Dean asked.

She nodded.

"That is a very interesting looking house. It would make great footage in a film."

"Maybe," Erin said. "But there's a big hole in the ground next to it now and more mud than we know what to do with."

"That's it," Digger interrupted. "Stop gawking and go back to whatever you were doing." He took Erin's elbow and led her to one of the patio tables. Erin sat down and Digger straddled the bench beside her. He was close enough to touch. She was glad for the closeness. She felt like a stranger in a foreign land and needed the one person who spoke her language nearby.

Luanne went into the house. "Is there something I can help you with?" Erin asked.

"Not at the moment. Why don't you get a drink? Owen and Dean will help me." She emphasized their names. The two men got up and followed her, with obvious reluctance, inside.

Digger got a beer from a nearby cooler and offered her one. She opted for a cola. The drink gave her something to concentrate on. Erin felt as if she were under a microscope. They all looked friendly, but she wondered what they were thinking about her. Except for Dean and Owen, who were definitely showing their admiration, the others' thoughts were hidden.

"Have you lived here long?" Rosa asked her.

"I'm a native," Erin said. "I grew up in Cobblersville."

"It's a nice town. I like little towns."

"But you live in New York."

"That's were the work is. They send me all over the world, but I've found I like the little places where people get to know each other."

She reinforced Erin's initial impression. There was more to Rosa Clayton than her good looks.

"You all look very different," Erin said. "I have three sisters and we all look enough alike to be mistaken for each other."

"That must have been fun in high school," Brad commented. He was the quietest one in the bunch, Erin thought.

"We did it a couple of times, but more often than not we'd get caught in something that was hard to get out of."

"We're all adopted," Digger told her.

She looked at him. "All of you."

"They were all part of the foster care system. Problem children, incorrigible, abandoned, the hardcore unadoptable. That's what Luanne says about herself," Mark explained.

Erin took in small breaths. She couldn't imagine someone abandoning their child. Children were so precious, it hurt her to think that people abused them or hurt them in any way.

"Most of us don't get a chance," Brad took over the story. "People don't understand how a child feels who's been abandoned. We were the lucky ones. We ended up in the home of Devon and Reuben Clayton."

Digger slipped his arm around her waist and took her hand. Erin squeezed it, glad of the anchor.

"They were wonderful," Rosa said. "They turned our lives around. I don't want to think what would have happened to us if we'd been lost to a system where people don't care."

"We didn't give them an easy time of it," Digger said. Erin could feel him talking. Her back was against his chest and his deep voice thundered into her. "I was thirteen when it happened to me. I lived on the streets, stealing food and sleeping in railroad cars. I was arrested three times and escaped twice. Mom and Dad did nothing but love us. They set up the rules, told us they would back us to high hell if we did the right thing, but they wouldn't live with people who didn't want to be loved or be there. Then they left us alone to think about it."

Erin knew what he'd decided. What any child would want—the love of a parent.

"When Dad died of a heart attack," Mark said, "the entire group decided to change their names in his honor. They were still under the foster care system and underage. Mrs. Clayton went to court and adopted six children of various ages and backgrounds. Only two of them even share the same bloodline."

Erin looked from one to the other. Then at the house. She was trying to figure out who resembled whom.

"Owen and I," Brad told her. "We come from the same biological parents." His voice told her he was still bitter over his fate.

"At the adoption hearing our names were legally changed to Clayton," Rosa finished.

Luanne came back with Owen and Dean in tow. Each carried a huge plate or bowl. "Time to eat," she announced. "Digger, are you going to change?"

He got up. Erin looked at him, letting him know she would be fine if he left her. "Do you need any more help in the kitchen?" she asked Luanne.

"Don't let her," Digger said, walking away. "She can't cook. That's why she came without a covered dish."

Erin picked up her empty can of soda and threw it across the lawn at him. He ran forward looking over his shoulder and caught it as if she'd pitched him a ball.

"He didn't tell me we were coming until he arrived today. I thought we were going to a restaurant."

"It's not a problem," Mark said. "Luanne always has enough food for everyone."

By the time Digger returned, all the food had been brought out and everyone was passing it around the table.

"Save some for me," he said, sliding into place next to her.

The meal went well. Erin enjoyed herself immensely. They welcomed her into the fold and, for a moment, it made her uncomfortable. She knew this wasn't Victorian times. This was modern-day Texas. Taking prospective brides home to meet the family prior to offering betrothal was something out of the dark ages. Yet she had the queasy feeling that she was being judged in this manner.

Shouldering it off, she let herself relax and enjoy the day. She ate and relaxed by the pool. While Owen, Rosa and Dean swam, Brad and Digger stayed close to the patio with Luanne and Mark. Except for Brad, the conversation was easygoing and comfortable. When Digger finally announced it was time for them to go, Luanne and Mark walked them to the car.

"Thank you for having me. I had a wonderful time," Erin told them and genuinely meant it.

"Please come back."

Erin smiled and got in the car. The sun was setting when Digger parked in front of her house.

"You have a wonderful family," Erin said. "You're very lucky to have found each other. And to live so far apart, yet have everyone come here. Was this a mini-reunion or something?"

"Kind of. Luanne was in the hospital earlier this week."

"I know."

"You do?"

"My best friend is an emergency room nurse. She was there when Luanne was brought in. I didn't know you had a sister," she paused. "So they all came to town to see that she was all right?"

"Basically." he nodded.

"That's wonderful. My family would never do that, not over a minor traffic accident." She smiled. "I like it. It's nice. I do have one question though."

"What's that?"

"Brad."

"Brad is an enigma to all of us."

"He was hurt very badly by the abandonment and he hasn't recovered from it."

"You don't recover."

"I meant, he hasn't gone on with his life. He's a children's doctor, isn't he?"

Digger shook his head. "Pediatric surgeon."

Erin could only imagine the trauma he'd probably seen.

"You're not going to analyze all of us, are you?"

Erin laughed. "Not a chance. You're all out of my league." She looked at him for a moment. He looked happy. One would never know he came from a background of abandonment and childhood hurt. "I had a very good time. Even though I didn't take anything for the hostess." Erin looked at him. The car was dark, intimate and she felt close to him.

"You're not going to let me live that down, are you?"

"I consider it my sole purpose in life to make you remember it every chance I get." She stuck her finger in his chest to drive her point home. Digger captured it and held it. The air turned hot. The smiles froze on their faces. Applying only a little pressure, he pulled her forward. Erin went willingly. He kissed her, letting go of her finger to run his hand around her neck and into her hair.

He held Erin's mouth to his as he teased her with his tongue, tasting her, savoring the sweetness as if it came in short samples and he had to continually open the next package. Erin reached for him, wanting to touch, feel the solidity of his chest, to hold on to his physical being, to have her hand rooted in him.

The kiss ended all too soon.

"You'd better go in," Digger whispered. "Or your neighbors are going to get a show."

Erin stared at her hands. She wanted to ask him in. Yet he'd dismissed her. After spending the day with her, inviting her to meet his family, kissing her until her toes curled, he wanted her to leave, spend the night alone. She wanted to spend the night with *him,* make love, feel him moving inside her. But she knew where it would lead, where it always led. She shifted in her seat and reached for the door handle. Digger hit the locking mechanism and released the door. She climbed out and headed for the stairs. He met her at her door. Erin stopped.

"Digger, don't you want to make love to me?"

"More than I want to take my next breath," he said.

"Then why—"

"Because you're the marrying kind. I don't want to be married. I've done that. It didn't work, and I can't do it again."

Erin was too stunned to say anything.

"I tried to stay away from you. I tell myself all kinds of things in the safety of my home, then I find myself here, with you in my arms."

"Digger..." She got no further. His hands cupped her face and his mouth took hers. He kissed her deeply, thoroughly, until she couldn't think, couldn't do anything but cling to him, hang onto him to keep from falling. His head bobbed back and forth as he tasted her mouth, devouring every area of it, dancing with her tongue in a rhythm so old, so primitive, so ritualistic that neither of them could stop the spirits that moved through their bodies, that spoke to them over the transom of heritage, ancestry and the beating hearts that pounded in their breasts.

Erin was pinned to the door, the jamb cutting into her back, yet the discomfort wasn't enough for her to push him away. She wrapped her arms around him, giving as much as she took. Erin let go of her reserve. She threw herself into the kiss, communicating, letting him know that she was his for the taking.

Then Digger wrenched himself free of her. He hurried down the steps and got into his car. He reversed down the driveway and headed away from her, leaving a layer of tire rubber on the pavement in his attempt to escape.

Erin slid down the wall and sat with her knees in her chest, tears blurring her vision.

Chapter Eight

The Child Welfare Department for Cobblersville, Texas was housed in the courthouse building. So were the Department of Fishing and Game, the Marriage Bureau, the Department of Public Works and Building Permits, the Birth and Death Records Division and Roads and Bridges. Luanne Rogers worked on the third floor of the only three-story building in Cobblersville. It had an elevator, but Digger took the stairs.

The building had been constructed in the 1920s. It was of the traditional Greek architectural style with Corinthian columns and a wide staircase. After the passage of the Citizens with Disabilities Act a ramp had been added to allow wheelchairs to reach the inside.

Luanne had left him a message to call her. He knew she wanted to talk about Erin. Digger didn't want to discuss her, but he knew he'd have to. He'd invited her to dinner, let her meet his family then he'd frozen. He didn't want to feel like this. He didn't want thoughts of Erin disturbing his sleep. He didn't want to remember how good she felt in his arms or how her body melted into his. He didn't want to fantasize about making love to her. He wanted to forget he'd ever met her.

But he couldn't.

He opened the door to Child Welfare. "You rang," he said, finding his sister standing on the other side of a brown counter.

"I didn't mean for you to come by," she said. "I just wanted to talk to you."

"Well, I'm here. Talk."

"Come on in."

He followed her to her office halfway down the hall. It had been nearly a week since dinner, and he had calls on his answering machine from most of his siblings. He hadn't answered any of them.

"Is this about Erin?" Digger started.

"I liked her. She was intelligent, fun. She fit in. Some of those stories she told about the kids at her school were just hilarious."

"I'm not seeing her anymore."

Luanne stopped. She stared at him. "All right. That's your business."

Digger knew it didn't stop there. Luanne had more to say.

"You two seemed good together, as if you wanted to get to know each other better."

"I can't do it, Luanne, and you know why."

"Isn't it time to put that to rest?"

"Yes, dammit. I try. I really try, but when it comes time I just can't go through with it."

"How's she feel?" Luanne asked.

"I don't know. I haven't seen her."

"You just dropped her off on her doorstep and never called, never said a word?"

He looked at her. "It wasn't quite like that, but that's the gist of it." That wasn't nearly the gist of it. He'd kissed her. She'd kissed him. But it felt more like she'd branded him. He could still feel the hot sweetness of her mouth and the thought of making love to her haunted him day and night.

"James Clayton, I'm ashamed to call you my brother."

"What do you want me to do?"

"At least tell her why."

"I can't."

"Why not?"

"I think I'm in love with her."

The kids were sitting in a circle on the floor. The blond teacher held up a flash card and the kids repeated in unison what was on the card. Sam saw him and stood up.

"Digger," she shouted and rushed across the room. He lifted her into his arms. The rest of the kids stood up and started toward him. The teacher tried to restore order.

"Everyone, please sit down," she said. "You know how to act when we have a visitor."

They stood back. Digger set Sam on the floor. She stayed by his side, holding his hand.

"Can I help you?" the teacher asked him.

"This is Digger." Sam spoke for him.

"I'm here to teach your class about the construction," he told her.

"I don't know anything about this."

"Ms. Taylor asked me to come by."

"This is Digger," Sam said again as if that was explanation enough.

"Ms. Taylor asked me to explain to the children how construction works."

"She didn't tell me anything about it."

"Why don't you go clear it with her while I wait here?" She looked indecisive.

"Don't worry. This one will watch me while you're away."

Another woman had appeared from a different classroom. She stood apart, but eyed him suspiciously. Digger felt uncomfortable, but he was glad to see they were protective of the children.

The woman nodded to the blonde and she went off. He walked to the windows and looked out.

"Anybody know what's going on out there?"

Every hand in the room went up. Digger pointed to a boy wearing a blue shirt and khaki shorts.

"They're adding room."

"Right." Digger smiled. "They are adding rooms to the back. Anybody know how we add rooms?"

Three or four hands went up. He chose a girl with a broken front tooth.

"The big machine digs up all the ground. Then men put walls up."

He smiled. "That's partly true. We do dig a big hole. It's called a foundation. Can you say that?"

In unison they tried to repeat it. He had to help them three times before they got it right.

"Anybody live in a house with a basement?" He didn't count the hands. There were a lot of them. "Anyone ever been in a basement?" The rest of the hands went up. "A basement is the foundation. It holds the house up."

"The hole will hold up the rooms?" Sam asked.

He nodded. "For the most part." Digger picked up a piece of paper and sat down in the middle of the group. He started drawing. "First we dig the hole," he said, drawing his rendition of a crane. Next to it he drew a circle to represent the foundation. Some of the kids stood up behind him. He felt tiny hands on his shoulders. He was only uncomfortable for a moment.

"Then we put these braces in." He drew long stalklike squares inside the hole.

"I can draw like that," one of the boys said.

"Then a big truck comes and pours cement in the brace. Do you know what cement is?"

No one said a word. "Cement in the stuff on the street that you walk on. You only walk on the sidewalk, right?"

"Only walk on the sidewalk." Sam repeated the phrase.

Digger looked up and saw the teacher and Erin standing outside the door. They were talking to each other. He assumed Erin had approved him. Her face showed relief when her eyes met his.

"You put the sidewalk in there?" Someone drew his attention back to his drawing.

He continued, "No we put the same kind of stuff in there that we use to make sidewalks."

"Oh," the kid said, clearly not understanding. The teacher slipped back in the room and nodded at him.

"Anybody ever make a Popsicle?"

"Me."

"Me."

"Me, too."

The last hand was directly in front of his face. "Remember you put the water in the little tray?" Heads bobbed up and down. "What happened after you put it in the freezer?"

"It froze."

"Good," Digger told the little girl who answered. "You put it in as a liquid, like water." He looked around for the bobbing heads. "When it came out it was frozen, solid."

More bobbing heads.

"That's what we do with the cement."

"You freeze it," a smiling four-year-old stated. Digger wanted to laugh.

"We freeze it." He looked at the teacher. "That's it for today. I have to go freeze some cement. I'll come back tomorrow to tell you about walls. And I'll bring some hard hats. How's that?"

A cheer rang out in the room. Digger stood up and met the

teacher at the door. "I apologize," she said. "Ms. Taylor has a lot on her mind, and she forgot to tell me to expect you."

"No harm done," Digger told her with a smile.

"You'll be back tomorrow?"

"We're going to talk about putting up walls." He turned to the group who repeated "putting up walls."

Digger had enjoyed himself. He had been scared to come and do this, but he found he liked talking to the kids. And he couldn't get Erin out of his thoughts. He'd wanted to do or say something to make her happy. He wondered if Erin had known the kids would be good for him? She didn't know about Josh. Did she think talking to the children would be therapy for his own emotional problems?

"I'd like to see Ms. Taylor before I go," Digger said to the teacher.

"You just missed her. She had some errands to run."

Digger wondered how suddenly these errands had come up. Her van had been parked out front all morning and as soon as he entered the building she had to go run errands. Digger wanted to talk to her.

And he was going to.

All her life Erin had tried to discover why people acted the way they did. She'd thought Digger's brother Brad had unresolved issues, but Digger had more than his share of baggage.

Erin had spent a week of nights wondering what it was she had done, why he'd acted as he had. She couldn't blow it off as just being a man. That was a catch-all phrase—*It's a guy thing.* Even guys used it as an excuse when they couldn't—or didn't want to—explain something. Erin knew there was more to this complicated man than his beautiful exterior.

She walked to the window of her office. Outside the crew worked. They'd squared off the area and would soon be pouring a foundation. Jackson had told her that when she took coffee to him this morning. Even though she'd looked, she knew Digger wouldn't be there. He only came at night. She knew that, too. He came at night to avoid seeing her.

Erin reclaimed her seat and stared out the windows. She saw nothing, not the moving machinery or the men in hard hats. He couldn't stay away from her, he'd said. She was driving him crazy, yet he'd kissed her like a man in love, a man fighting love.

Why couldn't she leave it alone? She had issues, too. She didn't want to be married. She *wasn't* the marrying kind. She was the kind that poured her heart out to a man only to have him leave her. She didn't want that kind of hurt. So why did she let Digger take her to dinner?

And why was she sitting in her office a week later still trying to figure out what had happened on her front porch?

There was a light knock on her door. Erin looked up as Wanda came in.

"I'm having a slight problem with my class."

"What is it?" Erin was on her feet. Wanda was young, but she was wonderful with the four-year-old class.

"There's a man here talking to the kids."

Erin ran. She grabbed her cell phone in case they needed to call the police. She stopped short at the door.

"Anybody know what this is?" Digger asked of his captivated audience.

Erin's heart had been beating so fast that the relief nearly made her pass out. Adrenaline raged inside her with no outlet. Erin's hand came up to her rapidly beating heart.

"I shouldn't have said it that way." Wanda tried to apologize. "I know now how it sounded. It's just that I wasn't expecting him. You didn't tell me he was coming."

She pushed Wanda back into the hall and closed the door. "I forgot," Erin lied. "I'd asked him to tell the kids about adding on to a building, and I forgot that he confirmed."

"It's all right, then."

"It's fine."

Wanda smiled. She stopped with her hand on the door. "He's really good at explaining to the kids and look how quietly they are listening."

Erin peeked into the room. For a hot moment her eyes met Digger's. She pulled them away.

"Wanda, I have some errands to run this afternoon. Could you stay and close up the school tonight?"

"Sure."

"Thanks. I'll be in tomorrow at the usual time."

In minutes Erin had gathered her purse and left the building. She didn't want to see Digger. She never wanted to see him again. She couldn't turn her emotions off. Their relationship had nowhere to go, and she might as well admit it and move on.

Erin drove straight home. She parked in the garage and went inside her house. It was unusual for her to be home this early. She felt at a loss for what to do after collecting the mail and throwing the circulars and advertisements out. She switched on the television and the phone rang.

"What's wrong?" Gillian asked without preamble. She always managed to call the instant something was out of whack in Erin's life. How could she possibly know?

"Nothing."

"I called the school to see if you wanted to go roller blading in the morning, and they said you'd left to run some errands."

"That's true."

"Then why are you home?"

"If you thought I was running errands, why did you call here thinking something was wrong?"

"It's unlike you to leave the school for errands unless it's Monday."

Erin waited a moment. She sighed and told Gillian, "Digger came to the school today."

"So?" Gillian held on to the single word as if it was the last note of a song. Erin had told her the details of Sunday's dinner and Digger's abrupt reversal from her porch.

"Gillian, this relationship…" she floundered for another word. "This nonrelationship has no future. I just want it to die a quiet death."

"Do you think it can?"

The doorbell rang. Erin tensed. She looked toward the door. Digger was standing in front of the window staring at her.

"I'm not sure," she said.

"Go away," she said as she opened the door. "I don't want to talk to you."

He pushed the door inward and came inside. Erin moved back as he slammed it closed.

"I want to talk to *you*."

"I have nothing to say to you."

"Good." He took a step toward her. She moved back. "I want to make love to you."

Erin was shocked, but she held herself together. "Too bad. You had your chance, now go."

This time he moved too fast for her. His hands were around her arms before she could sidestep him. "What is wrong with you?"

"Me?" She snapped her arms free. "You make all the rules and I'm just supposed to follow them? You don't talk. You take me to meet your family and then I don't hear from you for a week. You tell me you won't teach my classes, then you show up unannounced." She paused to take a breath. When she spoke again her anger was more under control. "I don't know much about you, Digger. Only that you had a poor childhood and you've found some people who love you, but there are issues you need to deal with and I can't help you with them. And I don't want just a few kisses and one night of lovemaking."

Suddenly she realized what she did want. It was a fairy tale. One that had a happy ending, an ending she knew she couldn't have.

"Please leave," she said. "And don't come back."

Digger said nothing. He looked at her as if she'd plunged a dagger into his heart. Erin kept her gaze level. She couldn't break now. She'd said her piece, and she stood by it. She couldn't tell him that the opposite end of that dagger was sticking in *her* heart.

He turned and went to the door. Without looking back he opened it and went out.

She listened for his truck motor to start and the sound to die as he reversed and drove away. Then, for the second time in a week, she crumpled to the floor and cried.

"Ms. Taylor, Ms. Taylor, Digger coming today?" Sam jumped up and down.

Erin looked over her head. Wanda stood there. "He said he was coming today to tell them about walls."

"Yeah." Sam jumped again. She ran across the room shouting, "Digger's coming" to everyone.

"It's all right."

"He was really good yesterday. The kids loved everything he said. Today he said he'd bring hard hats."

"I thought he didn't like kids." Erin didn't mean to say it out loud, but she'd heard it from more than one person. Sam seemed to be the only child he noticed.

"You should have seen him with them," Wanda went on. "He'll make a great father someday. He was patient and answered every question they asked."

And then he'd shown up at her house, Erin thought. She flashed Wanda a smile and went toward her office. She'd told him she didn't want to see him. Now he was circumventing her authority, and there was nothing she could do about it. He'd found her weak spot, the kids. She'd do anything to keep them happy. She couldn't fly out again today on the pretext of errands that needed running.

He showed up as she was serving coffee to the men. She saw his Bronco skid to a stop in the parking lot. Erin spilled coffee on the tray. She righted the cup and apologized to the man she'd planned to hand it to. Digger didn't even glance at her. He spoke to Jackson Wright, exited the lot and went around to the front of the building.

Erin was there to meet him as he reached the walkway. He stared at her. "If you want me to go, I will."

"You promised the children. You should never break a promise to a child."

She stepped back, and he passed her. She heard the cheering roar of the kids a few seconds later, time enough for him to cross the common room and go into Wanda's classroom. Erin stood in the doorway a second later. She couldn't get his words out of her head. He wanted to make love to her. How had she had the fortitude to tell him no when every cell in her body craved his? She wanted to touch him so badly it hurt.

Erin entered the room and saw Sam clinging to Digger. She regarded him as her own personal find and she let the other kids know it. He looked up at Erin, and she felt the electricity cross the room and shock her. How could he be this potent? No man should have that kind of magnetism.

"Sam, time to come back," Wanda called the little girl.

Sam looked up at Digger. She hooked her index finger, and he hunched down to her level. She threw her arms around his neck and kissed him. Digger lost his balance, and he and Sam sat down on the floor. Just like that first night, Digger protected the little girl.

Sam laughed with the high-pitched sound that penetrated the school on a daily basis then ran back toward her teacher. Digger got up. He looked at Erin again and went through the door.

She let out the breath she'd been holding. Straightening

her shoulders she told herself she'd made the right decision yesterday.

Erin returned to her office and spent the rest of the day going through the motions. She checked the stockroom for chalk and paper, went over the medicine log, cleaned out the refrigerator, looked at the broken toy bin to see if she could repair anything.

Finally, the parents started to show up and take their kids home for the night. Tonight, Erin would be glad for them to leave. She wanted to go home and nurse her wounds. Usually the kids were all gone by six. If someone was going to be late they called. Now, Sam was the only one left. She was happily playing with a hard hat Digger had provided for the whole class. She was building walls, using the school blocks.

By seven o'clock Erin was worried. She made a light meal for the little girl and called Sam's parents' house. Getting no answer she tried the school where they worked.

"Mommy coming?" Sam asked when she realized the other kids had been gone a long time.

"I'm trying to call her, Sam." The little girl crawled into Erin's lap.

By eight o'clock Sam had asked fifty times for her mother and father. She fell asleep at eight-thirty. Erin lifted her. She felt heavier than usual. All the cots had been put away. Erin would have to lay Sam down while she got her purse and locked up the building.

The door opened and she turned. Digger stood there.

"I saw the light. Are you all right?"

"I'm so glad to see you," Erin blurted out before she thought of what she was saying. She knew Digger came by at night to look at the construction. He came toward her.

"Sam's parents never came to pick her up."

"Is she supposed to stay with you?"

"We didn't plan on it. I've tried to reach them at their home and at the school, but no one answers."

"What about an emergency number?"

"I checked their application. There isn't an emergency number."

Digger saw her struggling to hold the child and he took Sam in his arms. "I was going to leave a note on the door and take her home with me."

"Go write the note."

Erin did as she was told. She got her purse and checked that everything was all right. They left, and Digger followed her to the van.

"There's a pull-down seat that converts to a bed." Erin set it up and Digger laid Sam on it. Erin strapped Sam in and turned to get out of the van. Digger was behind her. He moved back.

"I'll follow you."

Erin didn't argue.

He pulled out of the lot just as she passed it. She was home in a few minutes. She pulled into the garage. Digger's lights followed her. He was at her side as she opened the door. He went in ahead of her and brought Sam out.

Erin led the way to Sam's bedroom. She got a nightgown the child had left on an earlier occasion, then they dressed the sleeping child and put her to bed.

"She's so small," Digger said. "Rosa was about her age when she was abandoned."

"She hasn't been abandoned. There's a logical reason for her parents being late." She didn't know what it was, but she hoped it was something that would be cleared up by morning.

Digger lifted the small picture frame next to the bed. It held a photo of Sam's parents. He said nothing, but stared at the photo a while before placing it back where he'd found it.

He looked back at the sleeping child. Erin wondered what he was thinking. After spending Sunday with his brothers and sisters she understood a lot more about his feelings for children and what some parents could do to them. This was not Sam's fate. Her parents loved her to distraction. She was one of the happiest children Erin had ever met.

Digger continued to look at Sam. Erin could see the softness in his eyes. It was almost as shining as love. For a man who didn't want to be around children, he was certainly acting like someone who loved them.

Erin took his arm and led him from the room.

"Have you eaten?" Digger asked in the hallway outside Sam's room.

"I made a sandwich for Sam."

He took her hand and led her to the kitchen. She sat at the table as he rifled through her cabinets. Erin didn't know what he was looking for and she didn't ask.

"I'm supposed to call Child Welfare. I should have notified the police."

"Child Welfare is closed."

"There's an emergency number."

"Erin, you did what you had to. Sam is safe and tomorrow everything will be explained."

He found a can of soup in the cabinet and heated it in the microwave. Setting it in front of her he ordered her to eat. Erin did what he said without argument. She didn't know where he'd gotten the soup. It had vegetables in it and tasted homemade, but she didn't have any homemade soup. It was delicious and filling. She ate it all, along with some crackers, and drank the orange juice mixture he fixed, another concoction she couldn't identify as coming from her kitchen.

"You look tired."

She hadn't slept in three days. Not through the entire night anyway. She didn't tell him he was the reason she'd been awake. When she finished eating her soup, Digger cleaned the dishes and suggested she go to bed.

Erin went into the living room and sank onto the sofa. Digger followed her. "This isn't where you sleep. So you want me to carry you to bed, too?" The last was a joke, but Erin didn't laugh.

"I saw how you looked at her," she said.

Digger sat down.

"I watched you hold her, place her carefully on the bed. Even that first day when she jumped into your arms, the emotions were evident on your face. They nearly choked you. You hugged her, smelling her hair, and I saw the tears."

He didn't deny it as most men would have.

"She's so small, so vulnerable at this age."

"Wanda thinks you'll make a great father."

"Wanda?"

"The teacher of the class you interrupted."

He nodded absently.

"You're very good with kids, Digger. You should have one of your own."

Digger stood up then. He turned his back on her. Erin noticed the stiffness of his back. She got up and started for him. He whipped around as if he knew she was coming toward him.

"I had a kid," he said. "He died."

She was unprepared for that. She heard the emotion in his voice. It nearly choked him to say it. It knocked her back a step. She stood looking at him, lost for words. "I'm sorry," she finally said, knowing the uselessness of the phrase, how it couldn't convey her sympathy.

She took a step toward him, her arms raised to comfort him. Digger moved away in anger. He said nothing, only stared at her as if she'd accused him of something. Then he turned and left her.

What was wrong with her? How could she even think of touching him? He wasn't a child needing comfort. And after what she'd said to him just twenty-four hours ago, how could he interpret her actions as anything other than pity?

She knew his family background, knew he and his siblings

were abandoned as children. Tonight must have been heart wrenching for him, and he obviously didn't need her attempt at comfort.

The note was still on the door when Erin arrived in the morning. She snatched it down and went inside. Sam bounded into the empty school as if it were a typical day.

Erin had an uneasy feeling. She'd left more messages on George and Claudia Pierce's answering machines about Sam but she had yet to reach a person. They had never been late without calling or making arrangements. Something had happened that kept them from calling. Erin didn't like the feeling that skidded up her spine. They were conscientious, loving parents and would never abandon their daughter.

She kept Sam close, even allowing her to go outside when Erin served the men coffee. Sam thought it was wonderful to have a special privilege and see everything that was going on up close. No one else got to do it. And after Digger had spent two days at the school telling them about construction, in her four-year-old mind she knew it all.

Erin tried the phone at the university again when the children were eating lunch. At Claudia's office there was only an answering machine. The same was true of George's. Erin looked up the main number and dialed the switchboard. Someone had to be in the office by this time.

"Dr. George Pierce's secretary please."

She was connected and a voice immediately answered the phone.

"This is Ms. Taylor at the Country Day Nursery School. May I please speak with Dr. Pierce?"

There was a silence. Erin heard a muffled voice in the background as if someone was holding a hand over the receiver. Then a different person came on the line.

"Ms. Taylor, this is Dr. Anita Wize. I work in the same department with Dr. Pierce. Is Samantha with you?"

"Yes. I'm calling about her."

"Is she all right?"

"Yes, this is not an emergency. Sam is fine."

There was a sigh on the other end of the line. "I'm afraid I have bad news for you."

Erin was sitting down, but her heart sank anyway. She'd been expecting bad news, but hoping against hope that it wouldn't be anything serious.

"Go on," she said.

"Yesterday as Dr. Pierce and his wife were returning from a seminar in Austin they were involved in a car accident."

Erin gasped. "Are they all right?"

Again there was that sigh through the line. Erin felt Dr. Wize was struggling to get the story out.

"Dr. Pierce died in the collision. Mrs. Pierce was taken to a hospital in Austin. She died early this morning."

"Oh," Erin's comment was more a moan than a word. She was going to have to tell Sam.

"We didn't know how to get in touch with you," Dr. Wize went on. "We only found out an hour ago and everyone here is understandably stunned."

Erin understood. She was numb, too. What would happen to Sam now?

"Do you know if the Pierces have any relatives close by that I can call?"

"I don't know and since the news is so recent, no one has been able to discover anything."

Erin gave the doctor her phone number and asked to be contacted if they found out anything. She replaced the receiver and stared at the wall. On the other side of it the children were happily eating and playing. In a few minutes they would take naps. Sam was doing what she did every day, not knowing that her parents had left her and wouldn't return.

Digger had thought she'd been abandoned and Erin had rejected the idea. But that was exactly the effect of the accident. The child was alone.

There were procedures to follow for day-care providers in the event of child abandonment. Erin had books, supplements, rules she'd had to learn in order to get a license to operate the school. She'd never had to exercise them. Parents had been late in arriving before, but they always managed to call and alert her. Never had someone not shown up and not called. There had been no need to pull out the regulations.

Erin didn't want to pull them out now. She didn't want Sam sent to some stranger until relatives could be located. Telling her her parents weren't coming for her would be bad enough, having her go to strangers would be insensitive.

Erin jerked around at the knock on her door. None of the teachers ever knocked like that.

"Come in," she called.

A blue-uniformed policeman and a woman dressed in a gray suit came inside and closed the door.

"Ms. Erin Taylor?"

She nodded.

"I'm Officer Garland of the Cobblersville Police Department and this is Ms. Lawrence of Child Welfare. We're here to take Samantha Pierce."

Erin hugged the little girl. Sam had grown small in the last hour. "Don't be afraid, honey. It will be all right." Sam's eyes were the largest part of her face. They looked huge and frightened.

Erin insisted on going to Child Welfare and taking the little girl with her. Sam didn't know her parents were dead, and she might not even understand what death meant. Erin couldn't let these two people take her away with no explanation. After twenty minutes of wrangling, they agreed to let Erin drive Sam.

Outside the school the flashing lights of the police car were imposing and menacing to a four-year-old. Sam clung to her hand, squeezing her fingers.

"Where you going?" she asked from the car seat.

"We have to go downtown." Erin told her. "Don't worry. I'm going to be with you."

At the courthouse, Erin lifted Sam into her arms and took her to one of the park benches that lined the side of the building. She raised her hand to halt the policeman and the social worker.

"I have something to tell you, Sam." The big, trusting eyes looked at her. "What is your favorite movie?"

"Lion King." She said it quickly without having to think.

"Who's your favorite character in the story?"

"Simba." She stuck her chest out the way the lion does at the end of the movie and prepared to roar.

"Remember in the beginning of the movie when Simba gets in trouble and—"

"Mufasa comes." She smiled thinking this was a game. Erin hugged her tighter.

"You know what happens to Mufasa?"

"He died." An expression of sadness covered her expressive face. A lump rose in Erin's throat.

"Do you know what died means?"

"Go away, can't come back. Made Simba sad."

"That's partly right. He went away from Simba. Not because he wanted to, because an accident took him away."

Sam stared across the courtyard. The uniformed man watched her. "Last night your mom and dad had an accident when they were coming to pick you up."

"Gone away?" she asked simply.

Erin nodded. "They loved you Sam. They didn't mean to go away."

Tears started rolling down her face before Erin could finish. The four-year-old might not understand many concepts, but she'd already closed the gap between the story Erin was telling and why her parents hadn't picked her up.

"Gone away?" she repeated a little louder as she threw her arms around Erin's neck and cried in earnest.

Erin's throat was choked with tears. She comforted Sam while the little girl cried, not attempting to stop her. The officer turned away as did the social worker. Erin couldn't turn away. She felt the small child against her breast, felt her sorrow and her pain as she cried hot tears against Erin's neck. Tears ran down Erin's face and she tasted the salt as they reached the corners of her mouth.

Reaching into her purse, she pulled out tissues and wiped Sam's face.

"We have to go inside now and talk to some people."

"About what?"

"Where you will live now."

"Home." A stubborn streak that appeared occasionally popped up in the little girl.

"We'll have to find one of your relatives."

Sam didn't speak. Erin wasn't sure she understood. They went inside. The third floor corridor was full of people. Policemen, people waiting outside doors or lines waiting to get in. Child Welfare was at the end of the corridor where several benches had been placed. There were two other children sitting there. They looked about ten or eleven years old.

The social worker who'd come to the school went inside. The policeman stood a few feet away as if to keep the child from running away. Erin sat Sam on the bench.

"It's all right, Sam." The huge eyes looked unsure. "I have to go in there and talk to these people. Will you be all right here?"

"I come," she said, clinging to Erin's arm.

Erin shook her head. "I have to talk to them alone." Sam grabbed Erin's sleeve. "It's all right, Sam. I'll be back and then we'll go home."

She didn't know what she was promising, but Sam released her hold. Erin watched tears flood Sam's eyes. Erin fished in her purse for a game and handed it to the little girl. Sam took it but didn't find it as fascinating as she often did.

Inside, Erin was ushered to the back of the room where the gray-suited Ms. Lawrence worked. She explained what happened in circumstances where a child was left alone after an accident or abandonment.

"She was not abandoned. Her parents died." Erin stopped and took hold of her temper. "She's a child, Ms. Lawrence. She's four years old. She hasn't truly comprehended what is happening to her. You can't send her to a foster home."

"It's just until we find her relatives."

"No." Erin stood firm. "She's already had one trauma, and I'm not sure she understands the impact of it. To be sent to strangers, she'll really feel abandoned."

"Ms. Taylor, this is really none of your business."

Erin stood up. "Children are my business. I run a day-care center where we *care* for children. This child in particular." Erin took a breath. "I have an idea."

At that point another social worker appeared in the doorway. "Anything wrong?" she asked. Ms. Lawrence shook her head.

"Sam is used to staying with me. Why don't you just let her stay until you find her relatives?"

"This is outside of procedure. You're not an authorized foster parent."

"Then authorize me."

"It's not that easy. There are procedures that need to be followed. You have to have a—"

"Sam regularly stays at my home overnight. Whenever her parents are away I am their sitter. She has her own room, even some of her clothes are at my house."

"Ms. Taylor, you don't understand," the unidentified woman spoke.

"I understand that a child is out there," she pointed toward the door, "whose parents died yesterday and who is alone and frightened and you want to put her with strangers when she could stay with someone she knows and loves."

"That is not how things are done."

"Then change how things are done."

Luanne would be starving by now. Digger was late picking her up for lunch. He took the stairs two at a time. Turning into the hallway he was surprised to see it full of people. And equally surprised to see Samantha Pierce.

"Digger," she said without the usual pleasure in her eyes. She started running toward him. Instinctively he hunched down to receive her. She was crying. "What's wrong, Sam?"

"Gone," she sobbed and tightened her arms around his neck.

Digger carried her with him straight to his sister's office. Luanne looked up at the noise.

"What's going on?" she asked, standing up.

"I thought you could tell me. What is Sam doing here?"

"Sam?"

He tried to pull the little girl back, but she continued to sob on his shoulder and tightened her arms.

"Samantha Pierce. She's one of the children from Erin's nursery school."

Luanne looked at him. She walked around and tried to see Sam's face. The child hid it further in his shoulder. Luanne touched Sam's hand.

"Luanne?" Digger asked again.

"Sam's parents had an accident yesterday on the way back from Austin."

"That's why they didn't pick her up."

Luanne's knowing eyes flashed understanding that Digger had somehow been with Erin and knew about Sam's predicament.

"Are they going to be all right?"

Sam answered with her arms, squeezing tighter around

him. Luanne shook her head and without speaking he understood what the child meant when she'd said, *gone*.

"What are they going to do with her?"

Luanne didn't get to answer. A loud argument grabbed their attention, and they looked in the direction of the noise.

Digger recognized Erin's voice.

"We can hear you all the way to my office." Luanne Rogers stood in the door. Behind her was Digger holding Sam.

Erin sat quietly while Ms. Lawrence explained what happened to Sam's parents and Erin's unreasonable request.

"I can vouch for her," Digger said. Four sets of eyes went to him. "What she says is true. Sam does have a room at her house. I carried the little girl there last night. She stays often, and she loves Ms. Taylor."

"Thank you, Mr. Clayton, but—"

"Gemma, get the papers for foster care ready." Luanne addressed the woman in the gray-suit. "I know Ms. Taylor and I can also vouch for her." When Ms. Lawrence started to speak, Luanne cut her off. "We've done this before and we are here to look out for the best interest of the child. What better hands can she be in than someone who already knows her and loves her?" She turned to Erin. "Fill out the forms and leave them with Ms. Lawrence. We'll get everything else done as quickly as possible."

Erin silently thanked Luanne.

Chapter Nine

George and Claudia Pierce were laid to rest two days later after a simple ceremony. Erin wasn't sure if Sam understood any of what was going on. She clung to Erin or Digger, refusing to allow anyone else to touch her. She'd taken the photo of her parents from the nightstand in her room at Erin's house and carried it everywhere.

The university had hosted the burial meal. Erin and Digger attended with Sam. She ate only a small amount before she climbed into Erin's lap and fell asleep. Digger carried her to the car. The day had been exhausting, and she needed to sleep.

Digger also carried Sam into Erin's house and put her to bed.

Erin had noticed he'd eaten little at the funeral dinner. She placed a large glass of iced tea in front of him and warmed up some of last night's leftovers, lamb chops with mint jelly, mashed potatoes and peas. Sam usually liked lamb chops, but

Erin hadn't been able to get her to eat much and there was plenty left over.

She and Digger ate in silence. He finished first and pushed his plate aside. He finished his iced tea and got up to refill his glass. Erin watched the comfortable way he moved about her kitchen.

"Do you think she'll be all right?" he asked. She heard the concern in his voice. He'd been abandoned at thirteen, and he wore the scars to this day. Would Sam's be deeper?

"She's younger than you were. She doesn't understand a lot of what's happening now, but in time she will."

He sat down and linked his hands together, resting his chin on them. "It was nineteen years ago this August, and I remember the day my parents died with the same clarity as if it had happened yesterday. I was stunned at first. I didn't believe them when they told me. I thought it was all an elaborate trick someone was playing on me."

Erin reached over and placed her hand on his arm. He took her hand and by mutual agreement they both stood up and went into the family room. Digger picked up his glass of iced tea and held her hand with his free one.

"The school principal called me into his office and told me I had to go home, that someone would drive me."

Erin listened. She understood the fantasies that could build when people didn't know what was going on.

"The police were there when I got there and they immediately took me away."

Erin squeezed his hand and pulled him down onto the sofa.

"No one would explain anything. I kept asking questions and no one would tell me a thing. Finally, one of the neighbors, a man from down the block convinced the cop to let him talk to me for a moment. He told me."

Flashes of Erin's conversation with Sam as they sat on the bench outside the courthouse came back to her. She hadn't wanted Sam to learn of it from a stranger, someone she didn't know and didn't care about.

"It's good you were there with Sam."

"You care about her, don't you?"

He looked away from her as if she'd entered a secret place.

"She's hard not to like. She runs into you, puts her little arms around your neck and squeezes with all her might." Digger had a slight smile on his face. The kind that comes from pleasant memories. Erin knew he had terrible memories from his past. She was glad Sam had given him a good one.

"She's been at the school since she was six months old."

"She came that young?"

Erin nodded. "I've had her since she was practically born. I was working there when we had three infants. We could only take three because they required constant care. Sam was mine."

"She's still yours," Digger whispered.

"Only for a little while. I don't know of any relatives, but I'm sure Social Services will find someone. Then she'll be gone."

Erin had turned away from Digger when she said that. She didn't want him to see her face when she thought of Sam going away permanently, but he pressed her shoulder into the sofa so he could see her face.

"She's not mine," Erin said. "I know that. She's just been with me a very long time. I love Sam as if she were my own. I never imagined I wouldn't see her go to school, grow up, marry and have children of her own."

"Maternal instinct," Digger said.

"Call it what you will. I can't imagine going to work every day and not having her rush across the room and throw herself into my arms."

"I completely understand," he said simply.

For several moments neither of them spoke. Erin was alone in her own musings of what would happen next. She didn't know what Digger was thinking. He hadn't been around Sam as long as she had, but he seemed to like Sam just as much.

Finally, he got up. "I have to leave now," he said.

She got up, too. "Thank you for coming with me today. I'm sure it meant something to Sam even if she doesn't know it yet."

He nodded. It was a gesture he used when he felt embarrassed about a compliment. Erin had seen him do it several times, and she expected it now.

"If you need any help with Sam's adjustment, call Luanne. She's very good with children. She'd love to hear from you again."

"I will." Erin wanted to call *him,* but he'd passed her off to his sister. "I also want to say thank you."

"For what?"

They were walking toward her door. "Helping us. You told me you didn't want to be around us, but at every turn you're there." She looked up at him. "I appreciate it. I don't know what would have happened at Child Welfare if you hadn't been there."

He nodded again. Erin took a step forward. She knew it was a bad idea, but she didn't care. When Digger went through the door this time, she might never see him again, outside of the construction yard. She stepped into his arms and hugged him around the middle, resting her head on his chest.

The action surprised him. He went stiff for a moment. A lifetime of seconds passed before she felt his arms encircle her. Erin dissolved into him. She didn't care if he knew how she felt. He was leaving and this was farewell.

Digger's hands went into her hair. She felt his lips on her temple and a wave of passion coursed through her.

"Goodbye," he whispered.

Three weeks later Luanne was right on time for Erin's third home visit. According to regulations, a foster parent had to have three in-home visits. Luanne was accelerating the procedure. Erin opened the door Saturday morning to admit Digger's sister, and Digger was with her.

"I hope you don't mind. We thought Sam might want some of her toys and clothes from home. Digger brought them."

Erin stood back to allow them access. She hadn't seen him since the day of Sam's parents' funeral. Her eyes were hungry for the sight of him.

"Where do you want them?" he asked.

"By the stairs. Sam is asleep. I don't want to wake her yet." Erin stared at his back as he walked away. It felt like a lifetime since she'd seen him.

The addition was progressing. The foundation had been poured and the walls were going up. Erin had vacated her office since the outside wall was knocked down. If Digger still came at night she didn't see him. She left at closing each day and she and Sam went home to spend the evening together.

Erin took Luanne into the kitchen and poured her coffee. They sat at the table with a plate of cookies between them. Luanne wasn't here on a search and destroy mission, it was more like a get-to-know-you visit.

"How's she doing?" Luanne asked.

"She clings all the time. I can't go anywhere without her. I think she's afraid I'll go away and not come back."

"That's pretty normal. She needs time."

"She's not her old animated self. She doesn't talk like she used to, and she carries a photo of her parents all the time."

Digger came in then. He went to the counter and poured himself a cup of coffee. Erin wondered if his sister noticed how comfortable he was in Erin's kitchen. He didn't join them at the table, but brought the cup to the counter and leaned against it.

"How are *you?*" Luanne asked.

Erin's head snapped up. "I'm fine."

"That's not true," Luanne stated.

Erin hesitated a moment. She felt Digger staring at her

back. "I feel helpless. She's so hurt, and there's nothing I can do to help her."

"You *are* helping her," Digger said. "You're with her. She'll come around. Just keep being there for her." Who better to know than him, someone who'd gone through the same kind of loss?

Erin nodded and offered a smile. Luanne took one of the cookies. "Have you had any luck in locating a relative?" Erin asked. She hoped no one heard the quiver in her voice.

"Not yet. Apparently both her parents were only children and both their parents are deceased."

"What happens if you find someone?"

"Don't you mean what happens to you if we don't find someone?"

Erin dropped her head. She did mean that. She didn't realize how quickly she'd become attached to Sam. She loved the little girl and wanted to make sure she smiled again. Anyone who came along now would be another stranger. Sam needed stability in her life, but Erin wasn't a blood-tie. That meant something to families. If any of Erin's sisters died she'd gladly rush to take care of their children. Erin had to be prepared to give up Samantha.

"It's going to be hard to give her up."

Luanne reached across the table and took her arm. "You can have a family of your own." Erin noticed that Luanne slanted a glance at her brother when she said that.

Erin felt like telling Luanne the whole story of her life, but she held back. Erin would never have a family of her own. She knew that. She'd accepted it years ago. But with Sam she had something of her dream. Still, she didn't want to hope for too much.

"There is that option," she said, knowing there was no such option open to her. The roller coaster collapse so many years ago had sealed her fate. "How long before a search is given up?"

"Before she becomes a ward of the state?"

"That sounds archaic."

"There is no set time period. When the search is exhausted. When all possible searches and avenues are checked. When that's done and nothing more can be, we consider it over. She becomes a ward of the state. Until then, she's yours."

Until then. The words were like loosening the bolts of the sword over her head. She could have Sam but only for a short time. She'd fought the dragon of temporary custody. She'd won the battle, but invariably the war would be lost.

"I have to go now," Luanne said. She got up. Erin walked her to the door. "This was the final visit. You're official now." Luanne walked down the steps and toward Digger's Bronco parked in the driveway.

"Digger," Erin stopped him. "Thank you."

"For what?"

"Being a gentleman."

Digger's eyes met hers. They stared at each other in silence. Erin could smell him. She wanted to lean forward and touch him, kiss him. She didn't know what to make of the look in his eyes. Was it lust, love, regret, hurt, confusion? There were too many things it could be and he gave her no signal.

Finally, she fell back on something neutral. "Thanks for bringing the toys. I'm sure Sam will be happy when she sees them."

"Goodbye, Erin."

He went out the door. Erin caught the swinging screen and stopped it. He'd said goodbye. Erin didn't expect to see him again. There was no need. They had nothing between them, and she had Sam to take care of now.

Digger sat in his car, across from the school, a week later. He felt like a stalker. He wanted to see Erin one more time. He knew this was crazy, spying on her, watching her when she didn't know he was there, but this was the only way. He couldn't approach her, couldn't be near her. Each time he got close his hands found a life of their own; they invariably pulled her against him. After that he had no will that didn't involve his taking her in his arms and kissing her. He had to keep a lot of distance between them, but he also had to see her.

No other car had stopped in front of the school for the past fifteen minutes. She had to come out soon. She usually left at six. Checking his watch it was a few minutes before the hour. When she finally came out, he sat up in the seat. She was holding one of Sam's hands and she was limping.

"What's she been doing?" he asked no one. He watched as she slowly progressed to the van and settled Sam in the car seat. Then she limped around to the driver's door and got in.

When the van pulled into the street Digger was right behind it. He followed her home, pulling into her driveway directly behind her. He got out and walked to the driver's door just as she turned off the engine. Digger yanked the door open.

"What the hell is wrong with you?"

He was acting like a crazy man and he knew it, but he couldn't stop. "You only limp if you overdo. So what have you been doing?"

"Back off," she screamed, pushing him away. "I'm too tired to argue with you. Now go away and leave me alone."

"I can't leave you alone," he said. "I keep trying, but you're in my blood." He pulled her into his arms and kissed her, his mouth hot and seeking, devouring, punishing, his body instantly hard with a need that surpassed anything he'd ever known. Erin slumped, accepting the onslaught of raging emotions that forced him over the edge.

"Digger," she said breathlessly when his mouth slid from hers. "I can't stop you from following me, coming to the school or showing up at my house. I can't stop the way I feel about you. But I can't go on like this, either. Make up your mind. Either there's going to be a relationship or there's not. Stop playing me like a yo-yo."

"I know it's unfair. I don't know what comes over me. I saw you limping and something inside me snapped. You look tired, and you need my help."

"It's harder than I thought it would be—Sam, the school, grief. I spend the whole night talking to her, trying to get her to understand why her world has changed."

"Go in. I'll get Sam."

Erin headed for the inside garage door and hit the button that automatically closed the outside doors. Digger opened the van's sliding door and found Sam asleep. In her hands was a picture frame. He picked it up and looked at it. It was the one from the bedroom. Lying it down he unhooked her harness and lifted her out of the seat.

She woke up and saw him.

"Hi, Sam." He smiled. She started to scream, fighting in his arms, trying to get down. Digger held on to her to keep her from falling and hurting herself.

Erin appeared in the doorway. "Digger, her picture."

"What?" He couldn't hear what Erin said. Sam was fighting him for all her forty pounds were worth.

"The photograph."

Erin started down the steps. He saw the photo and grabbed for it. He showed it to Sam. She grabbed it from him, holding it to her small breast as if it would save her life. Digger breathed hard.

"What was that all about?" he asked when he got her in the house. Sam was holding on to Erin's arm as she sat at the kitchen table.

"She never lets it out of her sight," Erin explained. "It's like her security blanket. She needs it until she feels secure again. Right now she thinks the people she loves will go away and not come back."

Digger glanced at Sam. She was a different child from the one he'd met that first day, the one he'd caught in his arms many times since. She was sullen and lost. He recognized the symptoms. He knew where they could lead. Erin lifted her onto her lap and held her, stroking her hair and talking to her. That was the best that could be done.

"Take her into the other room and you both put your feet up."

"I have to get her something to eat," Erin said.

"I'll do it."

He went over and helped her up. Whatever she'd been doing for the past week was catching up with her. Her hip was in pain, and he felt like it was all his fault.

Back in the kitchen he fixed what he could find, mainly leftover dishes that he heated in the microwave. They came out too hot or not hot enough. Neither Erin or Sam complained. They all ate in the family room.

He tried to make Sam smile. She did several times but he could see her heart wasn't in it. At bedtime he gave her a bath, keeping the photograph in sight and put her to bed holding it.

Erin lay on the sofa where he'd left her. She was asleep too, but opened her eyes when he approached her.

"I didn't mean to wake you."

She sat up. "Is she asleep?"

He nodded. "What have you been doing?"

"Crawling over cases to find things. I had to move everything out of my office so they could break the wall down and I can't find anything."

"Why didn't you ask Jackson to do that?"

"They moved the heavy stuff. It's why I can't find anything. Then Sam is constantly clinging to me. Sometimes she wakes up during the night and cries."

"So you're not sleeping well either?"

She shook her head. "But I'm so tired now I think I'll go to sleep and never wake up."

"Not yet," he said. "I'm going to massage that hip. Stay here." He left her and went to the kitchen. While cleaning up earlier he'd seen the coconut oil. Bath oil would probably be better but he wouldn't go looking through her bathroom. This would do, and it had a nice soothing smell.

He poured it into a bowl and set it in the microwave while he went into the garage and collected some things he could use to construct a makeshift table. Then he gathered all the towels from the downstairs bathroom.

"What are you doing?" Erin called.

"I'm nearly done." The microwave bell rang, and he lifted the bowl of oil out and set it on the counter.

"I need you to come to the kitchen," he said, offering her a hand to help her up. Erin took it without argument and limped into the softly lit room.

"What is this?"

"This is for the pain. It requires a little trust."

"Trust?" She immediately became defensive.

"I'm going to have to touch you, massage your hip." She looked as if she were weighing her options. "I promise it will make you feel better." He tried to keep anything personal out of his voice. "Think of it as a doctor treating you."

"You're not a doctor."

"Tonight I just want your pain to go away."

There was a load of meaning in his comment, but none of it sexual. He could help her and he was willing—if she would trust him. He'd massaged her hip before, but this time would be different.

The bowl of oil was sitting on the counter and the smell of coconut wafted through the air. He'd lowered the shades, brought in some sawhorses and boards and used them to extend the kitchen counter to accommodate her height. He'd covered the counter and boards with sleeping bags he'd found in the garage. On top of those he'd spread the towels.

"I need you to lie down on this."

A pain must have caught her for she squeezed her teeth together and waited a moment before she said anything. "What do I have to do?"

"Just lie down here and put these over you." He offered her the towels.

"Without my clothes?"

"Yes."

The single word hung in the air as if he'd said sex instead of yes. He wasn't planning on sex. Not tonight.

"I kept my clothes on before."

"This time I'm using oil."

"You've done this before?"

He nodded. "In construction there are always aches and pains." That was the truth, but he'd learned massage to take care of his foster father. He'd had an accident that had left him bedridden for six months. Digger had massaged his legs and helped him exercise until he recovered. Touching Erin would be different, but she was in pain and he could help.

"I'll get a robe and change." She started toward the hallway.

"I'll get it. Where is it?"

"Bathroom, through my bedroom."

She seemed reluctant to tell him, but walking all the way down the hall and back was obviously more painful than him seeing her bathroom. Or seeing the sexy nightgown he found hanging next to the robe.

He handed her the robe, and she changed in the small bathroom off the kitchen. Digger turned the radio to a classical music station, then helped her onto the counter assembly and exchanged the robe for the large towels. He tested the heated oil and poured it into his hands. He began the practiced ritual.

"Ohhh," she breathed. "That feels good."

He didn't say anything. He kept the pressure even, stroking in one direction, elongating the muscles, relaxing them

and forcing them to release the pain that caused her discomfort.

Erin didn't want to concentrate on his hands. They were
too warm and sent too many signals to her body.

"Tell me about your brothers," she asked to keep her mind
off his hands. "Why aren't any of them married?"

"You're supposed to be quiet."

"I will be quiet. You're the one who'll do the talking."

He laughed.

"The last time you went to sleep. Sleep is good for you.
You already told me you were tired."

She yawned as if on cue. He added more oil to her side and
leg, pouring it over her brown skin, turning it a burnished
gold. He massaged her muscles, using long strokes from waist
to hip. With the music and the low light Erin eventually fell
asleep. He continued the massage, doing her back and hips and
legs.

Then he covered her with the robe and towels and carried
her to bed.

"Stay with me," she said as he lay her on the sheets.

"You're supposed to be asleep."

"You're supposed to be made of stone. Let's see if either
of those are true." She raised her head and her mouth met his.
Digger let her body sink into the mattress and he sat down
on it, taking her face in his hands as he looked into her eyes.

"I could hurt you," he whispered.

"Only if you stop now."

She slipped closer to him, bringing her mouth back into
contact with his. Digger held back. He didn't think he could
do this. She'd been limping badly. But her tongue crept into
his mouth and he was lost. He cradled her closer, deepening
the kiss, threading his fingers through her hair as the world
tilted.

For days, weeks, he'd dreamed of holding her in his arms,
of her naked under him, of their bodies joined. Now he

couldn't deny himself any longer. He wanted to know everything about her. He wanted to hear the sounds she made in the dark, wanted to taste her, learn her body inch by inch. He wanted to know the pitch of her voice when she climaxed and the way she sighed when she was truly sated. If he were to go on breathing, he had to have her.

Erin's hand reached for the buttons on his shirt. The towels fell away from her, leaving her exposed to him. He touched her hot skin. Waves of heat radiated through him as the shirt opened and she pushed it over his shoulders and arms. He shrugged out of it as if it were an enemy. His hands took hold of her. Her body was slick with oil and his hands slid frictionlessly over smooth skin. She smelled of coconut, reminded him of tropical beaches, palms swaying in the breeze, dark waterfalls and mysterious secrets to be explored.

He touched every part of her, sliding his hands over her arms and legs, tracing the zigzagging scar on her left leg, learning the contours of her waist and hips, outlining the length of her legs from her toes to her hipbone. Her skin was smooth, warm as wine and dark as the night.

Her breath was ragged as his mouth seized hers. Passion built between them, leading them to some quest neither of them had been on before. Digger shed his clothes while he watched her lying naked on the bed. Her eyelids were half-closed, a sexy, drowsy kind of look that took in everything he offered. She looked coquettish and wanton at the same time.

Digger closed the bedroom door. He snapped the lock into place and came to her, joining her on the bed and pulling her into his arms. Her mouth sought his as if he'd left her a hundred years earlier instead of the few seconds it took to discard his clothing.

The arms that enclosed him were in no pain. The mouth that found his, that burnished it with want and need showed no vestiges of being tired. And when he entered her, the legs that parted had no need for massage. Digger tried not to hurt her. He set the rhythm at a slow pace. He heard Erin moan, heard the guttural sounds that came from her throat.

He kissed her breasts, twin peaks that butted upward like brown cones. She raised her legs. He slipped further into her. Digger gritted his teeth and tried to hold back, but she arched upward into him, taking him fully inside her. Digger was lost.

He slipped his hands under her, massaged her buttocks and slammed himself into her. The need to do it again and again swept over him. She was beautiful. Being with her made him beautiful.

Erin met every thrust. Her back arched as her body accepted his invasion, craved it, thirsted for more pleasure. He rode her, rode hard and fast, as if something chased him, forced him to reach higher, go for something greater than he'd ever reached before. Erin seemed to understand. She was with him, reaching for the zenith, stretching upward. Her hands were on his back, raking down his skin. He could feel everything, his blood pumping, his nerves at skin level individually touched by the sensitized skin of Erin's fingers.

Digger had never felt like this, like there was a nirvana out there reserved for the two of them. That there was a quest he couldn't refuse. That he had to get there. He had to reach it, had to go with Erin and no one else. He heard his voice, the groans that mingled with hers, the uncontrolled force that pushed the two of them toward each other, that took the two of them and made a single individual of them.

Digger felt the wave begin, the trigger that flowed through his entire body, the rush that started near his belly and raced downward. He held back, holding it, keeping the rhythm going, continuing the pleasure he sought. He could feel it in Erin. She writhed under him, uncontrolled, hot.

Then it happened. The explosion, the discharged dynamite, the eruption, with volcanic proportions that sent them to the place they had been seeking, the place of pure and honest pleasure.

They clung to each other, breathing hard. Erin's arms were around him, and he was lying on her. The smell of sex surrounded them, keeping them high for a few more seconds. Digger wished he could hold on to the moment. Keep it, relive it, but all too soon they were floating back to earth, back to the softness of the mattress.

He rolled off of her, taking her with him as he removed any pressure from her hip. He kept her close, smelling her hair, taking in the sweet odor of their love and thinking that the reality of them together was so much greater than anything he'd dreamed.

Chapter Ten

Sunlight slanted across Erin's face. She opened her eyes. Digger was gone. Disappointment streamed through her. She wanted to wake up with him, crawl into his arms and have him make love to her again. She wanted to run her hands over his body, feeling the taut muscles under his skin and knowing there was a tenderness inside him that was reserved only for her.

She grabbed his pillow and inhaled the scent of him. He had been there. It wasn't a dream. She could smell him on the sheets and the pillowcase, feel that delicious stiffness between her legs that told her they'd made love, exciting love, the kind that changed lives.

Erin got up and went to the shower. The bed looked as if they'd danced on it and indeed they had. She couldn't remember a better dance. She got under the water. He'd been there. The shower was still wet and the air in the stall had the sweetness of soap and the tangy roughness that she thought of when she thought of Digger.

Is this how people fell in love? she wondered. With the love coming one slice of life at a time? He'd come to her rescue, taken her under his hands and removed her pain, then made love to her like no other, like she didn't know love could be made. Erin washed her hair and let the shampoo slide down her body in great bubbles. She should remember her vows, but she wouldn't this morning. The vestiges of last night lingered with her, lifting her heart and making her feel happier than she had in years. She wouldn't break the spell.

She dressed quickly in shorts and a top and kept her hair inside a towel turban. Checking on Sam, she found her bed empty. Where was she? Erin wondered. Since her parents died Sam had clung to Erin every minute.

Padding silently down the hall, she heard Digger's deep voice speaking lowly. Erin was glad he was still there, that he hadn't left her alone with another goodbye. She stood and watched them from the corner of the family room. Digger had Sam in his lap. She held the photo.

"Who is this?" Digger asked.

"Mommy," Sam said without sadness.

"And this?"

"My dad."

"What does your dad call you?"

"Sy."

"Who am I?"

She laughed. Tears clouded Erin's eyes. Sam hadn't smiled in weeks and now she was laughing.

"You're Digger, silly."

"I'm Digger Silly?" He acted surprised.

"No, Digger."

"Well, Sam, why don't we get some breakfast. Maybe then you can wake up Erin."

"Awake now."

Sam looked over his shoulder. Digger turned around and saw her. Erin left the wall where she stood and came into the room. She stopped next to the sofa where he sat. His hand touched her leg and tremors of excitement rushed through her.

"Good morning," he said with a sly smile.

"Good morning."

"Did you sleep well?"

"Better than ever," she told him. She had slept well, but neither of them were talking about sleep.

"Waffles?" Sam asked.

Erin returned her attention to Sam. "Sure, we can have waffles."

Erin headed for the kitchen. The makeshift massage table was gone; presumably Digger had put it back in the garage. Sam sat quietly in Digger's lap talking to him instead of clinging to Erin while she cooked. Erin had never seen a man as good with kids as Digger was. She wanted to ask him about his child, but she knew it would change his mood and she wanted to hold on to this moment.

Sam surprised Erin by eating a whole waffle, part of her eggs and drinking milk and orange juice. She wouldn't leave Digger's lap and the photo was placed on the table at the head of her plate. Digger didn't have a problem eating and holding the little girl. He put away three waffles, bacon, eggs, juice and coffee.

"How's your hip?" he asked when they were drinking their second cups of coffee.

"It feels normal."

"I didn't hurt you?"

She shook her head. Warmth rushed into her face at his meaning. Erin thought she was too old to blush, but thoughts of the wild ride they'd had last night were enough.

"I'd better leave." He stood up, lifting Sam with him. Small hands reached for the photo and toppled it over. It hit the table. Digger quickly retrieved it and handed it to her. Sam clutched it like a lifeline.

Erin got up and went with them. At the door, Digger set Sam on the floor. She immediately clung to Erin's leg.

They both looked down at Sam and knew they couldn't do what they wanted, be in each other's arms.

"I'd like to take you out to dinner tonight," he drawled. His eyes were bright and trained on her mouth. "But I guess we can't leave her with anyone."

"Not yet."

"How about I pick you up at six? We can all have dinner together."

"Will we be going to Luanne's or any of your relatives?" Erin needed more details this time. She didn't want to be surprised.

"Dinner will be at Chez James's."

"Your place?"

"My place. I'll get some kid videos and cook my specialty."

"Spaghetti or chili?"

He looked nonplussed. "Chili."

"Maybe I'd better drive. I have a car seat."

Sam was looking back into the living room. Digger grabbed a quick kiss and smiled. He said bye to Sam and went out.

"Well, honey, it's just us for the day. What would you like to do?"

Sam said the last thing Erin expected to hear.

"Go home."

Child psychology had been Erin's major, but she'd never gone any further than her Bachelor's degree. Sam was only four. Erin wondered if it would be harmful to take her to her home. It might help. Sam had left there one morning and never seen it again. The house was sitting empty. They were waiting to locate one of Sam's relatives. If no one appeared, the house belonged to Sam.

Erin called Luanne during Sam's nap and the two of them agreed it was all right to let her go back there, but to try and make her understand she could not stay.

"One more thing," Luanne said before she hung up. "You should take Digger with you."

"Why Digger?"

"She trusts the two of you. She's most likely to believe you. If you go to the house together, she'll have the two of you to fall back on when she discovers her parents aren't there."

"Luanne, that's an awful lot like a second father and mother waiting in the wings."

"It is, but under these circumstances I think that's what Sam needs."

Erin knew Digger's thoughts on a family. He didn't want one, but he didn't act like that when she and Sam were with him. Still, she thought asking him to go with them was manipulation on his sister's part.

"You're still looking for a relative." Erin said. "If you find one, they may not be married and she won't get surrogate parents."

"I'll leave the decision to you. I think the trust factor is more important. She's only four. She may not see you two as parents, but you're the only adults in her life that she trusts."

Erin hung up. She didn't like the idea of setting Sam up or of forcing Digger to be a parent. He'd rebel against it just as he had that first day in her office. He was an adult. He'd see the manipulation.

But Erin had to do it. She had to do what was best for Sam. And she needed Digger's help.

Adobe ranch houses were commonplace in this part of Texas. Digger's had distinction. The muted red and gold colors complemented the land around it, and the house sprawled. It had a center entrance and wings on opposites sides. Varieties of spiny cacti grew in his yard, some showing their colors and others hiding behind the green and straw-yellow of the season.

The double doors were black, lacquered smooth and shielded by full-screen doors that allowed the beauty to show through.

"We're early," Erin said the moment he opened the door.

"Three hours," Digger checked his watch. "Come on in."

Erin didn't move. Sam was clinging to her.

"What's wrong?"

"I need you to come with us."

"Where?"

"Sam's house."

Erin didn't know what his reaction would be, but she knew there would be one. It was something about children that was a point she touched each time she brought them up.

"Why?"

"Sam wants to go there, and Luanne and I thought it might be good for her if she gets to see it."

"Luanne said this?"

Erin nodded.

Some kind of understanding came into his eyes. She didn't ask what it was or try to understand it.

"I'll get my keys."

In seconds they were back in the van and heading for Sam's address. Erin had been there several times. She'd been very friendly with the Pierces and often attended holiday parties or summer picnics.

She parked in the driveway. Digger hadn't said a word since they left his house. He got Sam out of the car seat while Erin opened the front door. The three of them went in together, Digger carrying Sam and her picture, Erin following them.

Sam squirmed to get down and he set her on the floor. She took off running, calling "Mommy" or "Dad" as she went from room to room.

Erin and Digger stepped closer to each other. Their hands connected and held as Sam ran around. The house had been closed since her parents' deaths. It smelled a little musty, but someone must have cleared the trash away for there was no odor of decaying food.

When Sam rushed upstairs, Digger kept hold of Erin's hand as they followed her. For the most part, they were staying out of Sam's way, allowing her to find what she sought in her own time. When she discovered her parents weren't there, Erin and Digger wanted to be close by. They wanted her to know she wasn't alone.

Sam ran through each room, opening doors and looking inside. When she finally returned to the hall she looked at them standing by the stairs.

"Gone," she said.

Erin kneeled and opened her arms. Sam ran into them and clung to her.

Digger hunched down. "Can I carry you, Sam?" She went into his arms and he turned. The photo frame fell from her hands and bounced down the stairs. The glass broke, and shards sprayed over the stairs like small diamonds.

"It's all right," Digger calmed her before she could begin to cry. "It's only the frame that's broken."

Carefully, they went down the stairs. Erin picked up the frame and took the picture out. Sam grabbed it immediately, smoothing it out and holding it against her.

"Take her into the other room," Erin said. "I'll clean up the glass."

They left soon after. Sam's eyes were dry, but Erin thought Sam understood that her parents were gone forever. That they weren't hiding somewhere and they wouldn't be coming back.

"Are we still invited to dinner?" Erin asked as she went into the room where Sam and Digger sat. She wanted Sam to realize she wasn't alone.

Digger got up. Sam continued looking at her picture.

Digger came to Erin and kissed her, not desperately, but thoroughly. "Of course you're still invited to dinner. I might even want you *for* dinner."

On Monday morning Digger joined the building crew. Erin's heart jumped when she saw his truck already parked in the lot on her arrival. She headed around the front of the building where she'd parked since construction began. As she got Sam out of her seat he saw them and waved from across the yard.

"Digger here," Sam said, pointing.

"I see him, too," Erin told her.

Sam dropped her hand and the two of them went inside. It wasn't long before the other children arrived and the daily routine began. Erin was busy most of the morning as today's program was primed with mishaps, class disruptions and squabbles. Every toy had at least two kids claiming it.

Erin wanted to run to the windows and make sure Digger was out there. She hadn't been this giddy since she was sixteen and all dressed up, waiting for her first date to a dance, but the kids kept her away. At ten o'clock, she saw him when she and Sam took coffee outside. He had his shirt off and a fine sheen of dust and sweat coated his skin. Erin had never seen anyone look sexier.

She remembered their weekend, how that hard, muscled body had held her, how tender those strong hands could be. She imagined making love to him again. He didn't come for coffee, but kept working. She understood why. Silently they communicated, without words, with only a look. They were like dynamite and matches. If he got near her, they would explode.

The crew left at five. Erin and her shadow, Sam, left at six. At eight-thirty when she'd put Sam to bed and returned to the living room, Digger was at the door.

He took her in his arms and pushed her inside, kicking the door closed behind him. "Good morning," he said.

"It's not morning."

He kissed her again. "Good afternoon."

"It's not afternoon."

Again, he kissed her. "Good night."

"If I keep this up, how long will this go on?"

"As long as I can stand it," he groaned and deepened the kiss. Erin gave herself up to Digger. She wrapped her arms around his neck and pushed her aroused body into his. Digger's hands roved down her back and over her hips. Erin trembled as her nerve endings sprang to life.

Digger lifted his head. He kept his arm around her as they walked to the sofa.

"Do you want something to drink?"

He gathered her close to him as they sat down. "I already have a drink." His look was openly lustful.

Erin settled against him. She felt at home, happy, peaceful. For a moment, they said nothing.

"How's Sam?" he asked.

"She's still clinging. I'd hoped taking her back to her home would resolve some of the issues she's holding inside."

"She's only four, Erin. She'll come around. Children are remarkably resilient."

Erin wanted to ask him a million questions. She knew it would alter him, change his good mood to something unhappy. But she had to bring it up.

"Digger, what happened to your son?"

She felt him retreat. He didn't move; his body was against hers. He was holding her, one arm around her shoulder, the other draped around her waist, yet her question had separated them, drawn a line between them that became a gap. He shifted away from her, moving his arms, linking his hands and sitting forward.

"Don't go there."

"Why not?"

"I don't want to talk about that." He stood up and paced the room. He pushed his hands in his pockets. Erin had never seen him like this. She recognized hurt. She knew a lost child was something you never got over.

"Maybe if you did you could make peace with it."

"What do you know?" he snapped.

Erin sat back as if he'd hit her. She got up and went to him. She raised her arms and dropped them, unsure if he'd let her touch him.

"Don't you trust me, Digger?"

He faced her and she went into his arms. It felt good to be held.

"This has nothing to do with trust."

"It has everything to do with trust." The words echoed in her mind as if she hadn't realized what she'd said and it needed to be repeated back to her, reverberated as it gained strength and volume. Erin pushed herself out of his arms. She had assumed they were a couple, that they were developing a relationship. That there was a future for the two of them.

Together.

She should have known better. That wasn't going to happen.

"What's wrong?" Digger asked.

"I'm stepping over the line."

"What are you talking about?"

"I made an incorrect assumption." He was about to say something, but she continued. "It isn't you. You didn't do anything. I assumed we were on the road to a relationship. I forgot that neither one of us is looking for a relationship. Relationships require trust, commitment, a willingness to share. What we have is as simple as chemistry."

"Erin—"

"It's all right." She raised her hands, palms out, interrupting him. "I know some people equate chemistry with love.

I'm not one of them. But I was falling, Digger. I was well and truly on my way."

She crossed her arms, turned around, presenting him with her back. She was confused. Somehow she'd forgotten, lost herself in his lovemaking, in the magic they created when they joined. With him she'd lost control, forgotten to keep a tight rein on her emotions. She'd forgotten that this was not for her, not her life.

"Erin, I'm sorry."

"Don't apologize." She turned back to him. "I'm a hypocrite, too." She thought of the accident. He'd lost a child. She had lost the ability to bear one.

Digger moved toward her. Erin moved out of reach.

"Leave."

He didn't move. He look shocked as if she'd touched him with a stun gun.

"Erin," he said, moving to take her in his arms.

"There are a million things you don't know about me. Just as there must be a million I don't know about you. Things we will never know."

"I don't know what to say."

"Don't say anything. Just go."

He didn't move.

"Go!" she shouted.

He stared at her for a moment, then turned and left.

She waited. She knew the sound of his footsteps, knew how long it would take him to cross the porch, the walkway, reach the door and climb into the cab of his truck. She knew the second it would start up and how long it would take to back into the street. She waited that precise amount of time before she sank down onto the sofa and stared dry-eyed into the dying light of the summer sun.

The music was loud. The place was smoky. Digger sat at the bar, a glass of bourbon in his hand. He read the napkin,

Eddie's Bar. He was in Austin. He didn't remember how he'd gotten there. He'd left Erin's and drove. He didn't know where to go. He couldn't go home. Erin had been there, and he could remember her sitting in his living room, eating at his table, holding the photo of his Lego city, laughing at something he'd said and hugging Sam. He could remember kissing her at the door and in just about every spot in which the two of them stopped.

So he drove and drove.

He thought of her and what she'd said and what she hadn't said. He needed to get on with his life, not just pretend he was getting on. He needed to bury Josh and find new experiences in the world, new risks to take. His family condoned it. They all wanted him to be happy. He was the only obstacle.

There were things he hadn't told Erin. He was falling, too. Not just falling. It was too late. He was already in love with her. He'd fallen fast and hard. He wanted to know everything about her, from the moment she was born to the second he could hold her in his arms again.

But he'd blown it. She didn't want to see him again. She thought he hadn't trusted her enough to tell her about Josh. It wasn't trust. It was fear. He couldn't handle the telling. He'd bottled that little section of his life, corked it and stored it away, refusing to look at it, to even acknowledge that it still had the ability to render him helpless. He couldn't share that.

He just couldn't.

Digger raised the shot glass. It was full. Had he drank any of it? He didn't feel as if he had. There was no buzz in his head. Yet there was a check in front of him with several dollar bills lying on top of it.

"What's her name?"

Digger looked up. The bartender stood in front of him. She looked as if she'd battled the twenties to get to thirty. She had short dark hair and a tattoo of a rose on her left forearm.

"Whose name?" he asked.

"The woman who sent you here." She leaned on the bar. She had large breasts, but her shirt was buttoned high enough that none of her cleavage showed.

"How many of these have I had?" He indicated the full shot glass.

"One, and you haven't touched it. You've held it in your hand, looked through it, but you haven't seen it." She took it out of his hand and set it down. "She's got her hooks into you bad. Most men who come in here looking to drown their brains, drink till we have to pour them in a cab and send them home. They drown for a few days or a few weeks and they go on. That won't happen to you."

"What's your name?"

"Madame Sasha, seer, prophet, crystal ball reader." She smiled. She had a beautiful smile. "Theresa," she answered seriously. "Take it from me, I've seen them all. Leave the glass. Go find her."

If only it were that easy, Digger thought.

Chapter Eleven

The first room was nearly done. Two sides of it were enclosed and one side opened into the existing building. The last wall would meet the wall of the second room. The circular structure would complement the other side of the house, making it balanced even if Digger did call it a puzzle house.

Digger hadn't been back since the night he'd left Erin's house. Erin had looked for him the next morning, but he hadn't come. She didn't know if he'd reverted to his nocturnal visits, she had to stay with Sam at night.

It was better this way, she told herself. She knew she should never have allowed herself to get close to anyone. Doing so always ended in disaster and this time had been no different.

Erin placed the coffee cups on the tray. By now she knew which of the men took their coffee black, with sugar and with cream. Three of them liked the French vanilla flavor and two others preferred non-dairy powder to cream.

With Sam holding on to her photograph and to Erin, they

left the building. In the past week Sam had allowed Erin to move small distances away from her. But Erin leaving the building without Sam would cause the child to go into hysterics.

The men saw them coming and immediately gathered to meet them. Erin passed out the cups.

"Good morning, Sam." Jackson took one of the French vanilla cups and smiled. Sam took a step closer to Erin. Each morning Jackson tried to coax Sam into talking to him. So far he hadn't gotten her to say a word. "Can I see your picture?"

Sam answered by holding the picture closer.

Out of the corner of her eye Erin saw Digger. His eyes caught hers and held. Her fingers lost their ability to grasp the tray and it trembled. For an eternity nothing moved and no sound penetrated her ears. Then he turned away. Erin felt as if someone had cut her heart out.

Sam must have seen Digger, too. For the first time since her parents died, she moved voluntarily from Erin's side—headed across the construction yard.

"Sam!" Erin called. Sam was halfway to Digger when the alarmed note in Erin's voice seemed to penetrate Digger's mind. He turned back and saw Sam heading for him. She was going to cross several planks on the ground. Erin could see that the planks covered a hole, but Sam wouldn't know that.

Digger started for Sam at a full run. She got to the planks first. Erin dropped the tray and ran, too. Several men followed her. Sam reached the planks ahead of them all. She didn't weigh much, but it was enough for the planks to shift. Sam lost her balance. Erin could see Sam was going to fall. The photo went out of her hands as she flailed in the air.

Digger grabbed Sam and pulled her out of the air and out of danger. He held her to him. Erin stopped. The men behind her came to a halt. Dust flew around them. Erin watched the way Digger clutched Sam to him. It was the same as it had been that first day. His arms were protecting her.

Suddenly, Sam started to scream. She wiggled and pushed, trying to get out of Digger's arms. Erin looked around, scanning the ground. She knew what was wrong. The child had dropped the photo. Digger tried to hold on to the squirming child.

Erin spotted it on the planks where Sam had nearly fallen. She got it and ran back to the child.

"Sam, here. It's all right. Here's the picture."

Sam heard Erin's voice and stopped screaming. She took the photo, looked at it and clutched it to her.

"All right, the show is over," Digger announced. The men dispersed as if they'd been disciplined and dismissed.

When they were out of earshot, he sat Sam down, but held on to her hand. Then he turned to Erin.

"I told you I didn't want any children here. It was your responsibility to keep them out of this yard."

"Digger, it was an accident. She was running to you."

"She should be inside."

"I'll leave her from now on." She took Sam's hand and turned to leave. Digger stopped her with a hand on her shoulder.

"You'll do better than that," he ground out. "I don't want you out here either. No more coffee, juice, water, tea, sandwiches or pink ribbons. Nothing. There's a chuck wagon that comes by construction sites, including this one. If they," he gestured toward the crew, "want coffee and food they can get it there. They don't need your pampering."

With that, he left her and went to the hazardous planks. Erin was stung. For a moment she could do nothing. Then she decided to give him a piece of her mind. She took a step and came up against the pull of Sam's hand. Her concern for the child stopped her. She bent to pick up Sam.

"Put her down!" Digger's order was apparent. "You can't go around lifting heavy children."

* * *

Digger watched Erin walk away in a huff. He kicked the dirt the minute she rounded the corner. What was happening to him? Looking around, he noticed the men were staring at him.

"Jackson," he called. The foreman came over. "No one, I mean *no one* from that school is to be in this yard." Digger issued his order. "Except for the crew, this yard if off limits to everyone else. Understand?"

"Digger, she's all right, nothing happened."

"Understand?"

Jackson nodded.

Digger left. The men avoided his gaze. They all went back to work as if someone had shouted action on a movie set.

Digger got into his Bronco and drove away. He headed for another site, but abruptly changed direction and ended up outside Luanne's office. He cut the engine and sat in the parking lot. He was acting like a crazy man. He'd been harsh with Jackson. He'd never acted like that before. Jackson was the best foreman he'd ever had, and he wanted to keep him.

Digger hadn't seen Erin since he'd left her house thoroughly confused about what was happening to him and to them. He didn't know or understand what he wanted. For years, he'd told himself what he thought he wanted, but somehow Erin had destroyed his myths.

He didn't get out of the truck. He grasped the steering wheel tightly and stared past the building in front of him. Sam had scared him. His heart still pounded hard in his chest. It hadn't been her he'd seen in that yard. It had been Josh out there, running toward the gully.

He hit the steering wheel. Sam and Erin never should have been there. There was too much danger. He hadn't had a site accident in four years.

Erin's face jumped into his memory. He'd shouted at her. She'd looked hurt, as if he'd struck her. But he'd been scared.

She wasn't properly dressed and didn't know the dangers that lurked in a building site. She could have gotten hurt. Both of them could have. In trying to save Sam from harm she could have tripped. Any manner of harmful objects lay about the ground. She had no idea of the danger.

Yet he hadn't meant to be harsh. He couldn't help it. At that moment he had been so afraid of what could have happened that he couldn't control his words. Everyone stood around them and he wanted nothing more than to pull her into his arms and kiss her until he'd wiped away every angry word he'd said.

If Erin had had an office door to slam she would have, but the construction had robbed her of that. Her desk sat in a corner of the common room with boxes around it. Digger had humiliated her. She hadn't expected Sam to take off. When Sam saw him, the only other person she trusted, she naturally went toward him. She couldn't know there was danger.

Erin went to the school kitchen. Other than Sam, she was alone. She grabbed on to the counter and held on as the little girl kept hold of her leg.

"Digger mad?" Sam asked. Her huge eyes were orbs of concern.

Erin dropped down next to her. "He's a little angry, honey. But he's not angry with you. He thought you might get hurt in the yard."

"I sorry."

Erin hugged her. "He knows that."

Erin hoped she was right. His face had been as hard as granite. She'd never seen anyone so…afraid. That was natural, she thought, but his fear went beyond natural, especially since he reached Sam before anything happened. He was relieved, yet his face was sweating and his breathing labored.

"How about going to class?" Erin asked this everyday. She meant for Sam to go to class alone. Each time she'd received a quick shake of the little girl's head. This time Sam looked at the floor as if she were being punished for something. "It's all right, Sam. We'll wait until tomorrow."

Erin accompanied Sam to class and sat with the little girl, holding her hand and thinking about Digger.

The near accident in the yard seemed to be the jolt that Sam had needed. From the moment Erin entered the house that night Sam sat alone. She kept the photo with her at all times. The edges were frayed and torn, but she wouldn't part with it. Sam made sure she could see Erin. She sat at the kitchen table and colored in a book, no longer holding on to Erin's leg or hand. Sam continued to follow Erin from room to room, probably still afraid Erin might leave and not return.

The next day Sam truly went to class alone, but Wanda had trouble with Sam staying there. Several times she would come to the door to check on Erin or she would come running through the door when she couldn't see Erin immediately.

Digger returned to the site, too. He came day after day. Erin saw him through the windows. He never looked her way, and she told herself there was no reason for her to wonder about him. None other than the way she felt.

Erin never set foot outside the school during the day. She didn't bring drinks or do more than wave on her way into the school each morning. Her heart ached, though. She knew Digger was outside. For eight hours a day he was only fifty feet from her, but there were walls between them, fortress-thick walls that no tool or machine could tear down.

She missed Digger. They hadn't known each other long. They hadn't even liked each other on first meeting, but the way she felt in his arms and the way she felt when they made love wouldn't let her just walk away. How could he? Did he have no feelings at all?

Once, Erin had thought she would be satisfied with a child. And while Sam gave her a pleasure greater than anything she'd imagined, Erin also wanted Digger in her life. She wanted the family. She knew it was futile, that nothing could come of her association with Digger. When the addition was complete he would disappear from her life.

If he hadn't already done so.

Three o'clock in the morning. The blue numbers on Digger's clock radio mocked him. He'd been in bed for three hours and he hadn't slept for one minute. He kicked the covers off and got up. He couldn't go on like this. He'd only slept five hours in the last thirty-six.

Digger pulled on his jeans and a shirt. He got in the Bronco and drove through the streets of Cobblersville. There was no one on the street. The houses in Erin's neighborhood were all dark, including hers. He pulled into her driveway and cut the engine. This was crazy, he told himself, but he couldn't go on like this. He needed her. He needed her in his arms and in his bed and he wanted to stare into those drowning eyes, push his hands through her hair and take that mouth that always looked as if it wanted to be kissed.

He went to the door and rang the bell. She would be asleep. He was waking her up. But the light over the door came on too quickly. He only rang once. She would have to be awake to answer the door this quickly. He saw her face through the glass pane as she looked out to see who it was.

Then the lock was released and the chain removed. She opened the door.

"Digger?"

"I know it's late," he said. "I'm sorry I woke you."

"It's all right."

His weight shifted from foot to foot. "Can I come in?"

Erin stood back and let him enter. She had on a nightgown and the robe he had taken from her bathroom the night they made love. He almost pulled her into his arms.

She led him to the family room where she offered him a seat.

"I'll get us something to drink."

Digger didn't object. He listened to Erin moving around in the kitchen. She came back with soft drinks. Digger took his and drank most of it.

"I hope I didn't wake Sam."

"Sam is a sound sleeper. In the last few days, she's begun to come out of her shell."

"That's good to hear."

Erin sat in a chair opposite him. She said nothing for a moment. Then asked, "Why are you here?"

Digger set his glass on the table separating them. He didn't know what he wanted to say. He didn't know how to start. He'd never told anyone this story, but he needed to tell Erin.

"It was a few years ago," he started. "I lived in Dallas. I worked for a large building company. We put up office buildings, shopping malls or additions."

He stopped as memories flooded into his mind. He saw Josh smiling, saw Marita smiling that morning. That final morning.

"I was married then. My wife's name was Marita. She was the best thing that had ever happened to me and, in most things, I'd been lucky. I was a foster kid who'd found love with his foster parents. I found a beautiful wife and expected to spend the rest of my life with her."

Erin shifted in her seat. Her movement was slight, but he noticed it.

"Then things began to go wrong. They started with the accident."

"Accident?" The word was hardly audible. She sat forward, leaning into a listening position.

"I was the site manager. We were behind schedule. It was an office building. Thirty floors. Putting up the building was my responsibility. The entire steel and concrete skeleton was up. The foundation around it was huge. The building was surrounded by cranes."

Digger looked at her for understanding. "I've seen them."

"There aren't any at the school like the ones used in build-ing a structure thirty stories."

Erin nodded.

Digger linked his fingers together and looked directly at her. "It had rained for three days and the ground was soft. One of the cranes was stuck in the mud. We were trying to get it out when it happened."

"I thought they were designed to run on tracks so they could move through anything."

"That's the design, but it isn't always what happens."

Digger could see it. He closed his eyes for a moment try-ing to blot it out, yet it only intensified behind his closed lids.

"The crane jumped and lurched, then settled. At least we thought it settled. The ground was too soft and the big ma-chine too heavy. It was on the side of a mound. It started to slip sideways. Then it tipped."

Erin's eyes opened wide. Her forgotten drink sat on the table.

"There was a child on site that day. He stood on the other side of the yard, out of the way, a safe distance from the crane." He paused, took the glass and finished the drink. "But he moved. He sensed danger and was running to help."

Erin gasped. She said nothing, and Digger continued.

"He was only three. Who would have thought a three-year-old could be so surefooted? But he was. He started run-ning toward the tipping crane."

"Didn't anyone try to stop him?"

Digger nodded, "My best friend Jeremy saw what was happening and tried to get to him. They were both killed."

Her hands came up to her mouth. Then she moved from her seat. She came to the sofa and sat next to him, taking his hands in hers.

"My marriage fell apart after that. I couldn't do anything, even the simplest tasks were too much. I couldn't work, eat, sleep, even bathe. My wife left me and I spent two years in a bottle. When I finally crawled out, I had nothing. Luanne and my brothers saved me. They came and dried me out. I spent a year in Philadelphia with Brad. Then I moved here and started over."

"Digger, it wasn't your fault."

"It *was* my fault. He should never have been there. I should never have taken him. A building site is no place for children."

Digger felt it when her hand slackened. He knew she'd just connected the dots.

"Josh?" Her voice was low, almost reverent when she said it. "Josh was the little boy. He died at the building site." It wasn't a question. She spoke as if she knew, as if she had been there.

"He was my son."

If he expected her to react he was disappointed. She said nothing. Not an inch of her body moved. She could have turned to stone she was so still. Digger wondered what she was thinking. He wanted to know. Then her hand moved. Her fingers linked through his and tightened. He felt the tug of her arm as she pulled him. He leaned forward and her arms went around him. It was a comfort hug, not sexual, not motherly. He needed the contact of another human being, and she was there for him. Digger slipped his arms around her and held her.

He breathed in her scent, listened to the steady beat of her heart and felt the softness of this special woman.

"Digger." Erin spoke after a while. She didn't move, didn't release him or make any motion to look into his face. Her voice was muffled against his hair. "I'm sorry. I'm very sorry. I understand your concern for me and the children." She stopped to kiss him on the forehead. Her hand drew small circles on his back. "I'll make sure none of the kids go into the yard. And none of the teachers, either. That includes me."

Digger pushed her back. He looked into her eyes and knew

he was lost to her. He'd fallen in love. She'd gotten under his skin. There was nothing he could do about it. But he couldn't go on with it. He'd gone through the worst years of his life when Josh died and Marita left him. He couldn't do it again.

Digger stood up. He didn't have anything else to say and he couldn't continue looking at her. It hurt him too much. He could see what he was doing, knowing he had to leave her. It was self-preservation. He had to get away from her.

And he had to do it forever.

"Where are you going?" Erin got up and followed him to the door. She took his hand. There was a gentle tug, a quiet communication that said she wanted him to stay.

Digger had never wanted anything more in his life than to make love to her.

"Home," he said.

"Why?"

"Don't you think it's time?"

"No," she whispered. "There's something you haven't explained."

"What's that?"

"Why?"

"Why what?"

"Why did you change your mind about taking the job at my school? You knew the kids would be there."

He stared at her. She was the most beautiful woman he'd ever seen. He'd be lying to himself if he didn't admit she'd had a part in the decision.

"It has something to do with the kids, doesn't it?"

"I couldn't jeopardize another kid."

"What does that mean?"

"Allorca. I used to work for him. He cuts corners. He uses the minimum standards. If he built the rooms, I wasn't sure…"

"Wasn't sure of what?" she asked when he stopped talking.

"Whether he'd make sure the room wouldn't come down and kill another child. I couldn't take the responsibility."

"You also can't take responsibility for saving all the children in the world."

His eyes widened.

"Don't stare at me as if I'm against Mom, America and apple pie," Erin said. "I'm not. But I know my limitations and you have to know yours, too. What happened to Josh was tragic, terrible, beyond words. But you can't keep living it. Don't forget him, it would be inhuman to even try. But you've got to open your heart and stop trying to force yourself to have no feelings."

"It was my responsibility," he shouted. Quickly, he reduced his voice. "I have rules. I didn't follow them. And because of that two people are dead."

"Josh was young and innocent. I'm glad you had his well-being in mind. Your hurt proves you're human, and I'm sorry you have to live with this. But you did what you could. You *have* to live with it. It won't go away, but it doesn't have to take over your life."

He gave her a quick smile. Taking a long breath he walked away from her, then turned back. "You think I don't know that? That I don't wake up every morning and vow that today will be different? Then it happens. I see Josh running toward me. *I* was driving the rig. It was *me* he tried to save. At three years old he took on a thirty-ton piece of equipment."

"What are you taking on, Digger?" She stopped to let the impact of her words sink in. "Josh tried to save you, but he didn't. You died with him in that accident. It's why you push me away. Why you want to be with me, but all of you is never here."

He couldn't deny it. "I think it's really time for me to leave now."

She moved past him and pulled the door open. He looked at it and back at her. Then he walked to the door and stopped.

"There is one thing I couldn't control," he told her. "In all the time I was fighting you and trying to stay away from you." He ran his hand down her cheek. "It didn't work. I fell in love anyway. I love you."

He went through the door then, pulling it closed behind him.

Chapter Twelve

Erin didn't know how she got through the next week or how she managed to keep her depression from showing. How could she have let this happen? She knew better. Knew the danger. Yet she hadn't stopped it. She'd gone with Digger when she should have refused. They should never had kissed, never made love, never fallen in love.

By Saturday she was more miserable than she'd ever thought she could be. And the worst part was, she couldn't wear it. She had to hide it from everyone, including Sam and Gillian. She'd seen Digger every day; he'd come to the building site, worked side-by-side with the men, but the yard that separated her from him was as wide as the Sahara. They hadn't looked at each other, hadn't waved or even acknowledged that the other existed.

"I love you," he'd said. Digger's words still reverberated around in her head. "I love you." She heard it over and over. But it wasn't Digger's voice that disturbed her.

It was her own.

She was in love with him. How could she have let this happen? When she knew the consequences, knew the hurt falling in love would bring. This time it would be worse. Erin had thought she'd been in love before. She'd been prepared to marry Kent Edwards and spend her life with him. Yet he'd never inspired the fire Digger had.

I love you. Those three little words were as present as if Digger had only said them a moment ago, while nearly a week had passed, almost an anniversary.

Erin looked at Sam sitting on the floor. The television was on, but Sam seemed bored with it. Erin had a pang of guilt that she was neglecting Sam. Erin had problems, but she was better equipped to deal with them than a four-year-old.

"Sam, why don't we go for a swim?"

The little girl nodded and stood up. Together they dressed and headed for the backyard. Erin was glad there was a pool to distract them both. The water would be refreshing. She hoped it would lift her spirits as much as Sam's. Both of them were in need of a day without memories.

"You can lay the picture here where you can see it." Erin indicated the patio table. Sam looked at the photo then laid it down. Erin anchored it with a small rock. They sat on the side of the pool, their feet in the water.

Sam kicked the water. Erin closed her eyes and moved her head to avoid the playful splashing. She smiled at the little girl. When they jumped in, Sam kicked her feet and moved her arms as if she were swimming, though Erin propelled her through the three-foot depth.

"Swimmin," she shouted. Erin walked from side to side, carrying Sam as she mock-swam across the width of the pool. She was light in the water, but Erin gave her full attention to Sam to keep Digger off her mind. The two played for several more minutes. Erin pulled Sam into her arms and turned circles in the water. Sam laughed, a sound that was especially appreciated after weeks of sullenness.

Finally, Erin set her on the tiled edge of the pool and hopped up on it too.

"Again," Sam said.

"In a minute. I need to rest."

Sam kicked the water with her feet. Erin kicked, too. She liked the feel of the liquid against her legs. It wouldn't be long before the blistering heat sent them both back into the water or into the air-conditioned house.

"Where's Digger?" Sam asked, out of the blue.

Erin looked around quickly in case Sam had seen him. Erin was hungry for the look of him, hungry for the smell and taste of him. Her stomach dropped at the mention of his name.

"Honey, sometimes things don't work out with people. I don't think we'll be seeing Digger again."

"He not like us."

Erin put her arms around Sam. "Sure he likes us. He's just busy. When he finishes at the school he'll have to work at other places."

"We go other places."

"It would be dangerous. We could get hurt." Erin remembered how angry Digger had been the day Sam had run into the yard. And the story about his son dying at a construction site. She would miss Digger, but there was nothing she could do about the situation. She'd accepted her fate, and he'd be better off without her.

Erin slipped back into the water, taking Sam with her. The pool was deliciously cool and Sam loved the water. She was smiling, coming out of her shell. Each day she was a little closer to being the little girl Erin knew and loved. Sam had a full life in front of her. Erin would make sure nothing happened to her for as long as they stayed together.

She wondered if Luanne had contacted any of Sam's relatives. Secretly, she hoped Sam could always stay with her.

Sam had wormed her way into Erin's heart years ago. Having her around every day had been wonderful for Erin. She didn't want to think of Sam leaving, too.

"Are you alone?" Luanne looked behind Digger as he came in the door.

Digger arrived for Sunday dinner the same as he had for the past three years. He found Dean and Owen sitting in the living room, bottles of beer in front of them.

"Who were you expecting?" Digger asked as he dropped down in one of the wingback chairs that faced the sofa and love seat in Luanne's color-coordinated room.

"Erin and the little girl. Samantha."

"Why would you expect them?"

"Cause we like Erin," Dean piped in. "We drove all the way over here just to see her again." He indicated Owen, who sat in one of the deep living room seats.

"Sorry to disappoint you," Digger said drily.

"I thought you two were a couple," Dean said. "If you don't want her, can I have her?"

Digger threw him a laser-sharp look. "She's not a stick of furniture," he snarled. The smile on his brother's face froze as if they were in the frigid cold of Alaska instead of the blistering heat of a Texas summer.

"See, Owen, I told you he was in love with her. This proves it."

Digger accepted the bottle of beer his brother-in-law handed him and took a long swig of the cold liquid before coming back to the conversation.

"It proves nothing," Owen answered.

"Ask him then. Just ask him."

All eyes turned to Digger. They were waiting for an answer. He looked at them one by one.

"What Erin and I have is none of your business."

"We only want you to be happy," Luanne said.

"That statement assumes I'm unhappy," Digger pointed out, taking another drink and nearly emptying the bottle.

"By the look of you, you're miserable," Dean said.

He *was* miserable. He hadn't had a moment's peace in a week. He didn't know he could miss someone so much. Erin went to the school every day. He knew she was there, yet he never saw her. Some days it had been almost impossible *not* to find Erin, apologize for everything he'd said or not said and take her in his arms.

He wanted to go to her. The need built in him, growing stronger with each day until he thought he'd die, but each morning the sun rose and he dragged himself out of bed. He knew the pain would die. The job would end, and he would be plagued by images of her.

Even at his house.

She'd been there only once, but he remembered every detail of her visit, each chair she'd sat in, the glass she'd drank from. The house remembered her, too. He didn't seem to be able to get her out of his mind. Even the walls and furniture seemed to remember she had been there.

This couldn't go on.

"Wait a minute," Owen was saying when Digger's attention was drawn back to the family debate. "I know a way to tell for sure."

His gaze was steady, serious, as if he was about to say something profound.

"Did you tell her about Josh?"

Digger felt as if he'd been shot between the eyes.

"This is not a family meeting about me," he announced. "The entire family's not even here." He attempted to both lighten the mood and deflect the question. But Owen wasn't letting the subject drop.

"If necessary, we'll get them on a conference call. Now answer the question."

He nodded. "I told her." Digger paused a second, deciding if he should go on. It was obvious now. "I'm in love with her."

A whoop of joy rang through the small room as everyone moved to congratulate him.

"But—" Digger cut them off. "Nothing will be done about it."

"Why not? She's in love with you, too. Anybody with eyes can see that."

Digger wasn't so sure. He'd told Erin he loved her. She'd looked shocked, stunned, as if he'd announced he was leaving for the moon. She'd said neither of them wanted to be married. So that ended it. He didn't want to be married, and she agreed with him. His family couldn't change that.

"I don't want to talk about this. It's really none of your business," Digger said a second time.

"When did that ever stop us from talking? So spill it. What's the real reason?"

Digger looked at his hands, then at each of his family members. He knew he could tell them secrets, and they'd keep them. They had a special bond that existed in all families, but because his had been formed from the throw-outs of others their bond was especially close.

"I'm afraid," he said quietly. "I can't live through another Josh and Marita."

Luanne quickly held her hand up when Owen was about to respond. She cut everyone off with a look.

Coming to Digger she sat down on the coffee table and faced him. Her back was to their brothers who watched in silence.

"We support you," she began. "In whatever you decide. We are your family and we, too, share the loss of Josh and Marita. We wouldn't want you to go through that again."

"But living means risking," Owen joined in. He took a seat next to Luanne.

"Erin and Sam aren't Marita and Josh," Luanne said.

"We're close to finding Sam's great-aunt. Erin will be free and so are you."

"But if you're not ready to risk your heart," Owen said, "you'll have to wait until the time is right."

They weren't saying anything Digger hadn't already told himself. Except the part about timing. Would the time ever be right? Would this burning for her go away? He didn't know and, while his family could support his decisions, they couldn't go through the feelings for him. He had to do that alone.

Erin took Sam's hand as they crossed River Avenue and headed for the Cobblersville Hospital. The hospital wasn't large by big-city standards. Community Medical of Cobblersville was a two-story, 300-bed facility equipped to deal with normal surgery and minor emergencies. Anything major was air-lifted to Austin.

Erin had rarely entered the hospital for anything other than visiting maternity patients and meeting Gillian. Gillian was the reason she and Sam were here today. The two of them were meeting Gillian for lunch. Erin could have parked in the hospital parking lot, but there were no shade trees and the temperature was already in the nineties. Gillian had promised to meet her at the front door.

Erin had felt the humidity the moment they stepped out of the van, but inside, the building was cool and smelled of disinfectant. Ahead of them, past the stark white reception desk, was a long bench. Erin led Sam to it, smiling at the receptionist whom she knew only as Abby. Before she could sit down she heard her name called. The voice was enough to send chills up her spine. She turned around.

"Hello, Kent." She smiled brightly as if she was glad to see him. He'd just come through the door, a large bouquet of flowers under one arm. She glanced at Sam whose hand tightened in hers. "What are you doing here?"

"Jennifer delivered three days ago. She goes home today."

"Congratulations," Erin said. Sam climbed up on the seat and Erin put her arm around Sam to keep her from falling. "I take it the baby is a boy?" She looked at the blue ribbon on the roses.

He nodded and beamed. Erin felt inadequate. She wondered if Kent had stopped her to make sure she knew he was a father, and she would never be a mother. Once, she wouldn't have believed there was a bad bone in his body, but she'd learned better.

"Who is this? One of your school kids?"

He looked at Sam. A few weeks ago Sam would have been talkative, introducing herself as Samantha Yvette Pierce and telling him her father sometimes called her Sy. Erin so wanted to tell Kent the child was hers, but she couldn't. "This is Sam. I'm her foster mother," she answered.

"Mother," Sam said, perking up to the word. She hadn't spoken voluntarily in a while. Erin was glad to hear it and wanted to encourage her to continue, but the expression on Sam's face was reason for concern. She looked as if mother was a swearword and reminded her of something awful.

"Erin, that's wonderful," Kent said. "When did you decide to do that?"

"Not long ago." She glanced up at Kent then back at Sam.

"I'm glad." She looked at his eyes for some sign of insincerity, but he genuinely looked happy for her. "You're a wonderful woman and you deserve the best." He reached over and touched one of Sam's braids. She moved further behind Erin as if she were shy. Then he leaned down and kissed Erin's cheek.

She froze. Her throat closed off. She realized she hadn't any feelings for Kent, not like the feelings she had for Digger. She wouldn't have thought it possible a week ago, even a few moments ago, but she forgave him for his treatment of her. She wouldn't accept all the blame for their failed relationship. There had been a miscommunication, a serious one and she should have known better than to get involved. But he had taught her a lesson. One that was very valuable and that she would always remember. She *had* remembered— until she met Digger.

"I'd better get upstairs now," Kent said.

Erin nodded. "Give my best to Jennifer."

"I will."

As Kent moved out of sight Digger came into view. He stared at her. Erin had the feeling he'd been there a while, watching them. She knew he'd seen Kent kiss her. Why did he look as if he wanted to hit something? He'd left her standing in her living room with an epitaph that required further explanation. Erin hadn't asked for it and she wouldn't now.

The air in the room took on a charge. For a long moment neither moved or said a word. They only stared. Erin didn't know how long that would have gone on. She would never know. Sam dislodged her arm and jumped to the floor. She didn't speak or shout Digger's name the way she often did. She ran to him in silence, her tennis shoes making soft crepe sounds on the polished floor.

Digger opened his arms and she climbed into them, pressing her face against his shoulder. He held her, too, the way Erin was becoming used to seeing him do, as if she were a precious doll. He did it with his eyes closed, holding her carefully and taking in the baby-powder smell of her.

He opened his eyes and looked straight into Erin's. This time there was no mask to hide his expression, only his unguarded love.

It took all of Erin's resolve not to rush across the tiles and throw herself into the open space left by Sam. She'd never wanted anything more in her life. But she looked away, breaking the connection that held her in place. She could hear his footsteps. She would have known them in the dark, during a thunderstorm, with a full company from Lackland Air Force

Base marching in formation to camouflage the sound. When he stood directly in front of her she steeled herself for the emotional onslaught she knew would overtake her.

"Sam's missed you," she said. Her throat was dry, and her voice scratchy. She wondered if he heard the underlying message that she, too, had missed seeing him.

Digger glanced at Sam. Her arms continued to clutch his neck as if her life depended on it.

"I've missed her, too." His eyes never left Erin's as he spoke. "Is she all right?"

"She's coming around. She's back in her classes but she's still very quiet."

"Is she here to see a doctor?"

"No." Erin smiled quickly. "We're meeting a friend for lunch."

Digger nodded.

As if on cue, Gillian came through the double doors at the end of the hall. While a lot of nurses wore uniforms with pants and jackets, Gillian wore a dress, a short coat and white stockings. How she managed it in the Texas heat Erin didn't know.

"Hi," Gillian said, coming to stop in front of them. "I'm glad you're both here."

Erin knew then that she'd been set up.

"You're having lunch with her?" Digger asked.

"No, she's not," Gillian answered before Erin could say anything. "She's having lunch with you."

Both she and Digger stared at Gillian.

"Give her to me." Gillian reached for Sam, smoothing her hair back from her face. "Would you like to play with me?"

"Gillian, I don't—"

"Sam and I will be fine. We're going to the children's playroom. You and Digger have a good time."

Erin didn't know what to do. Sam looked at her, but made no fuss. The little girl hadn't been out of her sight in weeks.

Sam knew Gillian, who had come by the school and the house. The three of them had played together, tried to roller-blade, swam in the pool and baked cookies. Sam was some-what comfortable with Gillian, although she hadn't uttered a word.

Sam stared at Erin. "I'll be back, sweetheart. I wouldn't leave you." She knew Sam feared losing someone else. "It's all right to go with Gillian. She'll take you where there are lots of toys."

"And," Gillian added. "I have a surprise for you." She stuck her knuckle into Sam's stomach trying to make her laugh. She got a smile from the child who put her hands over Gillian's. "You two go. You have a reservation at Rosie's."

Gillian turned and started for the double doors. Sam looked over Gillian's shoulder. Erin smiled widely at her. She wanted Sam to feel safe and to know that if Erin left she would return. When Sam realized she was being taken away, she screamed and squirmed in Gillian's arms. Her shrill voice arched in the ceiling and bounced off the walls.

Digger's hands on Erin's arms stopped her from going to Sam and pulled Erin back against him. "You have to let her go," he whispered in her ear. "She's got to learn that if you leave you'll come back."

Erin knew he was right, but she hated to hear Sam scream. Sam had lost so much, and she was so young. Did she under-stand anything that was happening to her? Erin felt insecure. Was she doing the right thing? Sam's cries grew louder. They echoed off the sparse hallway and went straight into Erin's heart. Digger's hands were still curled around her upper arms when Sam and Gillian disappeared through the double doors.

Erin sagged against Digger.

"She'll settle down as soon as she sees the playroom," he reassured her, but Erin could still hear her screams. Each one seemed to rip through her. She turned around throwing her arms around Digger and holding on to him for comfort.

Digger didn't hug her. She felt his body tense as she pressed herself close to him, but his arms remained aloof. Erin knew she should pull back, but she needed human contact. She buried her face in his neck and closed her eyes until she could no longer hear Sam. Digger was right. Sam had to learn a lesson and, although it was hard on Erin, she had to be strong enough to let it happen.

Accepting this left her mind free to explore what was happening to her body. She was blending into him, becoming lost in the heat they generated, accepting the love she felt for him. At the moment she decided to move back, Digger's arms went around her. His hands slid up her back and he caressed her. She heard his breath expel as he bowed his head and leaned into her. He kissed her hair and sensations fluttered through Erin all the way to her feet.

She forgot they were standing in a public hallway. Erin turned her head seeking his mouth. Digger raised his head and then he was pulling her. She didn't know where. She went with him. A door opened and closed and she was being pressed against it as his mouth sought hers.

"God, I've missed you," he groaned as his mouth took hers. Erin had missed him, too, more than he would ever know. Digger's hands roamed over her as if he needed to reacquaint himself with every line and curve of her. Erin basked in the stirring emotions that sent rockets of sensation through her. He kissed her hard and roughly, until she was breathless. Erin didn't care about breathing. She only cared that she was in Digger's arms and she loved him.

Her body was hot as Digger pressed her closer to him. Erin was burning up. Digger lifted his mouth from hers, and she took in breaths in short gasps.

"We have to get out of here," he said.

Erin didn't quite understand. Her mind was muddled, still roaming somewhere in lovers-land.

"Are you hungry?" Digger asked.

"I'm starving," she said.

"So am I."

Neither of them were speaking of food. He took her hand and opened the door in almost the same instant. Erin didn't know what was happening, and she didn't care. In moments they were in Digger's car. They sped past Rosie's at twice the legal limit. Digger pulled into his driveway and cut the engine.

Both of them left the car at equal speeds. Inside they were back in each other's arms, continuing as if they were still in the small hospital room. They pulled at each other's clothes, refusing to break contact as they walked and twirled toward the bedroom. She pulled his shirt free of his pants and ran her hands over his slightly moist back. He groaned as her hands smoothed over sun-roughened skin.

Erin slipped out of her shoes. She felt Digger's fingers slip into the waistband of her shorts and push them down. They fell to the floor and he lifted her out of them. In a few steps he carried her down the short hall to the bedroom. The room was bright with huge windows and few curtains. Erin could see to the horizon with only cacti and trees to break the distance. He set her down and lifted her T-shirt over her head.

He kissed her neck, nibbled under her chin and licked the soft area where her collarbones came together. Erin felt her knees weaken. She clung to him, pushing his shirt off and making the effort harder by her own refusal to separate herself from him.

They tangoed over the clothes until they were both naked. Then they fell on the bed, panting for each other, unable to wait any longer. They had to have each other or cease living. Digger entered her, and she welcomed the invasion, expelling a breath of pleasure that had built inside her. Digger moved inside her, her body accommodating him. Emotion threatened to overwhelm her. Her eyes closed and pleasure rushed through her like silver moonbeams. Like a tidal wave it covered her, covered them both. Her arms wrapped around him and she held him as her body took on a life of its own. The two of them rocked and rolled on a sea for lovers, taking, giving, joining their souls, becoming one.

Erin heard the sound of her own voice, scratchy and low, full of emotion, before the scream broke through. For a long moment she and Digger hung on the wings of pure rapture. Then they fell back to earth, hot, wet and spent.

Digger rolled over, taking her with him, keeping her on top of him where her hair fell on his shoulders and she could look into his eyes. His breathing was as hard as hers. She could feel the rise and fall of his chest. He gathered her close, running his hands over her from shoulder to hip. Erin rubbed against him, watching his eyes close with the pleasure of her actions.

Like playful lovers she stayed there until her balancing act had her slipping to the side. She snuggled against him, loving the feel of his body. His arms circled her and pulled her spoon-style against him.

"I love you, Erin," Digger said.

Erin's eyes opened but she didn't move or speak.

"I told you once," he continued. "I know you're in love with me, but you've never said it." She turned to face him. "Let me finish," he said when she started to speak. "I told you about Josh. After he died I never wanted to fall in love again or have children. The pain nearly killed me. I fought hard against falling in love with you, but I lost. I love you desperately."

He skimmed his fingers over her and she shuddered at the pleasure he could evoke in her with such a light touch.

"You changed all that." He leaned forward and kissed her shoulder. "I want to marry you. I want children with you. I want two girls with your face and boys with your smile."

Erin put her hand on his arm and stopped him from the erotic nibbling. She got out of bed, searching for her clothes.

They were strewn all over the room and in various places down the hall. She remembered getting to the bed, urgent to remove the barriers separating their bodies. Now she regretted it. She found her bra and T-shirt. Discarding the bra she pulled the shirt over her head and remembered her underwear was on the floor with her shorts somewhere near the front door.

"Erin, where are you going?"

Erin looked back and forth, feeling lost as she searched the floor for other items of clothing. She headed for the door. Digger came off the bed, grabbed his jeans and followed her. She got to her discarded clothes and pulled the shorts and briefs on together before he caught her.

"What's wrong?"

"Nothing. I have to go to Sam."

"It's not Sam. I said I love you. I want to marry you and you run like a scared rabbit."

Erin wrenched her arm free. "I have to go. I have to get to the hospital."

She headed for the door, forgetting it was ninety degrees outside and her van was parked across from the hospital, nearly ten miles from where she stood. She was at a disadvantage. Digger lived too far out of town for her to escape.

"Tell me what I said. What I didn't say. I thought this was what you wanted."

"It's not you," she flung over her shoulder.

He caught her arm and pulled her around. "Then tell me what's wrong. I do love you. I want to marry you. Don't you love me? Am I wrong in thinking you do?"

She dropped her head and stared at the tiled floor. Blue flowers sketched out pattern blocks under her feet.

"You're not wrong, Digger. I do love you." She turned again and headed for the door. "Please take me back to the hospital."

"You can't just drop a bomb like that and calmly ask me

to return you to the hospital. We've altered the forces of the universe. There is no going back for us."

"Digger, please don't ask me any questions. Just take me back."

"I bared my soul to you. Don't I deserve at least an explanation for what is bothering you?"

She faced him squarely. Tears gathered in her eyes, but she blinked them away. Digger waited.

"You do deserve an explanation. You didn't want to fall in love. Neither did I."

"Why?" he asked.

"Because I've been down this road before." He looked confused. Erin continued. "When I told you about my accident I didn't tell the complete truth. The roller coaster collapsed and I was pinned under it for five hours. When they got me out my hip wasn't the only thing crushed. The entire lower part of my body was pinned. After the doctors put me back together there were things they couldn't fix, and they were life-threatening. I had a hysterectomy when I was seventeen years old. I can't have children."

She remembered every word he'd said in the bedroom. He wanted to marry her, have children with her. That would never happen. Digger stared at her as if she'd hit him. And she had. His reaction was no different than Kent's had been or the few other men she'd told about her accident. Some had continued to see her for a few weeks, but in time they had all left her alone.

She thought she'd protected herself, but she hadn't. Digger got under her skin, under her resolve, and she was going down the road of heartache again.

Erin couldn't stand the silence. She turned away, rushing for the door. If she had to walk back to town she would. Outside the heat was oppressive. The red clay and sand colored stones of the walkway did nothing to dispel the heat. As she neared the car she remembered Digger hadn't taken the keys with him. His truck sat in the driveway next to the sporty vehicle.

Impulsively, she got in and drove away. He knew where she was heading. He could pick his car up there. She had to get away from him. She drove fast.

She needed to restore balance to her life, she told herself as she checked the rearview mirror. She wanted him to follow her. She hoped she'd see his Bronco rallying behind her like some knight on a charger sallying forth to save his lady.

But she was disappointed.

Chapter Thirteen

For the first time since Erin bought Crossroads Country Day School she didn't want to go to work. Digger would be in the yard, and she didn't want to see him. She wished she didn't have to return until the addition was complete and he was gone from her life for good, but she knew that wouldn't happen. She got up and started her morning routine, waking Sam at the appropriate hour.

Sam had no ill effects from being left alone Saturday afternoon with Gillian. When Erin had returned to pick her up, she'd run to her with a smile and a ready hug. Then Sam dragged Erin across the room and proceeded to show her the painting she'd done while Erin was gone.

"It's us," Sam had told her as she pointed to the stick people. "You and me and Digger." Erin's heart dropped when the small hand pointed to the figure of a man. Her mind rushed back to Digger and her flight from his bed. There would be no man in Erin's life. If she hadn't learned that lesson with Kent, Digger had driven it home only a few moments earlier.

Sam brushed her teeth and returned to the bedroom for Erin to comb and rebraid her hair. She sat still and chatted to her doll. Her depression was nearly over. In the past week she'd been quiet in the morning, but perked up in the afternoon. Gillian and Digger had been right. She needed to know Erin would return for her.

Erin was lucky to have Sam. She smiled as she brushed the long hair and twisted the three sections into equal braids. Sam helped Erin keep her mind on something other than Digger and her sorrow.

"I can make breakfast," Sam announced when Erin finished her hair. The two of them had a light breakfast each morning, usually cereal. After they arrived at school, Sam would eat with the other kids.

"You can help with breakfast on Saturday. Today you need to put your clothes on. You can do that, right?"

"I'm a big girl." She stood up a little straighter as if she'd been insulted. Erin hid her mouth so the child couldn't see her smiling.

When she parked in front of the school she noticed that Digger's truck wasn't in the yard. She was relieved, she told herself, but her heart knew she regretted not finding him there with the other men. She'd gotten used to seeing him, even when he wouldn't talk to her. He would probably never talk to her again.

Erin helped Sam out of her car seat and wondered if he'd returned to get his car. Would he show up today? Would he ever forgive her for allowing them to fall in love? After the tragedy that took his son and cost him his marriage, she should have stayed clear of him. It was too late to think about that now. Both of them had known better. Now she assumed they were both miserable, but there was nothing to be done about it except to keep away from each other and let time heal them.

She was sure it would happen. She'd gone through it before with Kent, and Digger had survived his life without Marita. They would survive. No one ever died of a broken heart, she reminded herself, even though the pain appeared unbearable, one day she'd wake up and he wouldn't be her first thought.

But that day was somewhere in the very distant future.

The moment the kids arrived Erin had no time to think of anything except them. It took several hours before the place calmed down and she had a free moment. Erin was at her desk when the phone rang. She was afraid and anxious that it might be Digger. Her heart sang of its own free will. She hoped it was him, but she didn't know what she could say if it was.

"Crossroads Country Day School," she said. "This is Erin."

"Erin, this is Luanne Rogers from Child Welfare."

As quickly as her heart had soared, it dropped. A cold finger ran up Erin's spine. "Is anything wrong?" she asked.

"I have good news. We've discovered Samantha has a great-aunt in Wyoming."

"Wyoming?" Erin could think of nothing more to say. She didn't want to lose Sam. She loved her. Wyoming was so far away.

"Yes, I'm waiting to hear from Child Welfare in Wyoming that they've contacted her and let her know about the little girl."

"How…how long before you find out something?"

"I'm expecting a call today. I thought I'd let you know that the search is nearly over and that Sam will have a relative to go to."

"Thank you." Erin's voice was tight.

"Are you all right?" Luanne asked.

"I'm a little surprised."

"You sound a little out of sorts."

"I thought," she hesitated. "I thought Sam…"

"Would be staying longer," Luanne finished for her.

"Yes." She nodded even though Luanne couldn't see her.

"That happens often with people like you."

"Like me?"

"Fosters on the fly, we call them. You come to the aid of a particular child that you're already attached to. When it's time for them to go, you don't want them to leave."

"Will she go soon?" Erin was close to tears.

"I'm not sure. We'll know more when the call comes." Erin tried to pull her thoughts together. First Digger and now Sam.

"Erin, are you all right?" Luanne asked.

Erin almost laughed, but knew if she started she'd fall into hysteria. "I could use a mental health day," she answered.

Luanne laughed in her ear. "I know about those. Everyone needs one now and then." She changed the subject. "I thought we'd see you at dinner last Sunday. Digger seemed quite taken with you."

Erin wasn't sure what she should say. This was Digger's sister and while they were becoming friends, Erin couldn't confide in her. "Sam keeps me pretty busy," she said not really giving the real reason, which was that she and Digger weren't a couple and would never be one.

"Well, the invitation is open," Luanne said. "I'll let you go now. Take advantage of a mental health day if you can." Erin heard the smile in her voice. "I'll call you when I hear from Samantha's great-aunt."

"Please do," she said, but she didn't really mean it.

Erin had denied that Sam had any other relatives. She was the child Erin didn't have. The one she wanted and could never have. She wanted to keep Sam, watch her grow, take care of her.

But Sam had a great-aunt in Wyoming. Someone who loved her and would give her the kind of life her parents would want, who could tell her stories of her family and introduce her to other members of her bloodline.

Sam had to go to her relative. Erin knew she would take

her sisters' children if anything happened to her sisters. Families wanted to be together, stay together, learn their heritage and their history. She had grown up knowing that. Even Digger's family, who were only together by happenstance, were a bonded unit with shared experience. Sam's leaving had always been expected, even if Erin denied it. Luanne's department was searching for a relative. Everyone knew that. Why hadn't Erin believed it would happen one day?

By noon Erin was ready to pull her hair out. She dove into the activities with the children as a way to clear her mind from the belief that the phone would ring at any minute.

During nap time Erin had a moment to look outside. Digger wasn't there. The addition seemed to be progressing rapidly. There was still a crane in the yard, but from what Erin could tell it was no longer being used. The complete structure was up and the men were working on the roofing. Electronic hammers and screwdrivers made buzzing noises that the teachers had been competing with for weeks. Each burst of sound made her think of Digger.

As the last parent left, Erin remembered she hadn't received another call from Luanne. Maybe there would be a message on her machine at home.

Erin took hold of Sam's hand. "What would you like for dinner?"

"Pizza," Sam answered without hesitation.

"We'll stop at Mario's on the way home." Erin wasn't in the mood to cook. She wanted to retreat to her bed, but Sam was more active than that. Erin would have to listen to Sam chatter, watch television with her, maybe even have some of the neighborhood kids in, until it was time for Sam's bath and bed.

And maybe Luanne would call.

Erin locked the school door and happily swung Sam's hand as they walked to the van.

"Do you know what Trevor did today?" Sam asked as Erin settled her in the seat.

"What did Trevor do?"

"He had a banana for lunch."

Erin knew she was supposed to make the jump between Sam's thought processes and what happened.

"What did he do with the banana?" She spoke loudly, over the burst of an electric hammer. At first the sound didn't register. It was so natural to hear it. She took the photo of Sam's parents and snapped the seat belt in place. The burst came again. Erin stopped as she realized everyone should be gone.

She turned around and could see no one and nothing except Digger's truck.

"Sam, stay here. I need to talk to Digger."

She closed the van's door and went into the yard. He was on the roof. The hammer bursts came in regular intervals. Digger was concentrating. He wasn't looking at the ground or at her. Erin went closer, trying to call his name between the hammer's language. He never looked down.

Erin saw the ladder and went toward it. Realizing she was still holding the photo, she put it down on the edge of the crane and climbed the ladder to the roof.

"Digger," she called. He looked up startled.

"What are you doing here? Get down."

"I need to talk to you."

"I think you said everything that needed to be said yesterday. Now get off this roof before you have an accident."

"Digger, I'm sorry. I'll take all the blame. I should never have let things get out of hand."

"Stop!" he shouted. "We're both adults and we can share the blame equally. Now get off my roof."

Erin stepped back and lost her balance. Digger reached for her. His steady hand and better balance caught her, but the scream that reached their ears came from the ground. Both of them looked down.

"Sam!" Erin's shocked voice couldn't be heard by anyone

other than Digger. He pushed her down onto her hands and knees where she would have more control over her balance and left her. He rushed to the ladder and started down it. Erin followed as fast as she could.

Erin got to the child a moment behind Digger. He was examining her quickly, but not moving her.

"She's unconscious. I don't see any blood," he said. "Call 9-1-1."

The waiting room seemed to grow smaller the more Digger paced it. He'd sat with Erin and Sam in the emergency cubicle, but he couldn't remain still. Even when Erin reached over and held his hand, he wasn't calmed. Eventually he'd gone to the waiting room, but it was taking too long for anyone to come and talk to him.

He went back to the emergency room stall.

"How is she?"

Sam was awake.

"Digger." She smiled as if nothing had happened.

"How are you, honey?"

"I want to go to the playroom," she said. To her it was a game. To him he'd been scared out of his wits. He looked at Erin.

"The doctor said she has a mild concussion. They're doing the paperwork to release her. I'm going to have to watch her through the night to make sure she sleeps normally, but she should be fine." Erin ran her hand over Sam's arm.

"I had a V.I.," she told Digger. "And it didn't even hurt." She shook her head from side to side to emphasize how big a girl she was.

"Very good. Needles scare me."

The nurse came in then with instructions. She recited them to both Erin and Digger, looking from one to the other as if they were Sam's parents. He didn't correct her. He actually liked the idea.

"You be good now." The nurse smiled at Sam. "And no more riding cranes." She left them alone.

"Where's my picture?" Sam asked.

"The photograph." Erin realized what had happened. Digger waited for her to explain. "When I saw you on the roof I had the photo in my hand. I laid it on the crane."

"She must have been trying to get it," he finished.

"It's at the school, Sam," Erin told her. "When you fell and the ambulance came, we were thinking of you and forgot the picture."

"We'll pick it up on the way home, all right?" Digger asked.

"All right."

The three of them left the hospital four hours after arriving. Sam had only had a few crackers and a glass of water to eat, but she fell asleep across Erin's lap in the cab of the truck.

Digger looked at Sam nervously.

"She's breathing normally," Erin told him.

The school wasn't far from the hospital and they got there in no time. Digger climbed down. Erin reached for her seat belt.

"Stay," he said. "I'll take you home."

"I can drive," she told him.

"I know, but you were right. We need to talk." He paused, looking at Sam asleep. "I want to stay with her a while." His eyes came back to Erin's. "If that's all right?"

Erin nodded. Digger reached under the seat and pulled out a long flashlight. He touched Erin's hand then went toward the fence. The truck disappeared from view and Digger looked around the area where Sam fell. The dark and dirt of the yard had swallowed the photo.

Digger switched off the light. The darkness claimed him. The past took hold and he wanted to scream. She could have been killed. Another child's life he would have been responsible for. Sam, he thought. Four years old. Josh had been three, but they were so similar. They had the same happy in-nocence. The same unconditional love they poured over those they trusted to keep them safe.

He was going to lose Sam. He'd already lost Erin. It felt as if a hot poker was inside him. They were waiting for him. He needed to go back. Digger had switched on the light and headed back when he remembered Erin had said she'd set the photo on the crane. He climbed on the big yellow monster and looked around. The photo lay on the floor under the seat.

"Did you find it?" Erin asked as he returned to the driver's seat.

He handed it to her and watched the relief spread across her features. He started the truck and drove them, in silence, to her house. He lifted Sam and carried her to her room where both he and Erin dressed her and put her to bed.

Only the night-light illuminated the room.

"You must be tired," he told her when they stood looking down at Sam. "I'll stay with her while you rest."

Erin didn't speak. She nodded and left them. Minutes later she came back with coffee. Without a word she handed him a mug and took a seat on the floor beside him. There was only a rocking chair in the room. He sat in it. She leaned against the side with her own mug of coffee.

"They're so innocent," he said.

"I know. I'm going to hate losing her."

"Losing her?"

"Luanne called this morning. Sam has a great-aunt in Wyoming. Luanne expected a call from their child welfare department sometime today. I checked the answering machine here. There is no call from her. But it will probably be a short while before she's turned over to a family member."

Digger couldn't help but put his hand on her shoulder. They were both very still. "How do you feel about her leaving?"

"Like someone stuck a knife in my heart and they're pull-ing it out one inch at a time."

Digger's hand threaded through her hair and she leaned back into it. He sat there watching Sam's normal breathing and smoothing his fingers through Erin's hair. He didn't dare move.

"Digger," she called softly after a period of quiet.

"What?"

"You understand this is Sam."

"Sam?"

"Yes, Sam not Josh. She'll be fine."

His hand stilled in her hair. "I know."

"This wasn't your fault. I shouldn't have left her alone."

Digger came out of his chair and pulled her up from the floor. "It wasn't your fault either," he whispered. "It was an accident. Nothing more."

"And it turned out fine. She'll be all right."

"Yes." He expelled a breath. "She'll be all right."

She knew he'd been sitting there comparing them. Sam and Josh. Two children in his protection. And he'd failed them both. "Erin, go and get some rest. I'll wake you if there is any change."

He knew he wouldn't go into her bedroom. If he went there the jaws of life couldn't get him out. "She'll be fine," he whispered. She left him and he sat back down.

Sam slept soundlessly, her breathing steady and normal. Digger kept vigil, rocking back and forth in the chair until the rhythm of his own motion lulled him to sleep.

Josh was there, waving to him. He ran toward him. The sun was bright and the day was beautiful. They were in a field of long grass. It waved back and forth. Josh's head bobbed up and down in the long fronds.

Digger waited with open arms. Then the huge yellow monster came up from the ground. It was big, bigger than Josh. It towered over him. The child didn't see it as it opened its mouth. Digger shouted silent cries as he rushed to get to his son. If he could only reach him before the yellow monster... He could save him.

"Digger, wake up. Digger, you're dreaming."

He opened his eyes. Erin was leaning over him. Her hands were on his face and she was whispering. "It's all right," she said. "It was only a dream. A nightmare, but it's over now."

He sat forward. The rocking chair knocked her off balance and she fell onto him and the chair. Pushing herself back, she stood up. She wasn't wearing a robe, only a nightgown. Digger groaned at the need for her that surfaced the moment he came out of the dream.

"You need to rest. Why don't you lie down in the guest room? I'll watch Sam for a while."

He stood up. "I need some air. Give me your keys. I'll go get your van."

"That's three miles. You can't walk there."

"It's not that far." She stared at him, but went to get the keys and walked him to the door. "I'll be back," he said and turned away.

"Digger," Erin called. He turned to her. "Don't be long," she said and moved into his arms.

Erin went back to sit with Sam. She breathed normally. Watching Sam might prove a waste of time, but neither Erin nor Digger could get a good night's sleep. Erin hadn't been able to sleep. Digger was on her mind. As much as she wanted to stop seeing him, the moment he arrived she couldn't get close enough to him.

Tonight might be the last time she saw him. Tomorrow Sam would be back to herself and they would all go back to being who they were yesterday.

Erin rocked in the chair where Digger had sat watching Sam. Sam would be gone soon, too. The house would be quiet without her constant chatter. Erin could resume her morning skating routine with Gillian. And she could remember not to get so involved with the kids. They had their own parents, their own families.

Sam turned over and kicked the covers away. Erin put them back over her and stretched. She'd been sitting a long time. She wondered where Digger was. It was almost morning and he hadn't returned. Erin wouldn't let her thoughts go where she knew they were headed. She started another pot of coffee instead of thinking about how he didn't want to return. He'd told her he wanted children. With her there would be none. He'd lost a son. He wanted another child, the product of his own body. She couldn't help him, couldn't be the other side of the biological equation.

But she loved him. More than she thought possible. She wanted everything for him *and* wanted to be with him, but that wasn't possible. Erin hadn't felt sorry for herself in years, but tonight with Digger watching Sam she knew she wanted everything he'd offered her yesterday in his bedroom. She wanted marriage to him, children, all the trappings. She wanted to fight with him and wake up with him. She wanted to make love to him and grow old with him.

Erin didn't see a solution for them. It was heartache all the way around. They both wanted the same thing, but it couldn't work. Digger had the chance. He could find someone to marry and have his own children.

"Erin."

She'd been concentrating so hard she hadn't heard the front door open or Digger's footsteps. When she looked up he was standing in the doorway. He looked terrible. His eyes were red as if he'd not only been up all night, but had been crying.

"What is it?"

"I love you, Erin."

"I love you, too." Tears gathered in her throat and she could hardly speak. She stood up and stepped away from the rocking chair.

"I know yesterday I said some things that pushed you away from me. But I can't live without you. I want you to marry me."

He stood waiting for her to say something. Erin was confused. He was offering her the world. She wanted to rush to it, headlong, unthinking and uncaring of any consequences.

"I said some things, too." Erin took a step forward. She put her hand on the dresser. Her knees were getting weak. "I didn't mean to throw it at you in anger, but it remains the truth. I can't have children. You want them."

"I do," he said. "I've told everyone who meets me that I don't like children, but that's a lie. I think they complete a family. And I want a family, with you. I don't think I can go the rest of my life without you. If we can't have our own children are you opposed to adoption? There are so many foster children who need a home."

"Digger, this isn't a joke is it? Because if you're just dangling a carrot in front of me, it's the cruelest thing you can do."

"This is not a joke."

Erin stared at him. Tears washed down Erin's cheeks.

"Will you marry me?"

Erin didn't move. She was too stunned to move. Then she flew across the room and into his arms. "Are you sure?" she cried. "Are you sure about the children, adoption?"

"I'm sure that you're the only woman for me. I'm sure that whomever we take into our lives will be the best family we can have."

Erin tightened her arms around him and kissed him with all her heart.

"Can I take that as a yes?"

"Yes," she said and resumed the kiss.

Erin was surprised she could hear anything other than the blood rushing in her ears, but she recognized the sound of tiny feet. Pulling back, she saw Sam standing there holding her photograph and a teddy bear. Digger kept Erin close as they both turned to look at Sam.

"I'm hungry," she said. "I want my pizza now."

Erin and Digger burst into laughter.

Epilogue

The courtroom was full of family. Erin stood close to Digger. Sam between them held a hand of each of her new parents.

"Mr. and Mrs. Clayton, I don't often get to see happy couples in my courtroom. I love this part of being a judge. It is my pleasure to sign the adoption papers for Ms. Samantha Yvette Pierce."

"Sometimes I'm called Sy," Sam said out loud. The court laughed, including the judge. He pounded his gavel and restored order.

"Sy, I wish you a happy life." The judge spoke directly to Sam. She smiled back at him. Erin looked at Digger over her head. "Court is adjourned," he pronounced.

"I'm yours," Sam shouted and jumped into Erin's arms. She hugged her and dragged Digger closer to make them a threesome.

"Yep, you're mine." Digger knuckled her stomach, and she giggled.

"Welcome to the family, Sam." They all turned to look at Brad. Digger's entire family had flown in for the adoption ceremony. Erin's sisters were there and Sam's great-aunt.

She lived in a nursing home in Wyoming and couldn't take care of Sam, but she wanted to make sure the child had a good family. She sat in a wheelchair, smiling as the procession of family members walked toward the court's exit doors.

Erin stopped when she reached the place where Aunt Joyce sat. "Thank you for coming." Erin held Sam's hand.

"Do you know who I am?" Aunt Joyce asked Sam.

Sam looked up at Erin. She shook her head.

"This is your Aunt—"

"It's all right," Aunt Joyce interrupted her. "You will tell her as time goes by."

Erin took Aunt Joyce's hand and squeezed it. "I will," she said.

Digger put his arm around Erin's waist. She smiled at him. Her husband. Something she never thought she'd have. Her life couldn't be better. She didn't expect she would always be this happy, but she had everything she wanted, a husband *and* a child.

* * * * *

*Please turn the page
for an exciting preview of*

*LUCKY
by
Jennifer Greene*

*Coming in July 2005 from
Harlequin Next!*

Prologue

DAMNED IF HER HANDS weren't shaking.

Kasey sighed in exasperation. A year ago, she could never have imagined this moment—but then, a year ago, she'd believed she was the luckiest woman alive.

Thunder grumbled in the west as she hurried into the baby's dark bedroom. Tess was lying in her crib, gnawing on a teething ring, wearing nothing but a diaper. Michigan in August was often hot, but this intense, smothering heat just kept coming. Normally Tess would have long been asleep by now, but the looming storm must have wakened her.

Curtains billowed wildly in the hot, nervous wind. Clouds hurtled across the sky, bringing pitchforks of sterling-silver lightning and a hiss of ozone. When the first fat raindrops smacked against the windows, lights flickered on and off—not that Kasey cared. She wasn't worried whether the house lost power. She was worried whether she might.

She was born gutless. Pulling enough courage together to

leave tonight was taking everything she had, everything she was—and she was still afraid that might not be enough.

"But you're up for a little adventure, aren't you, love bug?"

The baby kicked joyfully at the sound of her mother's voice.

"That's it. We're just going to be calm and quiet, okay?" Well, one of them was. The baby softly babbled as Kasey swiftly changed her diaper and threaded on a lightweight sleeper.

A short time before, she'd stashed suitcases in the back of the Volvo, but she couldn't leave quite yet. Quickly she packed a last bag with critical items—not diapers or clothes or money—but the things that mattered, like the jewel-colored mobile, the handmade quilt, and of course, the red velvet ball.

She juggled Tess and the bag, taking the back stairs, her heart slamming so hard she could hardly think. She grabbed rain gear on the way out. The garage was darker than a dungeon, yet Tess—who should have been tired enough to pull off a good, cranky tantrum—settled contentedly in her car seat. Kasey tossed in the rest of their debris and plunked down in the front.

It bit, taking the six-year-old Volvo. It wasn't a car she'd paid for. It wasn't a car she'd chosen. But compared to the new Mercedes and the sleek black Lotus and the Lexus SUV, it was the cheapest vehicle in the fleet, and God knew, the Volvo was built like a tanker.

A sturdy car wasn't going to do her much good if she couldn't get it moving, yet initially her fingers refused to cooperate. Yanking and snapping on the seat belt seemed to present an epic challenge. Then the key refused to fit in the lock. Finally she started the engine—which sounded like a sonic boom to her frantic ears—and then she almost forgot to push the garage door opener before backing out.

Her gaze kept shooting to the back door. Waiting for it to

open. Afraid it would open. No matter how well she'd planned, no matter what she'd said, she was still afraid something or someone would find a way to stop her from leaving, stop her from taking Tess.

In an ideal world, she'd have made contingency plans—but she hadn't been living in an ideal world for a long time now. She had no alternate plans, no contingency ideas.

This was it. Her one shot to tear apart her entire life in one fell swoop.

That thought was so monumentally intimidating that she considered having a full-scale nervous breakdown—but darn it, she didn't have time. Her hand coiled on the gearshift and jerked it in Reverse. The instant the car cleared the driveway, she gunned the accelerator.

Rain slooshed down in torrents, blurring her vision of the house and neighborhood. For so long she'd thought of Grosse Pointe as her personal Camelot. It struck her with a flash of irony that it really had been. She was the one who'd goofed up the happy-ever-after ending. She'd not only failed to follow the fairy-tale script, she'd somehow turned into the wicked character in the story.

Kasey knew people believed that. For months, she'd believed herself at fault, too—but no more.

She leaned forward, fooling with knobs and buttons. The windshield wipers struggled valiantly to keep up with the rain, but the defroster was losing ground. Steam framed the edges of the windows, creating a surreal, smoky world where it seemed as if nothing existed but her and the baby.

Kasey spared a quick, protective glance at her daughter. In that tiny millisecond, her heart swelled damn near to bursting. She'd never imagined the fierce, warm, irrevocable bond between mother and child until she'd had Tess. Sometimes she thought that love was bigger than both of them.

It still struck her as amazing, what even a spineless wuss—such as herself—would do for her child. And for love.

Emotions clogged in her throat, welled there, jammed there. Even now, she knew she could turn back. It was hard, not to want to be safe. Hard, to believe she had what it took to take this road.

By the standards of another life—the life she'd been living a year ago—Kasey knew absolutely that others would judge her behavior as wrong. Dead wrong, morally and ethically wrong, wrong in every way a woman could define the word.

A sudden clap of thunder shook the sky. The storm was getting worse, lightning scissoring and slashing the sky over the lake. When Kasey turned onto Lakeshore Drive, Lake St. Clair was to her left, the water black and wild and spitting foam. There were no boats on the lake, no cars on the road. No one else was anywhere in sight.

Sane people had the sense to stay home in storms this rough.

At the first traffic light, she whipped her head around again, but Tess didn't need checking on. The baby was wide awake and staring intently at the car windows, where streetlights reflected in the rain drooling down the glass.

The look in the baby's eyes warmed Kasey. It didn't suddenly miraculously make their situation all right—nothing could do that. But it was so easy to think of the storm as uncomfortable and unpleasant. Through the baby, Kasey saw the night diamonds, the magic in rain and light. Her vulnerable daughter had bought her miracles in every sense of the word.

Whatever frightening or traumatic things happened from here, she was simply going to have to find a way to cope with them.

The instant the traffic light turned green, she zoomed through the intersection. Quickly the lake disappeared behind them. The long sweeps of velvet lawns and elegant estates turned into ordinary streets. Lakeshore Drive changed its name when it got past the ritzy stuff. Kasey started sucking in great heaps of air at the same time.

The extra oxygen didn't particularly help. She still couldn't make her pulse stop zooming, her hands stop shaking. But it was odd. She didn't really mind being shook up to beat the band. At least those feelings were real. She didn't have to hide being anxious, being afraid—being who she was—anymore.

Love had the power to change a woman.

Kasey would never doubt that again.

The trick, of course, was for a woman to be able to tell the difference between life-transforming love and the kind of love that could destroy her.

She ran a yellow light. Then another. Courage started coming back in slow seeps. Of course, she was nervous and afraid. Who wouldn't be?

She knew where she was going now. It was just hard to stop the questions from spinning in her mind.

How could she possibly have come to this point?

How did a nice, quiet, decent woman who'd always played by the rules get herself into such a situation?

How had the dream of her life become such a soul-destroying nightmare?

But the answers, of course, couldn't be found in this night. The answers were steeped in the events over the past year. In fact, the whole story began almost a year ago to the day….

Chapter One

"FOR GOD'S SAKE, KASEY. No one's killing you. You're just having a baby!"

"Yeah, well, they told me all the pain would be in my head. None of it's in my head!"

"Yelling and swearing isn't going to help."

Well, actually, she thought it might. She should have known it would happen to her this way. Breaking her water at a party—right in front of people she wanted to respect her, people Graham respected. Still, knowing she was going to die within the next hour definitely helped. It was a little depressing, realizing that people's last memory of her would be with bloody water gushing down her legs in the middle of a dinner party. On the other hand, she'd be dead, so what was the point in worrying about it? For the same reason, there didn't seem much point not to howl her heart out when the next pain hit, either.

As far as she could tell, she wasn't likely to live through the next pain anyway.

"You wanted this baby," Graham reminded her.

"Oh, Graham, I do. I do."

"So try and get a grip. We'll be at the hospital in fifteen minutes. Just stay here. I'll run upstairs and get your suitcase and some towels for the car...."

He was gone, leaving Kasey in the kitchen alone for those few minutes. She sank against the white tile counter as another contraction started to swell.

Something was wrong with her. It wasn't the stupid pain. They'd all lied about the pain—and she was going to stay alive long enough to kill the Lamaze instructor who promised that labor was simply work. It wasn't work. It was torture, cut and dried. Yet Kasey fiercely, desperately, wanted this baby, and had expected to feel joyous when the blasted labor process finally started.

Instead, she felt increasingly overcome by a strange, surreal sense of panic. Goofy thoughts kept pouncing in her mind. This wasn't her house. This wasn't her life. This wasn't really happening to her.

As the contraction finally ebbed, leaving her forehead flushed with sweat, she stared blankly around the high-tech kitchen. She realized perfectly well that anxiety was causing those foolish thoughts, yet the acres of stainless steel appliances and miles of white tile really *didn't* seem to be hers. She'd never have chosen a white floor for a kitchen. The doorway led to a dining room with ornate Grecian furniture that she'd never chosen, either. The dining room led into a great room with cream carpeting and cream furniture—Graham had chosen all that stuff before they'd married, wanting a neutral color like crème to set off the artwork on the walls. He was a collector.

But now, the more she looked around, the more she felt a building panic roaring in her ears. This whole last year, she'd basked in a feeling of BEING LUCKY so big, so rich, so magical that she just wanted to burst with it. She'd found a true prince in Graham, when at thirty-eight, she'd given up believing she'd find anyone at all. And living in Grosse Pointe was like living in her own private Camelot—which it was, it really was. It was just that this crazy panic was blindsiding her. Maybe it had all been a dream. She didn't live here. How could she possibly live here? She didn't DO elegant. Cripes, she didn't even LIKE elegant.

Not that she'd ever complained. Graham had said too many times that his ex-wife, Janelle, had been a nonstop complainer.

It wasn't as if she spent much time in the fancy-dancy parts of the house, besides. With the baby coming, the kitchen was the room that mattered, and all the high-tech appliances were a cook's dream. Still, the dishes were bone china. Heirlooms. Beautiful—but it was darn hard to imagine a baby in a high chair, drinking milk from a lead crystal glass and slopping up cereal from a 22-karat-gold rimmed bowl onto that virgin-white tile floor.

Shut up, Kasey. Just shut your mind up. Another pain was coming. This one felt like lightning on the inside, as if something sharp and jagged was trying to rip her apart. Then came the twisting sensation, as if an elephant were swollen in her stomach and trying to squeeze through a space smaller than a spy hole.

She opened her mouth to scream her entire heart out, when Graham suddenly jogged into the room. "All right, I reached Dr. Armstrong. He'll meet us at the hospital. You holding up okay?"

Of course she wasn't okay. She couldn't conceivably be less okay. She was wrinkled, stained, shaky, and positively within minutes of death by agony. Graham, typically, looked ready to host a yacht-club outing. Abruptly—and with all the grace of a walrus—she pushed away from the counter and aimed for the back door. "Which car are we taking?"

"The Beemer. Easiest to clean the leather seats if we have to. Although I brought towels."

For an instant she thought, *Come on, Graham, couldn't you think for one second about the baby instead of fussing over getting a stain in a car?* But even letting that thought surface shamed her.

Her attitude had sucked all day, when she knew perfectly well that Graham was unhappy about the coming baby. During their courtship, he'd been bluntly honest about wanting no children—he adored his nearly grown daughter, but that was the point. He'd done the fatherhood thing. At this life stretch he wanted Kasey, alone, a romantic relationship with just the two of them.

Maybe there was a time when Kasey fiercely wanted children, but even at thirty-eight, there were increased health risks with a pregnancy. More than that, she'd already settled into a life without kids—and she loved Graham and everything about her life with him, so it just wasn't that hard to go along with his choice.

Birth control hadn't failed them so much as life had. She'd tracked conception down to the week she'd had a bad flu and couldn't hold anything down—including her birth control pills. By the time she'd recovered, the fetus already had a grab-hold on life. If the problem had never happened, Kasey would undoubtedly have been happy as things were—but once she realized that she was pregnant…well, there was only one chance of a baby for her. This one.

She wanted this baby more than she wanted her own breath, even her own life. It was her one shot at motherhood. She just couldn't give it up.

And she totally understood that Graham wasn't happy about it—but there was no fixing that yet. Once the baby was born, she could work on him, make sure he never felt neglected, take care to shower him with love. Besides which, once the baby was born and Graham held the little one, Kasey felt certain the baby would win his heart. It'd all work out.

If she just didn't blow it in the meantime.

"I love you," she said in the car.

"I love you, too, hon." But immediately he fell silent, steering through the quiet night, his profile pale as chalk. Dribbles accumulated on the windshield. Not rain, just the promise of it. She heard a siren somewhere, the thunk of the occasional windshield wiper, and realized that she was doing better. The pains were easing up, not one galloping right after the other now.

Randolph Hospital loomed ahead. Graham pulled up to the Emergency Room door where a sign read No Parking Under Any Circumstances. The hospital looked more like an elegant estate than a medical facility, with security lights glowing on the landscaped grounds and garden sculptures.

Graham slammed out of the car. "I'll get a wheelchair or a gurney. I hate to leave you alone, Kasey, but I promise I'll be right back."

"I'll be fine."

But she wasn't fine. He'd barely disappeared inside before another lumpy gush of blood squeezed between her legs. How come no one ever said labor was a total-gross out? Certainly not that nauseatingly cheerful Lamaze instructor. And then another pain sliced her in half, so sharp, so mean, that she couldn't catch her breath.

Pain was one thing. Being scared out of her mind was another. She fumbled for the door handle, thinking that she'd crawl inside the hospital if she had to—anything was better dying here alone in the dark. She got the door open. Got both feet out. But then the cramping contraction took hold and owned her. She cried out—to hell with bravery and pride and adulthood and how much she wanted this baby. If she lived through this, and that was a big *IF,* she was never having sex again, and that was for damn sure.

The emergency room doors swung open. She didn't actually notice the man until she heard the clip of boot steps jogging toward her, and suddenly he was there, hunkering down by the open curb.

"You need help?"

"No, no. Yes. I mean—my husband's coming. It's just that right now—" The pain was just like teeth that bit and ripped.

"What do you want me to do? Get you inside? Stay with you? What? I can carry you—"

"No. It's—no. Just stay. Please. I—" She wasn't really looking at him, wasn't really seeing him. Her whole world right then was about babies and labor and pain. Still, there was something about him that arrested her attention. Something in his face, his eyes.

Their whole conversation couldn't have taken two minutes. She only really saw him in a flash. Background light dusted his profile, sharpened his features. He was built tall and lanky, with dark eyes and hair, had to be in his early forties or so. His clothes were nondescript, the guy-uniform in Grosse Pointe of khakis and polo shirt, but his looked more worn-in than most. *He* looked more worn-in than most. The thick, dark hair was walnut, mixed with a little cinnamon. The square chin had a cocky tilt, the shoulders an attitude—but it was his eyes that hooked her.

He had old eyes. Beautiful brown eyes. Eyes that held a lot of pain, had seen a lot of life. In the middle of the private hospital parking lot, mosquitoes pesking around her neck, panting out of the contraction, scared and hot…yet she felt a pull toward him. He exuded some kind of separateness, a loneliness.

She knew about loneliness.

Of course, that perception took all of a minisecond—and suddenly the emergency room doors were clanging open again. The man glanced up, then back at her. "Damn. You're Graham Crandall's wife? And you're having your baby in *this* hospital?"

His question and tone confused her. She started to answer,

but there was never a chance. Graham noticed the man, said something to him—called him "Jake"—but then he disappeared from her sight. The world descended on her. In typical take-charge fashion, Graham had brought out an entire entourage—a wheelchair, three people in different medical uniforms, Dr. Armstrong.

Graham was midstream in conversation to the doctor. "I don't care what you have to do. She comes first. No exceptions, no discussion. You make sure she's all right and gets through this. And I want her to have something for the pain. Immediately."

"Mr. Crandall—Graham—first, I need to examine her, and then everything else will follow in due course. I swear that I've never yet lost a father—"

"I don't want to hear your goddamn reassuring patter, and forget trying to humor me. I want your promise that nothing is going to happen to my wife."

"Graham." Kasey had to swallow. She'd never seen her husband out of control. Graham didn't *do* out of control. And love suddenly swelled through her, putting the pain in perspective, reassuring her like nothing else could have. "I'm just having a baby. Really, I'm fine. The pain scared me. I didn't realize it was going to be this bad—"

"I'll take care of this, Kasey." Graham cut her off, and rounded on Dr. Armstrong again. "I don't care what it costs. I don't care how many people or what it takes—you don't let anything happen to my wife. You understand?"

The next few hours were a blur of hospital lights and hospital smells. The labor room was decorated to look like a living room, with a chintz couch and TV and even a small kitchenette. Dr. Armstrong did the initial exam. As always, he was patient and calm and as steadfast as a brick.

"But I can't be only three centimeters dilated! You have to be kidding! I thought I was in transition because of the amount of pain."

"I'm going to give you something to help you relax, Kasey."

"I don't want to relax! I want to get to ten centimeters and get this over with! And I want to be able to see the fetal monitor! Is our baby okay?"

"Your baby's just fine," Dr. Armstrong said reassuringly, but he hadn't even looked. What was the point of being all trussed up with the fetal monitor if no one was even going to look at it? "You can have ice chips. And your husband can rub your back. And you can watch TV or listen to music…."

She just wanted it over with. But at least, once they all left her alone with Graham, she thought she could get a better hold on her fears and emotions. Later—an hour, or two, who knew?—she remembered the man outside, and thought to ask Graham who he was.

"Name is Jake McGraw. Used to be from the neighborhood."

"I thought you called him by name, so I was pretty sure you knew him."

"Yeah, I knew him. He's Joe's son. You've heard of Joe, used to be one of GM's high-step attorneys. Money from generations back. Joe had a heart attack a while ago, put Jake back in the neighborhood now and then to help his father."

"So that's why he was at the hospital?" God. Another pain was coming on. How many did you get before you'd paid your dues? And now she knew you didn't die from the little ones, because there were lots, lots, *lots* bigger ones after that.

"I don't know why he was at the hospital. Forget him, Kasey. He's a loser. An alcoholic."

"Really?" For an instant she pictured those old, beautiful eyes again.

"Was part of a big fancy law firm, wife from the Pointe, fast lane all the way. Had a wild marriage, and I mean capital *W* wild. Gave one party that started out in GP and ended up in Palm Springs. They both played around, until some point when Jake went off the deep end. Or so they say. He's got a teenage son, Danny, lives with his ex-wife. Doesn't practice law anymore. You hearing me? He's bad news all the way. Lost everything. And deserved to."

"You never mentioned him before—"

"Why would I? And it beats me why we're talking about him now."

And then they weren't. She'd only asked the question in passing. The man wasn't on her mind. Nothing was, as the minutes wore on and the night deepened and darkened. Somewhere in the wing, a woman screamed. A door was immediately closed, sealing out the sound. The nurse came and went. Graham survived for a while—at least the first couple hours—but then he started pacing.

"Do you want some more ice chips, Kase? Are you cold? Warm? Want to watch any specific show on the tube?"

His solicitousness was endearing—except that every time a pain ripped through her, he paced again, like a panther who wanted to throw himself against the bars. Anything—but be trapped in here. "Graham, go out," she said finally.

"No way. I'm not leaving you."

"I know you're willing to stay. But this is hard…harder than I thought. And to be honest, I believe I'll handle the pain better if I'm alone. I've always been that way. Go on, you. Go get some coffee, or something to eat. Don't feel guilty, just go."

He kissed her, hard, on the forehead, squeezed her hand. But eventually she talked him into leaving.

She'd lied about wanting to be alone. The truth was, she desperately wanted Graham to be with her, yet he was obviously miserable, seeing her in pain. And for a while, for a long time, the fear completely left. Medical help was just a call away, and so was her husband, so it seemed easier to relax. She inhaled the silence. The peace. The feeling as if there was no one in the universe but her and the baby.

She cut all the lights but one, shut off the television. In between contractions, she rubbed her tummy, talking softly to her baby. This was about the two of them. No one else. "You're going to love your room. I bought you a teddy bear the size of a Santa, and the toy box is already filled. The wallpaper is balloons in jewel colors, and over your crib, I set up real jewels dangling from a mobile—amethyst, citrine, jade, pink quartz. When the sun comes, you won't believe what brilliant crystal patterns it makes on the wall. And there's a wonderful, big old rocker. You and I are going to rock and sing songs, and I'm never going to let you cry, never...."

An hour passed, then another. Suddenly a pain seared through her that was different from all the others.

Finally, she thought, the transition stage. All the books claimed this stage was the hardest—but it also meant that they were nearing the end. Soon enough she'd hold the real baby in her arms after all these months.

Another pain. Just like that one, only worse. More of the fire, more of the scalding feeling of being ripped apart. She hit the button for the nurse, then hit it again.

No one came.

Now she realized what a sissy she'd been before, because these contractions were completely different. And possibly that's why no one was coming now, because they thought she'd been crying wolf? Only Graham...where was he? Surely they wouldn't leave her much longer without someone checking on her?

This wasn't pain where she could scream or yell like before. This was pain so intense that it took all her concentration to just endure. This wasn't about whining how she could die; this was about believing for real that she may not survive this. Agony lanced through her, again and again, not ceasing, not letting up, not giving her a chance to catch her breath. Her body washed in sweat. Fear filled her mind like clouds in a stormy sky, pushing together, growling and thundering. She wanted her mom. She wanted Graham. She wanted someone, anyone. She pushed and pushed and pushed the call button, but she had no possible way to get up out of bed and seek help on her own, not by then.

Finally the door opened a crack. Then a nurse's voice. "Good God." Then...lights and bodies and motion and more pain. "There, Kasey, you're doing good—it's going to be all over very soon." By then she didn't care any more—or, if she cared, she couldn't find the energy to respond.

They wheeled her into an unfamiliar room. Stuck her with needles. "Where's Graham?" she asked, but no one answered. Everyone was running, running. The baby seemed to be rushing, rushing. And the pain was there, but with that last hypodermic, the knife edges of pain blunted, and her mind started blurring.

Somewhere, though, she heard a woman's voice. One of the nurse's. Low, urgent. "Doctor, there's something—"

She tried to stir through the thick mental fuzz, recognizing that something was happening. Something alarming. She heard the doctor's sharp, "Be quiet." And then, "Get out of the way. Let me see."

"Is something wrong?" she whispered.

No one answered.

"Doctor, is something wrong with my baby?"

Still no one answered. But she felt another needle jab in her arm. And immediately came darkness.

HER DREAMS WERE ALL SWEET, dark, peaceful. She remembered nothing until she heard the sound of a nurse's cheerful voice, and opened her eyes to a room full of sunshine. "Are we awake, Mrs. Crandall? I'm bringing your beautiful daughter. There you go, honey...I have on your chart that you want to nurse, so I'm going to help you get set up. Can we sit up?"

She pushed herself to a sitting position, listening to the nurse, taking in the pale blue walls of the private room, the fresh sun pouring in the window, the washed-clean sky of a new day. All those sensory perceptions, though, came from a distance.

Once the bundle was placed in her arms, there was only her and her daughter.

OhGodOhGodOhGod. The pain and fear had all been real, but mattered no more now than spit in a wind.

The feel of her daughter was magic. Reverently she touched the pink cheek, the kiss-me-shaped little mouth, then slowly—so carefully!—unwrapped the blanket. She counted ten fingers, ten toes, one nose, no teeth. Without question, her daughter was the first truly perfect thing in the entire world. Love rolled over Kasey in waves, fierce, hot, compelling, bigger than any avalanche and tidal wave put together.

"She's all right? *Really* all right? I remember the doctor sounding worried in the delivery room. I was scared something was going wrong—"

The nurse glanced at the chart at the bottom of the bed, then quickly turned away. "She sure looks like a healthy little princess to me." Efficiently the nurse adjusted Kasey's nightgown, and finally coaxed Kasey to quit examining the baby long enough to see mom and daughter hooked up. "I'm going to give you two a few private minutes, but I'll check on you in a bit, okay?"

Kasey nodded vaguely. The nurse was nice—but not part of her world. Not then. She stroked and cuddled her miracle as the little one learned to nurse.

She and Graham had bickered about baby names for months. Boys' names had been tough enough, but girls had seemed impossible. Cut and dried, Graham wanted Therese Elizabeth Judith if the child was a girl. Kasey thought that sounded like a garbled mouthful...now, though, she found a solution to the problem in an instant. Graham could have whatever name he wanted on the birth certificate.

But her name was Tess.

Kasey knew. From the first touch, the first smell and texture and look…the name simply fit her. And it was hard to stop cherishing and marveling. The little one had blue eyes—unseeing but beautiful. Her skin had the translucence of pearl. The head was pretty darn bald, but there was a hint of rusty-blond fuzz. Little. Oh, she was so little.

Kasey thought, *I'd do anything for you.* And was amazed at the compelling swamp of instincts. How come no one had told her how fierce the emotion was? That mom-love was this powerful, this extraordinarily huge?

"Oh, Graham," she murmured as she caressed the little one's head. "Wait until you see how precious, how priceless your daughter is. She's worth anything. Everything. All…"

Kasey stopped talking on a sudden swallow. She looked up.

Darn it—where *was* Graham?

JAKE PULLED HIS eight-year-old Honda Civic into the driveway on Holiday, touched the horn to announce his arrival, and then walked around and climbed into the passenger seat.

He saw the living room curtain stir, so Danny heard the car—but that was no guarantee his son would emerge from the house in the next future. Rolling down the window—it was hot enough to fry sweat—he reached in the back seat for his battered briefcase. Sweet, summery flowers scented the late afternoon, but the humidity was so thick it was near choking.

He glanced at the windows of his ex-wife's house again, then determinedly opened his work. The top three folders were labeled with the names of suburban Detroit hospitals—Beauregard, St. Francis, and Randolph. All three hospitals had a history of superior care until recently, when they'd had a sudden rash of lawsuits, all related to rare medical problems affecting newborns.

Traditionally even the word *newborn* invoked a panic

flight response in Jake—yeah, he'd had one. He still remembered the night Danny had been born fifteen years ago—and his keeling over on his nose. So babies weren't normally his favorite subject.

But he'd accidentally come across one of these mysterious lawsuits when he'd been researching a separate story for the newspaper, and then couldn't shake his curiosity. Every question led to another dropped ash—a lit ash—and no one else seemed aware there was an incendiary pile of embers in the forest.

In itself, the increase in lawsuits didn't necessarily mean beans, because everybody sued for everything today. People especially freaked when something happened to a baby—what parent didn't suffer a rage of pain when their kid didn't come out normal? Although Jake was no longer a practicing lawyer, he knew the system. Knew how lawsuits worked.

He'd already told himself not to get so stirred up. What looked like a Teton could still end up an anthill. But it smelled wrong, this sudden burst of lawsuits—and this sudden burst of serious health problems for babies, especially when the affected hospitals had longstanding excellent reputations.

Momentarily a woman's face pounced in his mind. Kasey. Graham Crandall's wife. Crandall was one of those starched-spine controlling types—a silver-tongued snob, Jake had always thought, the kind of guy who'd give you the shirt off his back—as long as you gave him a medal for doing it. There was no trouble between them, no bad history. Jake didn't care about him one way or another, even back in the years when he'd hung with the Grosse Pointe crowd.

But it had been a shock to meet Crandall's wife. Coming out of the hospital that night, he'd only seen a woman in labor—she was crying. Who wouldn't? About to give birth to a watermelon? Yet her face kept popping in his mind. The short, rusty-blond hair. The freckled nose and sunburned cheeks.

She wasn't elegant or beautiful or anything like the women Jake associated with Crandall. Instead, there was a radiance about her, a glow from the inside, a natural joyful spirit. The wide mouth was built for laughter; her eyes were bluer than sky.

Pretty ridiculous, to remember all those details of a woman he didn't know from Adam—and a woman who was married besides. Jake figured he must have had that lightning-pull toward her for the obvious reason. It had momentarily scared him, to realize she was going into that hospital to have a baby—the same hospital where he'd been researching the lawsuits.

Now, though, he sighed impatiently and turned back to his papers. Kasey was none of his business. Hell, even these lawsuits weren't. For two years, he'd tried his best to just put one foot in front of the other, pay his bills, make it through each day, be grateful that the half-assed weekly paper had been willing to give him a job. Even the research on these hospitals he was doing on the q.t., his own time.

Jake had done an outstanding job of screwing up his life. Now he was trying to run from trouble at Olympic speed. He figured there was a limit to how many mistakes a guy could make before any hope of self-respect was obliterated for good.

The instant he heard the front door slam, he looked up, and immediately hurled his briefcase into the back seat. Quick as a blink, he forgot all about lawsuits and strangers' babies. His focus lasered on the boy hiking toward the car. Just looking at Danny made him feel a sharp ache in his gut.

At fifteen, Danny had the look of the high school stud. The thick dark hair and broody dark eyes drew the girls, always had, always would. The broad shoulders and no-butt and long muscular legs added to the kid's good looks. The cutoffs hanging so low they hinted at what he was most proud of, the cocky posture, the I-own-the-world bad-boy swagger…oh yeah, the girls went for him.

Jake should know. He'd looked just like the kid at fifteen. But there were differences.

Last week Danny's hair had been straggly and shoulder-length; this week it had colored streaks. The kid's scowl was as old as a bad habit and his eyes were angry—all the time angry, it seemed. The swagger wasn't assumed for the sake of impressing the girls, but because Danny was ready to take on anyone who looked at him sideways.

Jake understood a lot about attitude. What knifed him in the gut, though, was knowing that his son's bad attitude was his fault.

The boy yanked open the driver's door and hurled his long skinny body in the driver's seat. "You're late."

Not only was Jake ten minutes early, but he'd been waiting. Still, he didn't comment. If Danny hadn't started the conversation with a challenge, Jake would probably have had a heart attack from shock. "You brought your permit? And you told your mom that you're going out with me?"

"Like I need to be treated like a five-year-old." Danny fussed with the key, the dials, then muttered, "If I had any choice—just so we both know where we stand—I'd rather be anywhere but here."

That about said it all. Danny wanted to drive so badly that he was even willing to spend time with his dad—and then, only because no one else wanted to practice-drive with him. Even his mother valued her life too much to take the risk.

"I suppose you're in a hurry." Danny used his favorite world-weary tone as he started the car.

"Nope. I've got as much time as you want—although I assume your mom wants you back by dinner."

"Yeah. Maybe. Can I go on the expressway today?"

Maybe Churchill thought there was nothing to fear but fear itself, but the image of Danny on a Detroit expressway at rush hour was enough to make bile rise up Jake's throat in abject terror. The kid had just gotten his practice license. The last time he'd tried to do something as basic as making a right turn, he'd climbed over a curb. "I think you probably need to get a little more comfortable with the stick shift before we take on the expressway."

"That's what you said last week." Danny shoved the stick in Reverse, made the gear scream in pain, and then stalled out when he let up the clutch too fast. Red shot up his throat. "That wasn't my fault," he said furiously. "It's this old heap of a car. It's so old it doesn't respond to anything."

It was going to be one of their better times, Jake thought. Of course, as they aimed toward Lakeshore, the test questions began. *Can I play the radio. Can I drive by Julie Rossiter's house.* Can I this, can I that.

As far as Jake could tell, all the questions were designed to elicit a *no,* at which point Danny would instantly respond with a look of anger and disgust. Jake knew the game. He did his absolute best to say yes to any request that wasn't definably life-threatening. Sure, Danny could drive by the girl's house. Sure, he could play the radio—any station and at any volume he wanted. Jake encouraged him to drive exactly as he would be driving later, when he was alone, so he could see how distractions affected his concentration.

"Oh, yeah? Does that mean I can smoke while I drive?"

"No." Jake didn't elaborate, knowing how a lecture on smoking would be received. Besides, just then his right foot jammed on the imaginary brake and his pulse pumped adrenaline faster than a belching well. No, they hadn't hit that red Lincoln going through the intersection. No, scraping the tire against the curb wouldn't kill them. No, braking so fast they were both thrown forward didn't mean either of them were going to end up hospitalized.

"I'm going to be sixteen in another seven months," Danny said, as he turned onto Vernier.

"I know." Jake resisted holding his hand over his heart. Suburban driving wasn't too bad, but Vernier eventually turned into Eight Mile. Eight Mile was a Real Road. The kind that tons of people actually used. Some of them might not realize how close they were to imminent death.

"So, any chance you might buy me a car?" Danny rushed on, "Mom'll never let me drive the Buick. It's uncool, anyway. But she's already warning me that I won't be able to use her car all the time. I really need wheels."

"I can't afford a car, Danny."

"You could. If you were still a lawyer. If we were still a family. If you weren't a drunk."

There now. Every one of the accusations stung like a bullet, just as his son intended. Sometimes Jake wanted a minute with his son—just one damn minute—when Danny wasn't trying to wound him.

But of course he'd earned those accusations. And all he could do now was hope that time—good meaningful time together—could start to heal that old, bad history. "Getting you a car isn't just about having enough money to buy one."

"The hell it isn't."

"Danny, come on, you're a new driver. You know that you need more practice before you'll be safe—or feel safe—on the road. It's nuts to start out with a new car before you have some experience under your belt."

"You care about being safe on the road? You used to drive drunk."

"Yeah, I did. And I hope you never do. I hope you're way smarter than me."

"That wouldn't take much." Danny made a left onto Mack, where approximately five thousand cars were speeding toward home. Horns blared when the Honda accidentally straddled two lanes. Jake reached for an antacid. Then Danny tried another jibe. "Mom's going out with some guys. Three of them, in fact."

"That's nice."

"I'll bet she's screwing at least one."

Jake understood that this comment was supposed to be another way to hurt him. Danny assumed that he still cared what
Paula did. And even though Jake should have known better
than to bite, he couldn't quite let this one go. "Don't use
words like that about your mother."

"Oh, that's right. We're not supposed to tell the truth about
anything. We just lie and pretend everything's okay, right?
The way you lied about being an alcoholic. And about you
and Mom staying together, that you were just going through
a rough time but we'd all be fine."

Halfway through a yellow light, Danny gunned the engine
and it stalled. The light turned red while they sat clogging the
middle of the intersection. Sweat beaded on Jake's brow. He
said, "Take it easy. The other drivers can see you, so there's
no immediate danger. Just concentrate on getting the car
started and going again."

On the inside, Jake marveled at the epiphany he kept getting from these practice driving sessions with Danny. You
sure learned to value your life when it was constantly at risk.

Besides that—and in spite of Danny's sarcasm and surly
scowls—Jake still felt the wonder of being with his son. It
wasn't a given. Danny hadn't been willing to see him for most
of the two years since the divorce—and God knew, that
wouldn't have changed if Danny wasn't desperate to drive.

Jake realized he was riding a shaky fence. He fiercely
wanted to make things right for his son, yet there seemed no
parenting rule book for this deal. The kid was always egging
him on, pushing him to lose his temper. What was the right
dad-thing to do? Be tough? Or be understanding? Give him
the tongue-lashing he was begging for, or keep proving to the
kid that he'd never vent temper on him?

Hard questions surfaced every time they were together.
Jake didn't mind the kid beating up on him—hell, he had a lot
to make up for. But just once in his life, he'd like some answers.
Some *right* answers. He was already a pro at the other kind.

When Danny turned again, aiming down a side road toward Lakeshore, the boy suddenly muttered, "Julie's house is down here."

Abruptly the kid slowed to a five-mile-an-hour crawl—which was fine by Jake—until Danny made another left. Four homes down from Sacred Julie's house was the Crandall place. Jake spotted a BMW pulling into the driveway. Saw Graham Crandall climb out of the driver's seat. Saw the passenger door open.

And there was Kasey.

His pulse bucked like a stallion's in spring—just like it had the first time he'd seen her. The kick of hormones struck him as incontestable proof that a man had no brain below his waist…still, it made him want to laugh. The last time he remembered that kind of zesty hormonal kick, he'd been sixteen, driving Mary Lou Lowrey home from a movie, and 51% sure from the way she kissed him that she was going to let him take her bra off. Second base was hardly a home run, but sixteen-year-old boys were happy with crumbs. Even the promise of crumbs. At that age, the thrum of anticipation alone was more than worth living for.

Hormones were undeniably stupid, but damn. They made a guy feel busting-high alive and full of himself—a sensation Jake hadn't enjoyed in a blue moon and then some.

Temporarily his son diverted him from the view—primarily because he was doing something to torture both the gears and the brakes simultaneously. "Danny, what are you trying to do?"

Danny shot him an impatient look. "Parallel park, obviously."

"Ah." Perhaps it should have been obvious. They'd edged up the curb, down the curb, up on the stranger's grass, down on the grass, several times now. Ahead of them was a freshly washed SUV, behind them a satin-black Audi. In principle there was an ample ten feet between the cars. "Try not to go quite so close—"

"Well, this is hard," Danny groused. "How the hell are you supposed to know where the back end of another car is if you can't see it?"

But he could see her. Kasey, climbing out of the passenger seat, holding a small pink blanket. She hit him exactly the same way she had before—as if he were suffering the dizzying, stupefying effect of a stupid pill.

The darn woman wasn't any prettier than she'd been the first time. No makeup. Her rusty-blond hair was wildly tousled. She was wearing some god-awful green print that overwhelmed her delicate features. But the details just didn't matter.

The sound of her laughter pealed down the street. She didn't laugh like a lady; she laughed as if her whole heart and belly were into it, joyful laughter, the kind of hopeless giggling that it sucked in strangers passing by.

And the way she held the baby, it was damn obvious the kid was worth more than diamonds to her. As Graham crossed the car to her side, she climbed out, then surged up on tiptoe and kissed him. She looked up at him with a love so radiant and full that you'd think Graham was everything a woman ever dreamed of in a guy.

And there it was, Jake mused wryly. He got it, the reason he had such a hard time looking away from her. It was plain old jealousy.

He knew damn well no one had ever looked at him like that.

No one's fault for that but him. He'd grown up a spoiled rich kid, raised to be selfish, to feel entitled, to take whatever he wanted whenever he wanted it. God knew his parents only meant to love him, but that upbringing had still skewed his perspective. It had taken his losing everything for Jake to figure out what mattered. He'd run out of time. Either he got around to developing some character, or he was going to end up lost for good.

An alcoholic—at least an alcoholic who was serious about recovering—discovered certain things about life. There were things you couldn't do. Other people could. You couldn't. Life was as simple and mean as that. No one else had your exact list, but Jake knew what was written on the forbidden side of his sheet. Being attracted to a married woman—a very, very married woman—was as off-limits as it got.

He understood Kasey's tug on him. Something about her reminded him of what he once thought life could be—when he still believed in dreams, when he still believed in himself, when every moment of sunshine was a treasure. He understood—but he turned off the volume and the vision, promptly.

Danny had given up trying to parallel park. He took the first left turn, aiming back toward his mother's house. He didn't speed. His driving problems had never been about carelessness, but about having no natural sense for the stick shift and the car. The more impatient he got with himself, the more he tended to make mistakes. Jake tried to shut up. Time and experience were the answers, not carping. Besides, dads couldn't die from nerves, could they?

Danny accidentally hit the gas, pulling into Paula's driveway, tried to recover by slamming on the brakes, and then, of course, stalled. For the first time in almost two hours, the kid looked him straight in the eye.

"I suppose you don't have time to do this again on Thursday," he said disgustedly.

"I suppose I do."

It probably hurt the kid like a sore, but hope surged in those broody blue eyes. "Same time? Four o'clock?"

"I may be a little late."

"Yeah, so what's new? The question is whether you'll show at all, just because you say you will."

Jake said easily, "Damn right. You think I don't know how much I need to make up for, Sport, you're mistaken. And in the meantime, if you also want to take on a drive on Saturday or Sunday—there's less traffic early in the morning, so we could go for a longer trek."

"You mean get up early?" Danny's tone suggested that particular idea was as appealing as a snake bite.

"No sweat if you don't want to. I just know you're hot to get more driving hours in, and I can't get here during the work week until after four. Weekend mornings could give us more time."

Danny heaved out of the car. "I'll think about it."

"Okay." Jake got out, too, and crossed to the other side, conscious that his son hadn't used the word *Dad,* much less said anything as pleasant as "goodbye." This lesson, though, had been significantly more peaceful than the last one. Danny hadn't sworn at him. Hadn't hit anything.

"Hey." Danny stopped at the front door, key in the lock, turning back to offer one last belligerent look.

"Yeah?" Jake assumed the "hey" was meant as some kind of question.

"Thanks for taking me," Danny said stiffly, and then promptly disappeared in the house and slammed the door.

Well, hell. Jake was stunned speechless. The kid had actually thanked him? Maybe, just maybe, father and son did have a chance to mend their fences. Of course, earning the kid's respect was still an uphill battle.

Coming this July from NEXT™

Sometimes a woman has to make her own luck.
Find out how Kasey does exactly that!

LUCKY by Jennifer Greene

Don't miss the moving new novel by *USA TODAY* bestselling author Jennifer Greene.

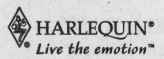

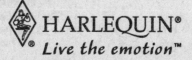

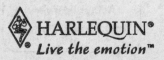

MINISERIES

From *USA TODAY* bestselling author

Marie Ferrarella

**Two heartwarming novels from her
miniseries The Bachelors of Blair Memorial**

THE BEST MEDICINE

For two E.R. doctors at California's Blair Memorial,
saving lives is about to get personal...and dangerous!

"Ms. Ferrarella creates a charming
love story with engaging characters
and an intriguing storyline."
—*Romantic Times*

Available in July.

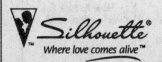

Where love comes alive™

**Bonus Features,
including:
Sneak Peek,
Author Interview
and Dreamy Doctors**